MORGANDALE

PIONEERS BOOK ONE

PETER RIMMER

ABOUT PETER RIMMER

~

Peter Rimmer was born in London, England, and grew up in the south of the city where he went to school. After the Second World War, aged eighteen, he joined the Royal Air Force, reaching the rank of Pilot Officer before he was nineteen. At the end of his National Service, he sailed for Africa to grow tobacco in what was then Rhodesia, now Zimbabwe.

The years went by and Peter found himself in Johannesburg where he established an insurance brokering company. Over 2% of the companies listed on the Johannesburg Stock Exchange were clients of Rimmer Associates. He opened branches in the United States of America, Australia and Hong Kong and travelled extensively between them.

Having lived a reclusive life on his beloved smallholding in Knysna, South Africa, for over 25 years, Peter passed away in July 2018. He has left an enormous legacy of unpublished work for his family to release over the coming years, and not only they but also his readers from around the world will sorely miss him. Peter Rimmer was 81 years old.

ALSO BY PETER RIMMER

∾

The Brigandshaw Chronicles

The Rise and Fall of the Anglo Saxon Empire

Book 1 - Echoes from the Past

Book 2 - Elephant Walk

Book 3 - Mad Dogs and Englishmen

Book 4 - To the Manor Born

Book 5 - On the Brink of Tears

Book 6 - Treason If You Lose

Book 7 - Horns of Dilemma

Book 8 - Lady Come Home

Book 9 - The Best of Times

Book 10 - Full Circle

Book 11 - Leopards Never Change Their Spots

Book 12 - Look Before You Leap

Book 13 - The Game of Life

Book 14 - Scattered to the Wind

∾

Standalone Novels

All Our Yesterdays

Cry of the Fish Eagle

Just the Memory of Love

Vultures in the Wind

In the Beginning of the Night

≈

The Asian Sagas

Bend with the Wind (Book 1)

Each to His Own (Book 2)

≈

The Pioneers

Morgandale (Book 1)

Carregan's Catch (Book 2)

≈

Novella

Second Beach

FOREWORD

～

Peter Rimmer died in July 2018 having written over thirty novels, several short stories as well as two plays. He began his writing career we believe in 1961, aged twenty-four. Peter's family were aware of the extent of his writing but not how early he had begun and this they discovered in letters from literary agents.

Unfortunately dates of when *Morgandale*, and its sequel *Carregan's Catch*, was written is unknown. However, based on the address written on the manuscripts, it's believed they were written in the mid-1970s. Nearly fifty years ago!

To that end, if you have already read any of Peter's later novels, you may find the style of writing and topic of *Morgandale* to be somewhat dissimilar, and different from present times where attitudes and perceptions are vastly changed to what they were in the 1970s.

We are proud to share with you *Morgandale* and we hope you will enjoy reading this novel.

Kamba Publishing
August 2020

PART 1

1890

1

"*Have* you ever seen a horde of heathens that have spent seven hours working themselves up for a fight?" asked Major Johnson.

"No, sir, I haven't," said James, "I have only just arrived in this country."

"And yet, having arrived at the civilised end of Africa, you immediately wish to go up north and pit your new wits against the wiles of Lobengula. What do you want us to do, carry you up there?"

James Carregan looked at Major Johnson and tried to keep down his temper. The interview had lasted five minutes.

"You haven't answered my question," said Johnson.

"You can hardly say," said James, measuring his words to keep them under control, "that travelling six thousand miles as crew on a clipper, cutting every trace with an otherwise leisurely future and irrevocably discarding the patronage of one's father is a whim of the moment. I am young, new and inexperienced, but I am also fit, healthy and able to learn. There must be a beginning for everything. There must have been a point when you were in the exact same position as myself and had not seen a Matabele impi."

They continued to look at each other until Johnson laughed.

"You know how to fight back with words, anyway," he said and leant forward over his desk, his hands clasped in front of him.

"This whole operation is not going to be easy, Carregan. I have promised Mr Rhodes to occupy the country on ninety thousand pounds and there isn't any more for the job. Many others say he needs an army of two and half thousand to either frighten Lobengula into keeping quiet or to defeat him. I have contracted to do the job with one hundred and eighty men with a similar escort of police. To win, I must pick each man. Preferably, I would like one hundred and eighty men with hunting experience and the bush knowledge of Selous, but if I found them they would all want to lead, so there can only be one Selous to show us the direction for the road. I require baggage masters to make certain that we do not run out of anything between the Sabi and Lundi rivers, and I have Captains Heany and Borrow for this job. I require scouts to constantly test the country for the advancing column, and I have Willy von Brand and Rhys Morgan. When we get there – and this is just as important, since my job is to occupy the country, not just to get there and come back again – I need architects, builders, lawyers, farmers, administrators, miners and engineers. I need something of everything to make a frontier country, and I need each of them to be tough enough to fight his way to Mount Hampden, and to cut a road through some of the hottest and most fly ridden country in Africa. Where does a newly made Bachelor of Arts in history fit into this? You tell me, Carregan; I'm only asking. I want to know what you can offer us."

There was silence in the large office.

"You also need men," replied James, after a moment, "with the determination and willpower to dig themselves into the new country; people who will not run home if the gold cannot be picked up in handfuls. We all know there is gold but has history ever shown men an easy way of making their fortunes? It is a vast country. The gold will not be everywhere; if it were, the blacks would have found it and sent it down to the Portuguese trading posts in Mozambique. History tells us that the Portuguese have been waiting for the flood of gold for four centuries. Doesn't this suggest that we will have to search for this gold, and that it will only be determination that will succeed? And, if the gold is not there, we will have to cut ourselves a farm to survive. No sir, I have no illusions as to easy gold. I want the opportunity to create something that is totally new. I can learn, and I want to learn."

"At twenty-one, Carregan," said Johnson. "you may be able to learn, but I don't know whether we have the time to teach you. It is a pity that you have not been out here for some years. Look, I have the address of your hotel. I have many more people to interview, and if nothing else it has been my pleasure to meet you. I hope you are wrong about the gold, as Mr Rhodes needs it to pay dividends to the many shareholders who have invested in the British South African Company. I think he persuaded the Queen to give him the Charter on the strength of the gold. Can you find your own way out of the building?"

They got up and shook hands. Major Johnson was once again engrossed in paperwork when James opened the door and let himself out into the corridor.

Outside the two-storey building, the February sun seared into his eyes but failed to produce any warmth in his body. He would go on to China with the *Dolphin*; that was it, he told himself; and he would find someone who wanted to use his services. If not, he thought with less confidence, he would go back and accept that he was only good enough to follow in his father's footsteps. He walked for ten minutes and came to the sea. A strong wind pressed at his body. From Liverpool, he had thought it only necessary to reach Africa to join the occupation force. There had been no question of coming this far and then being refused. His grandfather would laugh at him, and his father even more. Well, he told himself, there is not an easy path in life.

He thought of all the questions that Major Johnson had asked and tried to remember the ones he had answered incorrectly. He could do the job, of that he was certain. The voyage from England had proved to him that he did not break under hard conditions. He thought of ways of putting his case again. He became more determined as he watched the sea pound at the wet, grey rocks thirty feet below him. He was impatient with himself and turned abruptly, walking briskly, parallel to the sea, towards the hotel.

"COME, ME-LAD," said his grandfather, "we'll be off to the docks and the Harbour Tavern. The Cape brandies are good and the wines are even better. If ye prefer some gin, I won't stop ye. One way and another, we'll 'ave ye singing tonight."

Captain Carregan looked out of the window onto the road.

"The cab's here," he said. "Come on."

James followed him downstairs and out of the hotel.

"Do you think any other members of the column will be at the Harbour Tavern?" James asked his grandfather when they were inside the cab.

"If there are, I can find out."

His grandfather noticed the change in James's attitude and looked at him a second time in the bad light.

"Try and find out for me," asked James. "I want to meet as many as possible. Major Johnson may not make his decision for some days and in the meantime I want to have my name brought up in his company as many times as possible. He knows as well as me that he cannot judge a man in ten minutes across a desk, and that was why he was looking for the right background to prove that the person would fit his requirements. He was not judging the man but his history. If I can talk others into putting a word in for me, it will immediately take me out of the list of ordinary applicants. He can't be having it all his own way, as otherwise he would not waste his time interviewing people like myself. He had all the basic details on the application form."

"Ye've got a good point, lad," said Captain Carregan. "Right. We'll make it our business to meet these people. We'll find out where they stay and where they drink. I can get meself into conversation and introduce ye afterwards. If we do it right, they'll never see it as lobbying. 'Ave a Cape cheroot... they're strong, but ye get used to 'em after a while. I must have smoked everything that's been going in me day."

They lit their cheroots, and the pungent smell of green tobacco pervaded the cab and the red ends of the cigars glowed in the half-darkness as the horse trotted on its way towards the harbour. James looked out confidently over the night sea, its surface washed by the colourless light of the moon. He began to enjoy the taste and the smell of the tobacco.

ONE LANTERN HUNG above the entrance to the Harbour Tavern. As they swung into the yard in front of the low building, with the sheen of moonlight on the water behind it, James listened for the noise of drinkers, but there was no sound above the metallic trotting of the horse's hooves. He flicked the end of his cheroot out of the open window, and the red glow curved up and then down, and exploded on the cobblestones. The cab came to a stop and they opened the small doors and got out.

"Where can we get a cab to go back in?" said his grandfather to the native driver as he paid him off.

"I will go back here sometime later. There are others too."

"I'll take ye word for it," said the captain, not understanding the dialect, and they walked off towards the light from the lantern. Behind them, the cab turned and headed back into the night.

His grandfather walked strongly and without any sign of age. They lowered their heads and went in through the doorway and under the lantern. James followed down a narrow passage. At the end of the corridor they turned left into the bar. The voices were low and well ordered; the men sat in twos and threes at the long benches. James stood just inside the doorway and looked around the room. On his right, two seamen were playing cribbage. His grandfather put a hand on his shoulder and guided him between the dark wooden benches and tables towards the bar. Finally they leant on the bar counter and looked at each other. A row of lanterns hung above their heads along the length of the bar and gave a good light.

"What'll ye have?" asked his grandfather.

"What do you suggest?"

"Evening, captain," said the barman, pressing forward a little with both hands on the edge of the oak bar.

"Business looks quiet tonight, Hennie," said the captain.

"It will get better later. Full of people it was, earlier."

"Make it two mugs of red wine. A good one. I don't want me gut to start rotting at my age."

They looked around the bar and only turned to face each other again when the barman put the pewter mugs down in front of them. They picked them up carefully without spilling the wine, and glanced up at each other.

"Cheers, lad, and good luck," said Captain Carregan.

"Thanks," replied James. They drank together with their noses in focus above the rims of their mugs.

"Not bad, Hennie, not bad," said Captain Carregan, and lowered his mug onto the bar, his head tilted a little to one side in appreciation. "Do ye hear anything about Rhodes's column? I'd like to meet any of them that are going. If ye see any come in tonight, give me the nod. I've thought of taking the *Dolphin* round the coast to Portuguese waters, if they find all the gold they've been shouting about."

"There's none of them here now, captain," said Hennie, "but if I as see them, I'll tell you which ones they are."

"Have a drink," said the Captain.

"I will, but just a small one. These can be long nights, and it is bad enough when they get drunk."

"It had better not be any of my crew tonight," said the captain, and winked.

They drank in silence. James looked around the room. Tobacco smoke hung heavily under the low beams and the wine seeped comfortably into James's stomach as he drank it down in pace with his grandfather. He looked carefully into the faces of everyone who came into the bar. The place filled up and Hennie worked harder, and the level of noise grew with the flow of liquor.

Hennie leant his left arm across the bar and pointed with his forefinger for Captain Carregan to follow its direction.

"I think he's one of the officers," said Hennie.

"Thanks," said the captain, and Hennie turned to serve a new customer.

Holding his half full mug, James followed his grandfather towards the man sitting by himself at the end of a table; he was young and well shaven, and showed no surprise when the elderly seaman sat down next to him on the bench.

"'Ope ye don't mind," said Captain Carregan. "Me name's Carregan of the *Dolphin*. The barman tells me yer one of those going up country for Mr Rhodes, and I wanted to hear some more about it."

"What can I tell you? My name is Borrow. For the journey north I shall be an army captain; for afterwards I shall be a settler like the rest of us." His voice was friendly.

"What I was thinking," said Captain Carregan, "was that if ye find what yer looking for, ye'll need a port nearer than Cape Town or Durban from which to trade, and ships to call there. If I knew when there would be cargo, I'd bring me ship into one of those Portuguese ports. From what I know of where yer going, I'd say the place was Beira. It ain't much of a place at present, and they say there's a lot of fever, but the harbour's safe."

James listened to them. They ignored him, and he sat and drank his wine. The bar was full and the voices loud.

Slowly his own thoughts dominated the surroundings. He thought of the new spring in England, and the many angry words that his father would have spoken about him to his sister. Provided he was accepted for the column, he told himself, it would be worth his father's inconvenience and Ester would find herself a husband and be away from the house. She was pretty. She would have her own home to run. He had his own life to lead, and only himself to make it go forward in the way that he wished. He knew there were penalties to pay in any course that he set himself, and there would be no family in the new country and no women. He thought about women and hoped that by not seeing them he would not think of this need; when he had built his farm, he would go back to England and look for a wife; there would be good time enough for everything. He looked back and saw that women had never been a large part of his life. He had been a boarder at Wellington, and the holidays had seen the occasional ball at a neighbour's home, but he had met no one then, or afterwards during vacations from Oxford, who remained in his memory. He remembered seeing very little strength in any of them. He promised himself that when the farm was built he would go back and look properly.

"I think you are right, captain," Borrow was saying, "a railway line will have to be built to the Portuguese coast, but it will cost money, and there is a limited supply in the Charter Company."

"If ye find the gold there won't be any worry. My, we've been talking so much I've ignored me own grandson. This is Captain Borrow, James; he's one of the leaders of the column."

They shook hands.

"I wish I was his age," said his grandfather, "as otherwise I'd have been with him yesterday, seeing your Major Johnson."

"Are you going on the column?" asked Borrow, with renewed interest in James.

"I have applied," answered James. "My handicap is not knowing Africa. For the rest, I am confident, but the decision is out of my hands."

Captain Carregan again turned his back on James.

"Will ye mention me to Major Johnson," he said to Borrow, "I 'ave me agent in Cape Town and call here regularly. If the major is interested, I can write him the details and, if he has a cargo, bring up the *Dolphin* to get it out. It'll be like trading with the old *Mirtle* again, and with young James up there as well, it'll add a bit of family interest. When ye've built the railway line, I'll come and have a look at the new country meself, but you ain't getting me up there on an ox wagon. I've had me days of rough travelling. Now, look at that," he said, getting up and quickly shaking hands with Captain Borrow, but looking over Borrow's shoulder at the same time. "There's me bosun, and by the looks of 'im, he's been drinking. Now that's not nice for me bosun." He winked at Captain Borrow. "Come on lad," he said to James, and then to Borrow, "Everyone knows the *Dolphin*, so ye won't have any difficulty finding us. Bosun," he shouted over their heads, "where's the first mate?"

The bosun pointed, and James looked around the bar and picked out a number of the older members of the *Dolphin*'s crew.

"All being well," he said to Borrow. "I look forward to serving under you on the column."

"What do you want to do up there, mine or farm?"

"Farm," answered James.

Captain Carregan moved away and beckoned James to follow. "Same as me," said Borrow, smiling. "Maybe we shall farm near the same place."

"It is a big country."

"Come on, lad," shouted his grandfather, "the first mate's buying us a drink."

They nodded to each other, and James followed his grandfather. He had to squeeze past people to catch up.

"Never show yer too interested and without anyone else to talk to or to buy ye a drink," said his grandfather, as they joined the first mate. "The name Carregan will certainly come up next time he sees Johnson. That's my lad, Hal, a drink or two off duty never hurt no one."

The drink flowed quickly, and by the end of an hour no crew member of the *Dolphin* was fit for intelligent conversation. James occasionally saw Borrow through the throng of people, where he was surrounded by a group of men, some of whom were little older than James. They looked confident and at ease with each other.

A large man with a beard joined Borrow's party and James could hear his accented voice above the babble of the others. The man had been drinking, and even from fifteen yards, and through the crowd, James could see that he was rocking gently on his heels.

"We'll end up inside a vulture," said the man with a German accent, and drank hard at a brown spirit that James guessed to be brandy. The man's body swayed gently as he kept himself upright. He was in full control of himself, despite the slight rocking of his body. James thought him to be nearer fifty than forty.

"Captain Borrow," the man said, resting his left hand heavily on the other man's shoulder, "let us drink to the last journey of Willy von Brand. I see fat vultures, and my bones lying bleached by the sun."

"The birds will also be drunk," said a man with a Welsh accent, but James could not see the face through the throng.

"With your good guidance, Willy," said Borrow, "we'll make it in style. Since when have you become frightened of the Matabele?"

"Frightened, never, but realist, yes," said the German. "I can kill a large number before they gut me, but there are hordes of them, and none of them know fear. They have not been defeated in two generations and think no man their better. It is arrogance born of proof. They conquered by force, and have held down the country by force for sixty years. They will think nothing of attacking a few white men if they are sufficiently aroused, and if Lobengula cannot keep them in check; they like to fight. Lobengula is getting old and he's turned to fat and he's full of gout; he's had his fighting days, but there are others under him who thirst for our blood. If he doesn't let them fight us, the old bastard may find an assegai in his own back. They say his purges are becoming more frequent, which is a sure sign of a tired king. Kill or be killed. It's as old as history. We'll have to face the same problem ourselves before everything is done."

"But we only intend to occupy Mashonaland," argued Borrow.

"Certainly, but that's their larder; it's like taking their food and their recreation in one go; unless, that is, we are going to allow the Matabele raiding parties in to slaughter the Mashona, and loot their cattle and grain. But, once we're in there with our civilisation, we can't have black man killing black man. Lobengula knows this as well as you and I. He may be old, and past his best days with a spear, but he isn't any man's fool. He's kept control of them for thirty years, and even Shaka wasn't good enough to do that and not get himself murdered."

James felt their uneasiness in the lull that followed in their conversation, and then he heard the voice with the Welsh accent again.

"It's a question of everybody's principles. If we don't go in there and civilise the place, the Matabele will continue to go on the rampage at the end of every rains, and if we do go in, most likely someone will get hurt. It is probably better for our principles to limit the slaughter, so we'll use our principles to further our ends. We've got more right than Lobengula, so if necessary we fight, and if we lose, the Queen will have to send in the army to salve the British pride. Rhodes knows this. He's outmanoeuvred Lobengula before we've even left the base camp on the Limpopo."

"Yes, but that doesn't help us if we end up inside a vulture," said the German.

"Have another drink, Willy," said Borrow, "and stop being morbid. If we do our job properly, train properly, and keep to our discipline, the impis are not going to defeat Maxim machine guns with a few Martini-Henry rifles."

"And look who gave the guns to Lobengula – Rhodes," said the German, "part of the price of his concession to dig for gold. Makes you laugh when it's the likes of me and you who feed the vultures. But I'll tell you all something," he said, and gathered his large arms around the shoulders of Borrow and the Welshman, and grinned at each of them in turn, "I'll enjoy the fight." He bellowed with drunken laughter, and James felt a queer feeling go up his spine.

He looked closer at the German. The black hair that grew profusely from his face was flecked with grey, and the hairs on his arms were white, and there was white hair spilling out of the top of his shirt. James smiled to himself; he could not imagine any heathen looking worse than the German. The German looked up at James from his confidants, and slowly closed one lid over a red, watery eye and bellowed with laughter at his own effrontery. Then he stopped abruptly and slapped Borrow and the Welshman on their backs, which made Borrow take a pace forward and sent the German leering at him with satisfaction.

Suddenly, the German broke off and lunged his right hand out to catch the waiter, a native. The movement was fast and accurate.

"I will order and they will pay," he said to the waiter. "Three brandies, and make them large ones as I have that bad feeling I won't be able to get drunk so much in the future."

He let go of the waiter, who rubbed his arm as he went on his way to the bar.

James took a sip of his wine, and tried to think out how he could get into conversation with the group without making it obvious to Captain Borrow that he was pushing himself forward with a purpose. He went back to the bar, leaving his grandfather with the first mate and the bosun, waited for the barman to have a slack period, then beckoned him to lean across the bar towards him.

"Who is the man with the black beard talking to the man you pointed out to my grandfather?" he asked.

"Willy von Brand, the hunter. He's been going up into the interior for thirty years. A friend of Selous. The younger one with a beard is also a hunter; Rhys Morgan. He's been up there for ten years. When he first arrived in Cape Town, there was some story about him having been forced out of England because he'd got a peer's daughter into trouble. You can't tell how true the stories are, but that one's stuck a long time, as he didn't start it himself. If you go up into Lobengula's country by yourself, you must be running away from something. Seeing those two together, it wouldn't surprise me to see Selous himself in Cape Town."

James ordered another drink and watched the hunters for some time. Then he struck on his plan, and began to make his way towards the group. He pushed his way politely but firmly through the drinkers, who good-naturedly gave way. He had decided to chance his luck with the younger hunter. Within arm's length of them, he waited for his moment. When Morgan turned away from the others to put down his empty glass, James tapped him on the shoulder.

"Excuse me," he said, "but the barman tells me you're the hunter Rhys Morgan, and I need to ask you a favour." His voice sounded steadier than he felt.

"Go on then and ask it," replied Morgan. "You can always ask, though it doesn't mean to say that you'll get."

"My name's James Carregan and I'm trying to get on the column. I had an interview with Major Johnson this morning, which in some ways went well but in others went badly. You see, I've only been in Africa a week and the major told me that I didn't have the experience he needed. I can ride well enough and use a shotgun but I've never fired a rifle. I suppose you couldn't see yourself free to give me some tuition. I mean, not right now, but when you have a free moment."

Morgan looked at James and smiled at his nerve. He guessed his age at a little over twenty, and wondered how much girding it had taken him before he had been able to ask his question. He probably would not have done it without a few drinks, Morgan told himself.

"You must want to go on this column," he said.

"I have travelled six thousand miles and burnt all my boats at the other end. I suppose if I had thought carefully in England, I would have realised the difference between myself and the likes of you, but it wasn't easy as I did not have any comparison."

"And you think you'd be a marksman after a little tuition?"

"No. I don't think I'll be anything in a couple of hours, but at least it will be a start. Everyone has to start somewhere."

"We're camped just below Lion's Head. Get yourself a horse tomorrow and ride out. We always camp on the same spot, and a lot of people know us. If you get lost, ask your way. Six thousand miles is a long way to come on a wild goose chase," he finished, as much to himself as to James, and turned away to join his friends.

"Thanks," said James, "I'll be there." James stood for a moment, then began to skirt his way round to re-join his grandfather and his crew. He stood behind them for some time, sipping his wine and watching them and the people around him. The determination inside of him was a solid entity.

"How's the wine, lad?" asked his grandfather, noticing him after a while.

"It's going down well," said James.

"Want another?"

"Yes, I could drink another."

"You beginning to succeed or something? For the first time today you've a satisfied expression on your face."

"I invited myself to the hunter's camp tomorrow morning. I asked one of them to show me how to use a rifle. If I can bring those hunters onto my side, I can win."

"The Carregans always were a calculating lot," said his grandfather. "Now, why don't you go to the bar and get those drinks. The bosun is drinking brandy, but bring the first mate a mug of wine. Use your own money; if you run out, I'll give you some more."

2

In front of James, a granite kopje resembling a crouching lion looked over the port of Cape Town, with Table Mountain on its right and the pinnacles of the Twelve Apostles behind. At his back were the buildings of Cape Town, and in front the path gently sloped upwards through a series of camps.

James asked at the first camp and was told that the Morgan and von Brand party were a little further up the hill on the right hand side. He let the horse keep its own pace. The early morning sun had relaxed them both. He hoped that the hunters would have slept off the drink by now, having tried to judge the time when they would have had enough sleep but not enough time to leave camp on the day's business.

He saw Morgan first. He was peering into a cooking pot and prodding the contents without enthusiasm. James dismounted and led the animal by the reins towards the camp. They stood a few paces behind Morgan and waited. The horse lifted one hoof and put it down again. Flies collected around the animal's nostrils; it snorted and flicked its tail at the same time. Morgan turned and looked at them.

"You're a bit early," said Morgan.

"I didn't know what time you'd be going into town," said James.

"Have you had breakfast?"

"No. It took me some time to hire this horse."

"Tie up your horse over there," said Morgan, pointing to a stunted tree, "and then come and stir this stuff. It's meant to be porridge, but it doesn't look too good at the moment. It said on the packet to keep stirring."

James did as instructed and took up his position in front of the cooking pot.

"Can I try some more water?" asked James, looking at the porridge.

"You can try what you like. It can't be any worse than usual. Here, put this on the fire." He handed James a pot full of water. "If it boils, at least we can have some good coffee."

James hung the pot from the spare hook over the fire, and Morgan piled more wood on the flames. Little by little James added water to the porridge and stirred, scraping the bottom of the iron pot as the flames grew hotter, to prevent the porridge from burning. Morgan watched with interest as the texture grew nearer to what he remembered his mother had served him in Wales. He noticed that James concentrated completely on his task and was oblivious to the surroundings.

Willy von Brand came out of his tent and blinked at the sunlight.

"Funny," he said, "how you have to sleep in a tent when you get near to civilisation. What's this, Rhys? Have we got a cook or something?"

"Or something," said Morgan, and they both watched James as he stirred the porridge and added the water.

"Have you got milk and sugar?" said James, without turning round. "You can eat it with salt, but that's how the Scots do it."

"No, we've got milk and sugar," replied von Brand, and continued to look at James's back with interest. "You wouldn't like an apron or anything like that?" he asked.

"No, nothing like that," said James. "I think this porridge will be all right in the end. It's a matter of patience."

"Something Morgan never had," said von Brand.

"Your cooking's just as lousy," said Morgan.

"I never said that it wasn't."

"You got a hangover?" asked Morgan.

"The older I get," said von Brand, "the bigger they get, but at the time it always seems to be worth it."

They watched James for some time and then the water boiled. Morgan made coffee by pouring the boiling water into a pan that contained a layer of ground coffee at the bottom. The smell of coffee was strong. James poured the porridge into three tin plates, and they took the food over to a rock and sat down.

"Fresh milk every day," said Morgan, "what a luxury."

They ate the porridge and drank their coffee in silence.

"I can't remember your name," said Morgan, when he had finished.

"James Carregan."

"This is Willy von Brand."

They shook hands and James winced as his knuckles were crunched. The German smiled, and let go. James flexed his fingers.

"Carregan wants to be taught how to fire a rifle," said Morgan.

"Why? Are you thinking of killing someone?" asked von Brand.

"No," said James, "I want to go on the column."

"Another one trying to feed himself to the vultures," said von Brand, looking up to the heavens. "Why don't we take him as a cook, and then we'll have porridge like this every morning and be fat for the vultures."

"Can't you think of another joke?" asked Morgan.

"It's not a joke," said von Brand, and got up off the rock and went and poured himself another mug of coffee.

"We'll have to take the horses up around the back of the mountain and fire into rock," said Morgan. "I expect they have rules against it, but that can't be helped. Hitting a moving target with one bullet is a combination of natural talent and years of practice. Selous is uncanny. He never hits an animal except where it kills. Willy is the same. If they weren't, they wouldn't be alive now. We'll take a Martini-Henry rifle, since that's what we'll be using on the march."

"I really appreciate your help," said James.

"If you don't ask you don't get, and you asked," he replied. "Do you want to come with us, Willy?"

"I'll come," said von Brand, "the gun blast will either kill my hangover or me."

AN HOUR LATER THEY DISMOUNTED, and Morgan set up a tin can in a crevice with a good screen of rock above and below to absorb the bullets; there was nowhere dangerous for them to ricochet. They withdrew a hundred yards, and the sun picked out the target. Morgan explained the gun in detail, showing James the correct position in which to hold the butt into the shoulder. There was a consistent wind from the left, and he suggested aiming slightly to the left of the can.

"When hunting or fighting in the bush," said Morgan, "there is rarely time to find a rest for the gun, so you may as well start by firing without support. Lean well into the rifle, and sight without closing your eye. There is no resemblance between this kind of shooting and a rifle range. It is a question of sighting and firing in the same motion. Try it a few times without a bullet in the breech."

James tried and felt awkward.

"Lean more into the gun, and grip it as though it was part of you. Find the stance that gives you the most balance. I stand with the left foot forward, but Willy fires with his big fat feet planted almost parallel."

James brought the gun up to his shoulder, sighted and pulled the trigger, and then did it again.

"Now let's make some noise," said Morgan, taking the rifle from James. He loaded a full magazine, worked the action with his thumb, and put one bullet automatically into the breech, pushed back the safety catch, and handed the gun to James.

"Never hand anyone a gun, loaded or otherwise," said Morgan, "without putting the catch to safety. Now, get yourself comfortable, push forward the safety catch, and make that tin can jump."

James concentrated completely, registering his mind on the glint of the tin can.

"Breathe normally," said Morgan.

James brought up the gun, and fired.

"That was damn close," said von Brand, with surprise.

"Work the action," said Morgan, "and try again."

James pulled down on the lever below the trigger, and a bullet was pushed into the breech. He brought up the gun and fired a fraction further to the left.

"Your height is exactly right," said von Brand, "but the wind is stronger than you think."

James fired again, and saw the rock break on the left this time. He held the gun by his side, and relaxed. He worked the action, brought the gun to his shoulder, and fired.

"Got the bastard," shouted Morgan and von Brand at the same time.

"Now we'll go back another fifty yards," said Morgan.

As the sun rose higher they stretched out to three hundred yards. James's ears had ceased to function. They spoke little, and the tin was replaced many times.

"That'll do for the first lesson," said Morgan finally. "If we go on any more, you will neither have a shoulder nor an eardrum."

"If they all learn as fast as you," said von Brand, "the vultures are going to go hungry for white meat."

They went back to camp, and James cooked them a lunch of grilled chops, fried eggs and beans. After the meal they sat in the shade of a tent and smoked cheroots.

"What is it like in the interior?" asked James.

"You tell him," said von Brand to Morgan. "I don't notice it so much as I used to."

"It varies considerably," said Morgan, "from the lowveld to the highveld. Where we're going is the highveld, which has the best climate and the least disease. There's plenty of water up there too.

The rains start in November, and in December and January you wish it would stop. I've seen four inches of rain come down in half an hour. There were new rivers everywhere, and it was impossible to move around. When the sun comes out the humidity is almost suffocating. By March, the main rains are over, and from the end of April until November, there's no rain at all, and the sky is permanently like this, blue, with pocket handkerchief clouds that just stay up there and do nothing. During the day the sun is warm and good, and the nights are cold and invigorating. The campfires are home at that time of the year, and the night skies so clear that you feel you're looking to the end of the universe. When spring comes in September, without rain in the previous six months, the trees bud, and the leaves of the msasa trees break out into every colour of red and orange. It is like a miracle, coming out of so much dryness. I've seen it year after year, and have never grown tired of its beauty."

"Is there much human life?" asked James.

"Not a lot. Lobengula has seen to that. What's left of the Mashona live in the most inaccessible places, and run like hell at the smell of a stranger. There can't be more than a hundred thousand in Mashonaland, which is the same size as the British Isles. Whether there's gold there or not, it's certainly an El Dorado. Farmed properly, the soil will be richer than any Welsh farmer's most vivid dream. Over everything, there's a blanket of peace and wellbeing, which is only shattered by a Matabele impi. I loved my Wales, but I am married to this new place up there. Once you've been there you want to stay, and you always return. To love a woman is satisfying, but it doesn't compare with the completeness of loving a country. With human life there are too many frailties. Too many manmade obstacles and manmade people. A country can kill you, but it never throws back your love into your face. Hunters are nomads, going from one hunting ground to another, so when two wish to stay still you can be sure that they've found a kingdom of heaven on earth. If we succeed in this journey, we'll have founded a truly beautiful country. If one lives in the right setting, so many bad things in life seem tolerable, and the good are better, and it is very difficult to remain in a bad temper."

"You're right, Rhys," said von Brand. "If we get there, it will have been worth the chance, and if we don't we won't know any better. That's the one thing about death – everything stops; the world ceases to exist. But as it does exist at this moment, I suggest we mount our horses and ride them down to the Harbour Tavern. My horse knows the way so I'll lead. Until Borrow and Heany have decided what baggage they want us to escort up north, we're well paid gentlemen of leisure, and as such we should drink. Never miss an opportunity in life, Carregan, to enjoy yourself. We can resume your tuition tomorrow, if you would be so kind as to be here again at the same time to make my porridge. Not only would I have had to eat a badly cooked breakfast tomorrow, but I would also have had to cook the stuff."

"I must call in on Major Johnson for instructions," said Morgan, "and I intend to take a dip in the sea with the weather like this and the opportunity so rare, so I'll meet you in the tavern at sundown. Maybe Carregan prefers the drink to the fresh air, but for me I can't drink as much as you, Willy," he said, and turned to James. "Why not meet us both there at sunset, or you can come for a swim."

"I'll join you for a swim," said James.

"Fine," said Morgan.

They closed up the tents, untethered their horses and walked with them to the next camp.

"Will you watch our tents till we come back sober?" called von Brand.

An old prospector came out of his tent.

"Sure, Mr von Brand. It will be a pleasure."

They mounted the horses, waved to the prospector, and let the horses take their own speed. The prospector watched their receding backs for a while, waved, and then went over to sit on a rock which had a good view out over the ocean. The colour of his eyes and the sea were identical.

"The fairest Cape in all the world," said Morgan to James, who was riding Indian file between the two hunters.

James looked out and down the gently sloping hill, with fir trees over to his left, the clusters of buildings that made up the town and port of Cape Town to his right, the power of Table Mountain behind him, and in front, the sparkling blueness of a calm ocean. A three-masted schooner was making slow progress towards the harbour. James breathed in the fresh sea air as they went on down the path.

They split up in town, von Brand going on to the Harbour Tavern, Morgan going to Major Johnson, and James to the hotel to collect a bathing costume. The town was full of noise and people. Everyone seemed bent on an urgent purpose that would allow nothing to stand in its way.

MORGAN KEPT his horse at the same walking speed. He flexed his shoulder blades. He looked forward to getting back into the interior, and was impatient with the planners for the delay. He appreciated the task of kitting out one hundred and eighty men with provisions to live in the new country for a year, and he was glad it was not his task. Despite his law degree from Liverpool University, he had never enjoyed organised planning and, after eleven years in Africa, he had no wish to revert to the problems of civilisation. He wondered about Annie and his son briefly, and then put them out of his mind. Over eleven years, he had forced himself out of such thoughts as soon as they came to him.

He tied his horse to the hitching post outside Major Johnson's office, and went inside.

"Good morning, Frank," he said.

"Morning, Rhys," replied Johnson.

"When are we off?" said Morgan, sitting himself in the leather chair that stood in front of the desk. He accepted a cheroot from the box that was offered to him. They cut and lit their cigars, and then sat back and looked at each other.

"Are you finding a life of leisure and luxury too much for you?" asked Johnson, smiling.

"I'm not one for doing nothing," said Morgan.

"I hope to have everything ready by Friday," said Johnson. "You'll entrain to Kimberley and then Mafeking. You pick up the wagons and oxen at Mafeking, and take everything through to the base camp on the banks of the Limpopo. I'll explain in detail exactly where it is. The police detachment are camped on the Macloutsi. During the training period, I don't want the two camps to mix. You train at the Limpopo camp for two months, and we begin the march at the end of April, if the imperial officer sent to inspect us agrees that everyone knows what he's doing. We will know, as we are not being bawled out by some English gentleman who has never seen a Matabele. I will follow you to Mafeking next week, as I intend to supervise the training myself. We will have a number of raw hands, and by the time they go forward, they have got to be experienced. For the sake of the BSA Company, I agree with Mr Rhodes that we need some sons of influential men who'll kick up sufficient fuss to force the home government into sending help if it's needed, but it makes our task that more difficult."

"Have you completed the numbers?" asked Morgan.

"Not quite."

"Are you taking Carregan with you?"

"Hell, what is this, Rhys? You're the second man this morning who's asked that question. I had Borrow in here an hour ago, talking about Carregan and his grandfather. The old man has an idea to bring his ship into the port of Beira, as he rightly says Durban and Cape Town are too far away for regular traffic."

"I think we could use Carregan," said Morgan. "He has the kind of determination and perseverance that won't let the bush swallow him up. He's a naturally good shot, as well. Willy and I gave him a lesson this morning, and in the end he could hit a tin can at three hundred yards from a standing position."

"He's too damned inexperienced," said Johnson, "and though his father is rich, it's very new money and he hasn't any influence.

We can't afford any passenger that can be avoided, and you know that as well as I, Rhys."

"I don't think this one will be a passenger, but I won't try and influence your decision. You have to make up the column, and accept the responsibility if anything goes wrong."

"Do you think he would make a good settler?" asked Johnson.

"I have the feeling he would. He's one of those people you can't help liking, which is always an asset under adverse conditions."

"Maybe we should give him a try. I liked him myself," said Johnson.

"I don't think we'll be doing him a favour. After two months' training, I'll have him married to a Martini-Henry. Can Willy and I give you any help with the job on hand?"

"No. It's better for one person to do it from start to finish. I think I have its measure. Come in on Thursday and I'll give you both your written instructions. You and Willy will be responsible for guiding the column from Mafeking to the Limpopo. Borrow will be in overall command, but he doesn't know that part of the country."

"How is the political front? Is there anyone deliberately trying to stand in our way?"

"There are the usual problems at Gu-Bulawayo, but Maguire and Thompson are looking after our interests, and so far the Matabele inDunas have not come to the boil. There is a nice piece of confusion in everyone's minds as to exactly how far the Rudd-Rhodes concession allows us to go. Basically, it says we can only dig for gold, but to do this properly we need so many other things – like land to live on, for instance. I think they will still be talking about our intentions when we hoist the Union Jack at Mount Hampden. We have it very clear in our own minds, and with everything legalised in the Royal Charter, it is merely a question of cutting the road and occupying the place. Rest assured that when it comes to politics, there is no one better equipped than Cecil Rhodes. However hard you try to go against his will, he will convince you otherwise."

"So it looks as though we will really go forward," said Morgan.

"I've had the fear for weeks that someone would stop us. I will be here at nine o'clock on Thursday. Thanks for the cheroot."

They shook hands briefly, and Morgan let himself out of the office. He was convinced now that they would go.

His horse looked up when he came out onto the street. He unhitched the reins and swung himself up into the saddle, and headed the animal for the beach where he'd arranged to meet James. The day was good, and 1890 felt to Morgan like being a good year.

They took the sun on the beach all afternoon, swimming in the ice cold Atlantic every ten minutes. The contrast of the water and air temperatures was extreme. All through the afternoon, Morgan made no mention of his conversation with Major Johnson. James left the beach first, and rode his hired horse to the hotel. He ate a meal with his grandfather, and when it was sufficiently digested, they ordered a cab and proceeded to the Harbour Tavern for the second time in twenty-four hours.

Inside the tavern, Willy von Brand greeted James with an appearance of soberness.

"This is my grandfather, Captain Carregan," introduced James.

"Nice to meet ye," said the captain. They shook hands. "I believe you've been showing the lad how to use a gun. I had the job of knocking the first edges off him, on the way out in the *Dolphin*."

Morgan came into the tavern and was introduced. They ordered drinks, and three hours later they were talking rubbish, and the yarns of the bush and the sea grew taller with each drink. Captain Carregan began the singing, and they sang at the tops of their voices in drunken waves of undulating sound. The evening was a great success.

JAMES WAS ASKED to report to Major Johnson on the Wednesday afternoon, and he presented himself promptly on time.

"Sit down, Carregan," said Johnson. "You seem to have made a lot of friends in Cape Town, and they all want you to go on the expedition. I must congratulate you on not having wasted any of your time. I presume you set about making these friends deliberately, so that they would mention your name to me?"

"Yes," said James.

"I am glad you are honest. I can see you have a great deal of determination, as you most certainly would not have been asked to join us following your last interview in this office."

"This I guessed, as I had nothing concrete to offer you," said James.

"We will be training for two months on the banks of the Limpopo River. Rhys Morgan says he will have you married to a Martini-Henry rifle by then. I hope he is right. If you report to the railway station at nine o'clock on Friday morning, there will be a ticket to Mafeking waiting for you. There will be a number of your new friends at the station."

Major Johnson stood up and held out his hand.

"Welcome to the Pioneer Corps," he said.

"I will do my best," said James.

"We can't ask for more than that. I think you know your way out by now."

James left the room, without being conscious of anything apart from a powerful excitement in the pit of his stomach.

JAMES ARRIVED AT THE STATION, together with his grandfather, half an hour before the train was due to leave. Morgan was already there, and handed James his one-way ticket.

"By the looks of things," said Morgan, "Mr Rhodes has sent along the town band. The place is also crawling with newspaper reporters. They certainly intend the home newspapers to remember us. I expect Rhodes will arrange for newspaper reports all the way along our line of march, so that if anything goes wrong he'll be able to stir up an immediate outcry for help. It will be to our advantage if we find ourselves cut off, so we shouldn't complain."

They walked onto the platform that was crowded with people.

The train and seven coaches were waiting. James saw von Brand and Borrow standing back from the crowd.

"We've kept a place for you in our compartment," said von Brand to James as they joined them. "Hello, captain, when's the *Dolphin* sailing?"

"With the tide tomorrow morning," said Captain Carregan. "I've just been waiting to see the lad on his way, and then we set sail for Singapore and Shanghai. I don't think it's done the crew any harm having a rest."

"When the railway line goes into Beira, I hope the *Dolphin* will be the first to enter port," said Borrow.

"The confidence in our success is remarkable," said Morgan, and they laughed.

James put his belongings into the compartment, and got down onto the platform again. He and his grandfather moved up the platform, and the others let them walk out of earshot.

"Well, lad," said his grandfather, "yer really on yer way this time. Yer on yer own, too, but I'm sure ye can handle yerself. I really will come up there and have a look at yer new home, when they've put in a railway line. If ye need any help, ye know where to come for it. My port agent at Liverpool always knows where I am. If ye don't mind, I'm not going to wait around and hear that band play. I get a bit sentimental at times like these. Yer taking a good name up there, so don't ever forget that yer a Carregan."

"Thanks, Grandfather. I'll try not to let you down."

They shook hands and the older man turned and walked away. James stood and watched him go and saw him wave to the others and heard him wish them good luck. What a pity his father had not been more like his grandfather, he told himself, and slowly walked down the platform to join the others.

3

_J_ames was used to his uniform: the coarse tunic, brown corduroy trousers and yellow leather leggings above heavy army boots. He wore the brown bush hat and bandolier of bullets with comfort.

"The general will see the exercise at five o'clock," said Morgan as they marched across the well-trodden parade square that the police had cut from the virgin bush. "He's a cunning bastard – he wants to see if we can hit those targets at dusk."

The first light showed them the surrounding bush as they marched towards the flagpole on the far side of the parade ground. Trooper Carregan carried the Union Jack, and marched precisely in step beside Morgan and Trooper van der Walt, who carried the trumpet. The morning was cold, and the glow of red above the left bank of the Macloutsi River grew stronger as they approached the flagpole. The sun rose from the direction of Gu-Bulawayo and Lobengula. No word had reached the camp that Lobengula was aware of the size of the column. This had surprised the scouts, and in particular von Brand. James knew that the next day, if General Methuen passed them as fit for the job, they would move across the Macloutsi River into the country disputed over by Lobengula of the Matabele and Khama of the Bechuana. In this stretch of country, they thought they would be safer than in Matabeleland.

"De-tach-ment," Morgan shouted into the morning, breaking the syllables in time with their feet. "Halt." They came to a stop as one sound.

James took two paces forward, left turned and marched the ten paces to the flagpole, where he attached the flag to the outside rope. He held the inside rope and waited for the command.

"Bugler... sound the reveille."

The notes went out to the column and further still to Africa, and as the notes took command over the dawn chorus of birds, James pulled the Union Jack to the top of the flagpole, where it stayed, untouched by the slightest breeze. "Detachment... fall... in." The last word was crisp. They re-formed in lines of three.

Before they had reached the other side of the parade ground, the camp was astir. The smell of wood fires rose into the African dawn. The sun rimmed itself above the clear outline of the mopane trees that stood like sentries along the ridge of hills in Lobengula's country. The rising sun was reflected in the water that ran smoothly along the centre of the riverbed. The nostrils of hippopotamuses rested on the fire of the reflected sun, but the big bodies of the animals remained invisible below the flowing water of the river.

Koos van der Walt started the fire. It took quickly, the sticks dry from the lack of rain. The main rains had finished a month before. James attached their mess can to the metal tripod that straddled the fire, and watched as the mess of beans and bully beef heated up and bubbled stickily.

Van der Walt came back from the river with a can of water which he hung in the flames with the food.

"*Ja*, man, we can't complain with the food," he said, and squatted down to watch their breakfast cook. James prodded the flames with a stick, sending ash into the water and food.

"It'll give it some taste," said James.

"Tell me, *kerel*, what do you think are our chances?" asked van der Walt.

"It depends on whether Lobengula can keep his inDunas under control," replied James. "A successful kingmaker would need a conspiracy, and this will be difficult. The only way might be a general uprising of the impis against his policy towards us, and if this happens our chances of reaching Mount Hampden are negligible. We're taking a gamble, and we've taken as many precautions as possible, but if more than ten thousand heathens attack the column at once, it will be every man to kill as many as possible before he has his gut split open by an assegai. They're the best fighters in Africa, so they won't run at the first sound of the Maxims."

He stirred the breakfast with a clean stick and saw he'd burnt the pan, which went against his image of being a good cook. He unhooked the mess tin and poured the food onto tin plates, helping it out with a stick. He sprinkled ground coffee into the boiling water in the other tin and the strong smell flared his nostrils. They ate in silence though their thoughts were centred on the same subject. The weeks of waiting had built up a hard knot in James's stomach that he hoped would go when the march began. He looked over the bush, over the thorn thickets and mopane trees, to a distant line of hills and the sun, bright and vicious, just clear of the earth and throwing its first yellow light of morning at the bush. The softness and the killings of a night in the bush had given way to the hard reality of day. The bare, stark need for survival was visible.

They finished their food and prepared to fall in on the improvised parade ground. James slung the bandolier of bullets over his shoulder and fastened it at his right side. He picked up his Martini-Henry rifle and marched with Koos van der Walt to join 'A' Troop.

Major Johnson marched to the improvised dais and saluted General Lord Methuen.

"The Pioneer Corps and police detachment are ready for your inspection, sir," said Johnson.

Methuen and Johnson began their inspection and walked along each line of troops and police. General Methuen reached James in the line and looked him up and down but even if he had intimately known the young man who had come down from Oxford five months before, he would have found no resemblance. Along with Willy von Brand and Rhys Morgan, James had grown a beard and the flesh above his eyebrows and below his eyes was burnt mahogany from the sun. The remaining resemblance was in the slate blue eyes that confidently looked back at the general.

"Where are you from, trooper?" asked Methuen.

"England, sir."

"Which part?"

"The Wirral of Cheshire."

"You will find this new country very different to Cheshire."

"That is to be expected, sir."

"We shall see, we shall see," said Methuen, as he passed onto trooper van der Walt. "And your name, trooper?"

"Van der Walt."

"And what makes you join a British Expedition? I assume you are either from the Orange Free State or from Kruger's Transvaal."

"*Die Vrystaat, meneer.*"

"Ah, and you still prefer to talk in the *Taal*. I welcome your joining with us British in this venture. It is a pity that we cannot all get along so well together. I wish you good luck, trooper van der Walt, as I do Africa."

It took the general half an hour to complete his individual inspection, and then the tests got under way. First the seven pounders fired at set targets in the bush, firing in batteries of three. The African bush shrieked back and the snouts of the hippopotamuses disappeared completely. Then the Maxims fired in short bursts.

That evening, at dusk, 'A', 'B' and 'C' troops fanned out and moved into the bush. The thorn thickets took on the shapes of men, and the waving elephant grass became the ostrich feathers of Lobengula's impis. The first target dropped and hung from its rope in a tree some thirty feet from Morgan, who drilled it neatly through the middle, as did two of his men. The shadows moved, and the targets fell from their concealed hides as the dusk came down to an almost darkness, and the only clear line of light was of a target between the gun and the orange fire of the setting sun. The native bearers, pulling the release ropes, kept well down in the holes they had dug for protection.

When the one hundred and fifty targets were brought in for the general to inspect, only three were blank of holes, and most had two marks near the centre.

The column was drawn up informally to hear the verdict. The last hint of light was fading from the sky. The dais had been moved nearer the tents and the contingent squatted on the ground. The final, orange glow of the set sun silhouetted the general. Major Johnson stood beside the dais. The crickets screeched in the long grass, and the African night took up its noises.

"Officers and men of the Pioneer Corps. Officers and men of the British South Africa Company Police," began the general, his voice clear and carrying far into the bush, "you are making history and it is my prayer that it should be good history, and that in its beginning it should not be marred by any incidence that might jeopardise its future. You are at the frontier of the greatest empire this world has ever seen. The flag we stood before at the beginning of this ceremony flies proudly and justly over one fifth of the land surface of the world, and the Royal Navy holds peace in its power throughout the waters that join the Queen's empire. It is a great heritage. In the past, empires have come and gone because they were built on a selfish greed. The British Empire has been built on trade, and trade by its nature must be mutual. It is not surprising, therefore, that we find you going north under the control of a trading company.

"In any system there is good and bad. Because he was not made perfect, it is the tragedy of mankind that these two must always go together, and it is the tragedy of life that harshness and unhappiness must be used in the furtherance of goodness and justice, against evil, and no man, now, or in history, will ever be able to write that the good of our empire was weighed against by evil. It has been our hope, and our success, to give to all the people living within the shade of the Union Jack a better life. I challenge any man to go out and question each of these people, and prove on a balance other than what I claim.

"For man to prosper, he must be led, and to be led is to forfeit some of his unneeded freedom. In our modern world, strong government is essential, or else the jackals of unrest and dissatisfaction, the jackals who know so much better, because they have never faced the problems of leadership, come snapping to destroy the shelter and order of their fellowmen.

"Once again we are setting out to develop another great tract of country, and by our immediate presence we will bring good. Can those who will shout at us for extending our empire deny the rights of the Mashona people to live outside the shadow of the sword? The Matabele will not like you for this, and will say you are stealing what is rightfully theirs, but has any man the right to kill? When the Mashona have forgotten their fear, they will forget their thanks, and some may even clamour to be 'free'. What is freedom? Freedom is peace and prosperity, and no man can deny us our success with this commodity. We do not wield the fire of an invader, we wield the future which will bring through our government peace, prosperity and the right for each man to live without fear for his life. This is the meaning of our empire. We are proud, of that we have the right. It has been said we are arrogant, but that always by the people who envy us. But above all we are just, and it is just and right to see among you today members of the Boer people, who, with us, have placed civilisation at the feet of Africa. May this be the first of many ventures joining our two peoples together in one cause. There are many differences between the British and the Boer at this moment, and the best way to alter this difference is to mingle amongst each other, man to man, and in this way discover that we are the same. The differences of men are made by men, and they can only be solved by the same people.

"A good army is not built to wage war but to prevent war, and to protect those of us who go in peace. It has been prudent to arm you in your venture, but God be your witness if you ever use those arms for other than your own protection or the protection of others. The civilisation to which we belong, and of which we are justly proud, must be remembered by you in the darkest corner of the jungle. Humanity is frail, and will, without strength of mind, revert to its easy course. The course of justice, civilisation and Christianity is not always the simplest path to lead. It is easy to be drawn away from and only to be remembered at damnation. Humility is a virtue; be humble, but do not be frightened to be justly proud of that way of life that you are once again taking into the hinterland. Having a superior civilisation and brain is something to be thankful for and something to be used to the benefit of the less privileged. Someone has always been needed to lead and for the past hundred years it has been the privilege of the British people to provide this leadership. If in the future we are unable and unworthy to govern, then it must be then that we shall pass this burden of leadership to other hands. You are tough, well-trained and led by experts. Acquit yourselves well."

There was no light in the sky. The small sliver of the moon gave up no shadows and the stars had not reached a brilliance. The parade stood up and came to attention.

4

The shouts of the ox drivers could be heard a long way from the crossing on the Macloutsi River. Sixteen oxen strained at the traces of each covered wagon, and the long whips of the drivers stung harshly at the dumb animals. The river was low, and the passage made easier by the well-placed, close-knit rocks that they had put on the riverbed. Scouts were ordered ahead into the bush, and the first to cross the river was Morgan. With a single companion, he rode out into the new country.

"I've been through this country more than a hundred times, Michael," he said to Trooper Fentan, "but this is the first time the place feels still and unfriendly. They must be watching us from somewhere, even if it is only out of curiosity – yet there are no fresh tracks of men. There was buck here last night and that spore just to the left of your horse is warthog and very fresh. Game, but none of Lobengula's heathens. Strange in itself. We were camped on the other side of the Macloutsi for three days, and that's time enough to move up a Matabele army. These bastards can dog-trot fifty miles in a day." He looked around himself. "We'll go and look up to and just beyond those farthest hills," he said, pointing them out. "It's probably a guilt complex, but I feel I am being watched, and yet all my knowledge of the bush tells me that this is impossible. Watchers leave tracks: it's a basic law."

"Maybe the witchdoctors have put the spirits onto us," replied Fentan, without enthusiasm.

"That is probably the answer," agreed Morgan, and he meant it.

They rode on through the outcrops of vast rocks, under the tall mopane trees, and through the long elephant grass of the *vlei*. The sun had not got up over the hills, and the air was cool and fresh, and the night's dew soaked their yellow leggings and the bellies of the horses. Morgan stood up in his stirrups and scanned the surrounding bush with slow, methodical care. There was bush, and the two white horsemen, and nothing else. He sat back in the saddle, uneasy, and let the horse pick its own path through the thickening trees. The smell of dry dust was pleasant and familiar, but the feeling of tension would not go away.

He could hear the column breaking camp behind him. Some of the words drifting out into the still morning were intelligible. There was more comfort in the sweating proximity of the struggling wagons than alone out front. Morgan felt naked, and he had to force down his fear and reintroduce the precision of the tracker. He would be glad when Selous joined them at the Shashi River, as once they crossed the Shashi they would be into the humid lowveld of the Matabele. Morgan knew of a hundred places for the impis to stage a perfect ambush, places that would put them straight among the pioneers, where the guns would have less effect than the stabbing spears. The pioneers each carried an axe for felling the trees that stood in the path of the new road, and Morgan could visualise an axe swinging, hacking, a black-mingling-white kind of sweating slaughter which would slowly subside into a one-sided massacre. It would be academically interesting, he thought to himself coldly, to discover whether the Viking battle axe was a superior weapon to the Roman short sword. Willy von Brand would enjoy the debacle right up to the last moment, of that he was sure, but it gave Morgan no comfort. He thought of Annie and their illegitimate child, the small boy who had not been allowed to carry the name of Morgan, and this made him angry. His upper lip rose slightly on one side, and his fear left him.

At the foot of the hills, before even the horses had to strain their hind legs in the climb, they found human spoor, and they followed it up into the hills.

JAMES AND KOOS VAN DER WALT, stripped to the waist, and up to their knees in water, strained their shoulders at the heavy wooden bar at the back of the wagon, and pushed. The wagon remained stuck with the left wheel wedged between two rocks. The river flowed swiftly between the wooden spokes of the wheel.

"Make the bloody oxen pull together," James shouted at the native driver, who did not speak English. It relieved James's irritation, even though he failed to communicate. The driver stopped using his whip and let the animals rest. On the renewed crack of the whip, man and beast sensed the purpose, and they heaved together – the wagon lurched forward and the animals plodded their way to the bank and up the well-made, rock strewn path of the first few yards of the pioneer road.

The wagon came free of the water, and dripped off the river water. James and van der Walt went back for their horses, and led them into the river. The animals stumbled on the underwater rocks, but crossed safely to the other side. They mounted, and caught up with the wagon, and escorted it through the bushveld for a mile and a half to where they stopped behind the seventh wagon and waited for the remaining fifty-eight to take up their positions for the trek to begin in unison.

Each wagon took up fifty yards. The column, from one end to the other, was over two miles long, and as compact as practical. The few trees in the line of road had been removed by the front working party. The heat rose with the sun, and the flies, attracted to the ox dung, became incessant and buzzed at the corners of James's eyes. He would never get used to the flies, he told himself.

The police detachment took up their positions on either side of the column, at two-hundred-yard intervals. The seven pounders were mounted on the tailboards of four of the wagons. It was up to the scouts to give the column enough time to laager and throw up the defences. If attacked without warning from both sides, they would last a few minutes. The scouts roamed out on all sides of the column, and as the two miles of oxen, wagons, horsemen, spare oxen and horses moved forward, a scouting party hung back to cover their rear. The Matabele fought on foot, and under this system a theoretical hour's warning was possible. The column went forward at the speed it took the pioneers to make a clear path for the road.

The first few miles were sparse of trees, and it was not until the sun was high in the sky that James took his turn felling trees. Like the others, he stripped down to his breeches. First he dug out the earth around the roots of the tree, making a hole twelve feet in diameter around the mopane. The tree had a strong tap root going straight down, a year-round supply of water. James dug down to a depth of four feet, to bare the tap root. While he worked, with the sweat stinging his eyes, van der Walt stood guard with the two horses saddled and the spare Martini-Henry rifle protruding from the saddle holster of James's horse.

After an hour they changed over, and James slung the bandolier of ammunition over his bare shoulder and fastened it correctly. His skin was almost the same colour as the mahogany brown of the leather bandolier – both shone in the sun, one from polish, the other from sweat and health. With van der Walt's cartridge belt over his right shoulder, he stood to with his rifle. His eyes looked through slits made by his eyelids, but there was enough room for his contracted pupils to scan the depth of the bush all around him. Van der Walt took up the shovel and climbed into the hole.

The mopane was one of the largest in the line of road and four other troopers were detached to assist. After half an hour, the roots came bare and van der Walt took up the axe and, aiming his blows at the secondary roots, joined his rhythmic chopping with the rest of the pioneers who were spread out for a mile along the new road with the wagons bunched up behind them. The police patrolled the line constantly and the movement never stopped. The scouts came back at intervals to report and the big trees crashed over, were roped up and pulled away by a chain of men and the hole filled in with rocks and soil on top and the road took up a definite shape.

FENTAN SAW them first and quickly pointed them out to Morgan. Morgan counted eleven Matabele in full battle order; shields, assegais and ostrich feathers. He scanned the bush behind and to the side of them, looking for the main impis. Apart from the eleven jogging Matabele there was no sign of life in the bush.

"Go back and warn the column," said Morgan, "I will stand my ground. The way the bastards always come when the sun is going down gives me the cold shivers. Don't get lost on the way, Michael my boy, or it might be the death of the lot of us."

Fentan turned his horse about carefully, checked the position of the setting sun and put his 'salted' horse into a gallop. Instinctively, he put his head down over the horse's mane, and made his back as small a target as possible. Morgan sat his horse. With his back to the sun, he was clearly visible to the running Matabele, as was his intention. He kept his horse perfectly still and waited as the shields came round to face him. He made no move towards his rifle, which showed its butt clearly behind the horse's neck. The rhythm of their bodies was perfect, and they moved over the broken ground with the minimum of effort. Their speed never varied. As they drew closer, Morgan was able to see from their shields that they were from the Babambeni regiment, the personal bodyguards of the king. Morgan dismounted before they reached his horse, and held his empty hands out towards the Matabele. Their spokesman did the same and was immediately recognised by Morgan as one of the king's inDunas. They watched each other and no one moved.

"I see you, Morgan," said the Matabele in Ndebele.

"I see you, Nugeli," answered Morgan in the same language, and waited.

"I bring a message from Lobengula, and this message is for Rhodes."

"Rhodes is not with us."

"Then give this message to the inDuna of your impis. 'Has the king killed any white men that an impi is on the borders, or have the white men lost something they are looking for?'"

They stared at each other. Morgan looked at each of their expressionless faces.

"I will give our inDuna that message," he said.

The eleven Matabele turned about and quickly took up their previous pace, but in the opposite direction. Morgan waited till they were out of sight. With the light fading, he searched the surrounding bush with his eyes, section by section, but found nothing. Then he remounted his horse, turned it about and put it into a gallop to cover the ten miles back to the column.

When he found the wagons they were in perfect laager on the banks of the Shashi River. In all, they had covered twenty miles from the Macloutsi River. The laager was diamond shaped with the seven pounders at each point. The wagons were in the exact line of the diamond with the spare oxen, the horses and the men behind the stockade. He drew rein half a mile from the laager, and for the eighth time stood up in his stirrups and scanned the bush behind him. The light was almost gone. There was no wind and nothing moved.

The laager was quiet as he rode up and through the small gap that they made for him. He delivered the message to Major Johnson, who shrugged his shoulders and gave more attention and interest to the detailed report of the possible enemy action.

"You don't think there is a powerful impi close at hand?" asked Johnson.

"If there is, they have taken great care not to show themselves," Morgan answered. "I do not think they will attack us in the disputed territory. When the column crosses the Shashi River into Matabeleland, then they must show their strength or let us pass."

"Selous will be joining us in two days," said Johnson. "He will have definite information. For tonight, we will stand prepared and tomorrow we will mount the guns carefully to protect the crossing. It is our intention to build a fort on the other side of the river. This will hold the line of communication if we are to go on, then we do so and we ignore Lobengula. There was never the intention of turning back."

As they spoke, the dynamo started, and the searchlight began to play its beam of light into the bush from on top of the most prominent wagon.

THE KING WAS SEATED in a red armchair just outside his sleeping hut. Gathered around him were the inDunas of many of his regiments. They were squatting on their haunches, watching him. They were a nuisance to him, and a source of irritation. He argued with them, but when they did not agree they just sat there and said nothing. By their silence, he could not bring his wrath to bear on any one of them, and they hoped that this way the king would not be able to purge them all at once.

"They will only dig in the ground," Lobengula said yet again. "They will not steal my cattle. They have come for the gold, and with the gold that they will give us as payment I will buy more cattle, and I will be stronger... It is a big country – they will not bother us."

There was silence, and then the inDunas shuffled on their haunches.

"If we let in a few," said the inDuna of the Siziba regiment, against his better judgement on the matter of speaking his mind to the king, "there will be many more of them coming in afterwards. Look what they did to the Zulus, and when the great Zulu nation drew up its strength it was too late; there were too many of them in the country, and the white queen sent her soldiers, and soon after this the great Zulu impis were defeated."

"And you think," said the king, telling himself to be rid of the inDuna of the Siziba regiment and all his family, "that the white

queen will not again send her warriors if we kill this white impi that
is approaching the belly of our country? You are fools, all fools. If
they dig for the gold in peace, then we will grow rich at their
expense. This is sense. There will be many more cattle and it is a
big country. Go away, all of you, and leave me in peace before I lose
my temper."

One by one, the inDunas got up off their haunches and made to
move from the king's indaba.

"And how will you fight their eye, that watches you even in the
night?" the king threw at their backs.

They looked at him uneasily, and he leered at them, sensing
that he had scored a point.

"We will attack them during the day," said the inDuna of the
Siziba regiment with confidence, as he was as much frightened as
the rest of them of the light that shone out at night, that was neither
the moon nor the stars. "We are not afraid of what we can see. Many
from our impis will die if we attack in the day, but this has always
been the price of war. We are not afraid to die."

"And when you kill one white impi, there will be another,"
shouted Lobengula.

"Then we will die again," said the inDuna of the Siziba
regiment.

"You are ignorant fools and you have made me lose my temper. I
am the judge of your ills, and I say it is a false policy to attack this
white impi."

The king continued to sit in the big armchair that a white
concession hunter had given to him. He did not know which one it
was, as there had been so many. He had a hut full of an assortment
of useless trivialities. They had all wanted the same thing, and now
that he had given it to one of them, he had hoped they would not
bother him anymore. It was a big armchair, but the bulk of the king
had broken the springs, and on the one side the red frills hung in
the dust. The colour of the heavy fabric had faded in the sun. The
king was tired. The inDunas shuffled away but without enthusiasm.
They looked back at Lobengula, and talked amongst themselves.

They were not satisfied, but they were too frightened for their own lives, and the lives of their families, to voice any more of their opinions. They could see that Lobengula was close to violence.

"Get out of my sight," Lobengula shouted at them. They made a hasty departure, each one of them trying not to be the last out of the narrow gap that stood in the thatched grass wall that surrounded the king's huts.

Lobengula put his fat arms along the sides of his chair, let his head drop onto one side, and prepared himself for a pleasant snooze in the sun. He waited, but he could not sleep. If it was not the white men bickering amongst themselves, it was his own inDunas. If they were all going to be like this, he thought, maybe it would be better if they killed each other and left him in peace. It was too hot, and he was too tired to think about it anymore, and still he could not sleep. He would kill the inDuna of the Siziba regiment, he decided, and this gave him satisfaction.

It was good, he thought to himself after a while, that he had sent his scouts to watch the white men. The reply to his message had not been satisfactory, in that he had received nothing back, but then nothing was satisfactory. The white impi had crossed the Shashi River, and now they were cutting this road into his country. Maybe his inDunas would take it into their own hands and attack. He tried putting his head on the other side, but this did not make him sleep either. Slowly it came to him as he tried to sleep that for the first time in twenty years his power was being challenged. He sat up in the chair and faced the fact. The old power and strength began to warm the inside of his belly and it tried to stop the process of decay that had taken hold of him in the past three years. He was king, and for this he had a responsibility to his people. He again began to sift all the problems through his mind and began to search for a strong and lasting answer.

JAMES AND MORGAN saddled up and mounted their horses. They rode out of the camp on patrol with the sun halfway down the afternoon sky. Morgan saw that the rock walls of the fort were high enough and only needed the tin roof that had been brought up for the purpose. They would move out tomorrow, he thought.

The country was thickly populated by thorn thicket and rock outcrops. It was impossible to check the ground for more than a fifty-yard radius. There was a rich smell of humidity.

After half an hour, Morgan smelt game. He reined in his horse and signalled James to stop. Morgan dismounted and bent down to the dry, sun-scorched earth between the dry, twigged and thorned thickets, and picked up a handful of the fine topsoil. He straightened up and let the earth trickle from the bottom of his clenched fist. The slight wind took the tail of the falling dust out towards James. The wind was steady and from a constant direction.

"We are upwind of buffalo," said Morgan. "It's a big herd... about a mile, over there. Can you smell that rich, powerful smell that comes in waves every few minutes?... There it is. A good fifty buffalo." All the signs of care and worry had gone from his face. "To hell with the Matabele," he said, getting up into the saddle, "let's go and get some buffalo meat. In this kind of country, we are just as likely to flush a ten thousand impi by mistake. You must shoot the buffalo just below the big horns or in its heart," he continued, pursuing his main subject, "they are brave animals, and as clever and dangerous as the Matabele."

They moved off into the wind and towards the buffalo. Regularly, Morgan dismounted and picked up a handful of dust to check the wind's direction. The rich smell grew stronger. They kept the horses to a walk. The excitement of his first buffalo hunt gripped James. For the first time in four months, he forgot the existence of the column.

"We'll dismount and hobble the horses," said Morgan in a low voice. "From here, we go forward by foot. The cover is good and, if luck is with us, we can get to within thirty yards. My estimate is that they are over there, about a quarter of a mile. They stand quite still in the heat of the day, usually amongst trees. Unless you know, it is difficult to tell when the black mass of thorn thicket ends and the buffalo starts."

They pulled their Martini-Henry rifles from the saddle holsters and dismounted. They tied the ropes to the horses' legs to prevent them from straying, and took the safety catches off the guns. Morgan took another sample of the wind and, bending himself double, began to stalk the buffalo. It was a slow process; James kept behind Morgan, imitating his actions. The smell of buffalo was strong, and constant. Morgan kept the rocks and heavy thorn thickets between himself and where he expected to find the buffalo. His pace grew slower.

"They must be just over there," he whispered. "If we wait, one of them will move, and we'll be able to see the others."

They waited but saw nothing. The sun burnt at the back of James's neck. Morgan began to move carefully forward again, and he followed. They went ten yards, and Morgan held the palm of his hand back towards James. They poised, motionless. James searched the bush for buffalo, but without any success. Morgan's hand directed him to move behind a rock.

"There are more than a hundred," breathed Morgan, when they were behind cover.

"I can't see them," said James.

"They are quite motionless. Lean forward slightly behind that bush growing out of the rock crevice. Now, over to the right. That big thorn thicket. Watch it carefully. It's a very sparse thorn thicket – the black depth is buffalo."

James watched carefully, and slowly the head of an animal took shape from the thicket. He followed back from the head and made out the body, which merged with another buffalo. The animals were huge. He made out more animals. The whole thorn thicket was interspersed by buffalo, and he saw how easy it would be for the Matabele to hide themselves in ambush in such country, and his fear returned.

"Make up your mind which one you can hit best, and we'll fire together," said Morgan. "Make sure of your aim, because if you don't kill him the first time it means a long business to hunt him down. A wounded buffalo is never left alive, because it will wait and kill, and it may not be you or me but another member of the column. Go for the heart, the brain is too difficult a target from here. That one over there is mine."

James found his target, tapped Morgan on the shoulder, and pointed it out to him. Morgan nodded his head in approval. He indicated that he would fire kneeling, and that James should fire standing, keeping the explosion as far from Morgan's eardrums as possible. The guns came up.

"One," breathed Morgan, "two, three, fire."

From out of the silence, the double explosion deafened them both. The bush crashed into life, as the herd stampeded away from them. James's animal tried to run with the others. It took a few bewildered paces, stopped, shook its great head, the horns heavy, and sank down onto its front knees. James watched with anguish. Morgan ran out to cover his dead animal just in case it found enough life to run off and thwart him. Through the buzzing in his ears from the gun shots, James could hear the live members of the herd crashing their way deeper into the bush. The earth shook with the pounding of their feet. He lowered his gun, and stepped out from behind the cover. Thirty yards in front of him, Morgan knelt on one knee beside his animal.

"Instant death," he called back to James, "and yours didn't live much longer. It was worth giving you all that shooting practice," he laughed. "If any of the Matabele saw that piece of ironmongery, they'll keep away."

James walked out towards his dead buffalo, crossing the thirty yards of bush. He looked down at the carcase. It was no longer an animal, but meat. The soul of its living had gone away, leaving it like the other meat that James had eaten every week of his life. It was the law of nature. It left James with a great respect for the departed soul of the beast.

"Now we have the big job," said Morgan, taking out a hunting knife with a foot long blade. "This is Morgan, the butcher," he said, and plunged the knife into the animal's rump. "We take back the good meat now, and send the natives out for the rest. Our patrol is not due in till midnight, so we'll camp here and eat. We can gather as much information about our friends here as anywhere else."

It took them an hour to cut out the rumps and the choice sections of meat. Morgan knew the ants would get to the carcasses during the night, but it was up to the natives to wash the remaining meat clean. Ants did not create disease. When they finished, Morgan cut the small kidneys out of the inside of the animals and put them to one side, together with a large piece of fillet. He cut two half-inch-thick, forked sticks from a sugar bush tree, and another much longer, straight stick to go across the fire to make up the spit.

Their fire burnt rapidly, and then the flames died down, and left behind the hot embers of the wood. Morgan put the straight stick through the meat and balanced it between the forked sticks over the fire. He sat back on his haunches to watch. Night came down, and their world was that of the firelight, and the shadows of the mopane trees and the thorn thickets. One baobab tree stood sentinel, its girth more than fifty feet round, and its giant head a disaster of wasted growth, a growth that had dissipated its strength in the trunk, and had had no power left but to leave the arms of the giant stunted and tapered to a pathetic nothing.

To James, the hole at the base and the old, hunched-up witch were all that was missing. In the dark, the tree reminded him of England. He thought back to Halmeston, and pondered on whether his father had replied to his letter. He had received no mail in Africa, having been on the move ever since his arrival. England, to James, seemed a whole life away. Even Camp Cecil, on the banks of the Limpopo, was a far distance of time in terms of toil and fear. He looked around himself at the dark, new country. The moon was a week away from being full, and the pale light threw ethereal shadows through the bush. He felt content. The fat from the meat dropped onto the embers, hissed and flared. He felt the great space around him, and relished the feeling of total freedom. There was no convention here. Morgan turned the spit and the fat hissed and flared, cooking the buffalo meat in its own juice. The smell sent saliva up into James's mouth.

"You know, Rhys, I could make a farm right here," he said.

"Wait till you get up onto the highveld. There is too much fly here. By the tone of your voice, you've found the feeling we have for Africa."

"I suppose so. Let's hope we reach Mount Hampden, as this is going to be a great country to live in."

"You are right."

They both watched the meat slowly cooking, and neither of them spoke for some time.

"Jim, will you do something for me?" said Morgan, as he turned the spit. "If I don't live long enough, will you make sure my son inherits the farm I am going to carve out of the highveld?"

"I didn't know you were married," said James in surprise.

"I am not," said Morgan. "Gavin is a bastard."

"Who is the mother?" asked James, slowly.

"The Honourable Annabel Levenhurst. We thought it was the only way that that father of hers would let us marry. We thought if we disgraced ourselves enough, he would kick her out." He took the meat off the fire. "The kidneys are cooked," he said, and pulled one of them off with the point of his hunting knife and offered it to James. "Have your first buffalo's kidney and may the animal's strength be yours."

James took the meat and cut the kidney in half with his own knife, and nibbled a piece. The flavour was stronger than any meat he had eaten before.

Morgan threw more wood on the fire. The flames sprang up and the shadows danced out further into the endless bush. James did not prompt him. It was Morgan's conversation. James remembered the rumours of Levenhurst's daughter, but little else. The affairs of the big Cheshire families were of great concern to his father. If Ernest Carregan had been invited to dine at the home of Lord Levenhurst, he would, James thought, have considered his life fulfilled. James had been a boy at the time of the scandal, and had given it no attention. The conversation with the barman in the Harbour Tavern came back to him. He put the two rumours together.

Morgan threw more wood on the fire. He cut the fillet in half and gave one piece to James, together with the other kidney.

"There is one thing I cannot tolerate in this life," said Morgan, "and that is snobbery. How the man managed to produce such a daughter is a mystery to me. I never met the mother – she had been dead some years, so it could be there. I didn't set about looking for a titled girl to put in the family way, if that's what you're thinking. I didn't need another man's name and money to give me my chance in life." There was both scorn and bitterness in his voice. "We met at the university theatre – one of those charity evenings. I was moving scenery, and had been invited to the champagne drinking afterwards. She had sold more than ten tickets at charity prices, and had been invited as a result. The only mistake we made was to fall in love with each other."

He paused and the night sounds of Africa and the sounds of the crackling fire took over for a moment.

"Talk of love must sound strange coming from me, sitting here in the African bush, with an unwashed beard and wearing last week's clothes, but I was still the same person in those days – younger, but the same inside. I told myself, at first, that it was a case of wanting what I couldn't have, but the relationship was not tied up with property and names and impressing my friends. It was a friendship of she and I, to the complete exclusion of everything and everyone else. We were as we truly wanted to be when we were on our own, not talking, but close enough to touch, and to be with each other. This was the knowledge that we completely loved, and accepted the other without reason. It went on during my final year of law at Liverpool University. We met regularly, but never officially."

He lapsed into silence. James let him think.

"I would not be telling you this, Jim," he went on, "if I did not have a great trust in you. I must protect Gavin. At the moment, he is being brought up by foster parents in Liverpool, but in another seven years, when he is eighteen, he will be free and able to join his father. Annie married in the end, and I don't blame her for this, as it wasn't much of a life for her in Levenhurst's home, constantly being told that she was a whore. After my final, we thought it possible to go to her father. We both knew exactly what he was, but had one of those stupid notions of youth that the sight of the two of us together would melt the old bastard's heart.

"'And what,' he said to me," Morgan mimicked, "'is your father?' 'A sheep farmer,' I replied. 'You cannot, young man, imagine that I can allow my daughter to marry the son of a sheep farmer; and a Welsh sheep farmer at that. I am sure you have had lots of pretty little conversations together, about all these new ideas of empire that all these people go to universities to talk about, but I suggest it ends there and now. My daughter is a Levenhurst, Morgan; though it seems as though you have forgotten.'

"I knew we would have a problem getting him to agree, but I thought the world of 1878 was a little more enlightened than when the Queen first ascended the throne. We left it at that, but thereafter it was very difficult for Annie to get out of the house without an escort. She pleaded with him for six months, and then we struck on the only solution we thought would work. If he would not have me, then he must be forced to throw his daughter out of the house. We thought that to save his name, he would have to act in this way. People, Jim, never act to form.

"She was four months pregnant when she told him, as we didn't want him trying any accidents with our child. I think he enjoyed the even greater power that it gave him over her. He instructed her not to leave the house and told her, without emotion, that when the bastard was born and weaned, it would be given to foster parents, after which she would be made to find a husband, if she now found it impossible to control herself in the company of men. I cheated and bribed, but I have no idea how many of my messages reached her hands. I received few scattered messages, and pieced together what was happening from these. The only time she went out of the house in ten months was when he himself took her for a drive.

"I received one letter from Annabel during this time and it reached me with the approval of her father. When I had read the letter, I made plans to leave England, and shortly afterwards I sailed for Africa. As I want you to be the trustee of my will, you had better read the letter. I know it word for word; be careful with the paper, it is very flimsy at the creases."

James took the pieces of paper that Morgan carefully took from his wallet, opened it up, and began to read the letter by the light of the fire.

 My Darling,

Our child was a boy and I have called him Gavin. They took him away two weeks ago, to his new parents in Liverpool, and I have cried nearly all the time since. He was a strong boy and you would have been proud of him. They will not tell me where he has been sent, so we will never know.

Darling, even though these last ten months have been the loneliest months of my life, and having Gavin without you close to me was a torture I could never endure again, I do not regret a moment. Our love will go to the grave, and they will never be able to take this away from either of us. There is much life ahead, and many things may happen to you and me, and Gavin.

Darling, the joy of seeing him the first time. I yearned to enjoy him with you. I just wanted the three of us so much that even the old nurse began to cry with me. I have done a lot of crying, and I'm sorry, and I know you don't let yourself cry like that. He will be a strong boy, like his father. I think my father was purposely torturing me by letting me keep the child for five months. I want my baby. As all is my witness, I will hate my father for the rest of my life. He has used words like 'I do this in your best

*interest' but how can he have been so cruel to his own
daughter. If mater had been alive, this would never have
been allowed to happen. He will read this letter, and what
I have said is my heart, and what I am about to say is
why he will let me send you all of this letter. It is our little
bargain! I can say what I will, provided I make it clear to
you that I am shortly to be married.*

*Married, my darling, I will be – they have had their
way for so long – but in love, never. They can have my
body, because that is physical, but they have no means of
finding my love or my heart. Edgar Crichton was the only
one up to Father's so called standards who would accept
the stigma of Gavin and still go ahead with a marriage. I
don't know him very well, but I fancy he is as much
interested in marrying the daughter of a wealthy peer as
anything else. After ten months of this solitary
confinement, and losing Gavin, and with no chance of
being with you again, I have lost all my will to fight. It
cannot be worse, submitting to Edgar Crichton, than
Father. I will have a house to run, and things to do, and a
little less time to think about you and Gavin.*

*What else can I do, my love? I cannot stay in this
house forever. This is my only way out. I know how much
you have tried to reach me, but it is not possible. I am not
myself. I have been tortured by my solitude, which is a
million times worse now that I neither have Gavin inside
of me or close to me here in this room. Forgive me, my
darling, but may all our dreams be fulfilled in Gavin. Find
him. Find our child.*

Annie

It took James some moments before he could fold the letter and
give it back to Morgan. He kept looking at the pages even when he
had finished. He had no words except questions: Why hadn't she
run away? Why hadn't she waited until she came of age? Why did

she have to marry? But James was certain that Morgan had asked himself all these questions. They were very young, was probably the fatal answer, and moreover, they'd had no one else to turn to.

"I found Gavin," Morgan went on, taking the letter and folding it back into his wallet, "by sheer bloody determination, but the people with him had all the right papers, and by all the laws, they had more right to my son than myself. I struck a bargain with them, as even if I had my son I had no means of bringing him up, and then again I was going to Africa, and what could I have done with an eight-month-old child out here? They agreed to send him to a school of my nomination, with my money, and, when he reached the age of eighteen, to tell him the correct story and to allow him to make up his own mind. The man had agreed with Levenhurst never to divulge the secret, but the woman had a good heart, and so did the husband. They had no children of their own, and I could see they would look after Gavin to the best of their ability. When I have it, I send them money outside of his school fees, which I fixed in a trust fund with my father's money before I left England. They don't have much, and Liverpool is a cold place in the winter."

He got up and went to the horses and gave them some water.

"Will you do what I ask?" he said, when he had finished.

"Yes, of course I will, Rhys, but nothing is going to happen to you."

"It may be you, it may be me, both or nothing, but there is a good chance of any one of them, and you know it as well as I. You don't have any bastards of your own tucked away, so that I can do the reverse?"

"No," laughed James. "I haven't the knack for that one."

"Right, then let's pack up the meat, and begin our night patrol for those ostrich-feathered heathens."

They struck camp, and within five minutes were making their way through the bush, climbing the kopjes and looking for fires, smelling the night air for woodsmoke, and listening.

When they rejoined the column at midnight, they had seen nothing, but the meat was welcome. They gave directions and instructions for the carcases to be found in the morning, and went to their respective tents.

James dreamt of England that night. Ernest Carregan and Levenhurst seemed to merge into the same person, and they were chasing James, and laughing at him, but there was only cruelty in their laughter. When he woke with the dawn, he felt uneasy and as if he had had no sleep.

"You were having a nightmare, man," said van der Walt, as he opened the flap of their tent. "Were you dreaming of Lobengula?"

"No, Koos, a man called Levenhurst. I hope I didn't disturb your sleep."

James got up, still wearing his breeches and boots, as they all did at night, and looked through the flap of the tent. Vivid colours of sunrise shrieked out from the horizon behind the hills and trees in front of him. He walked out of the tent, and the fresh, clean air of the morning bathed his face and the hot palms of his hands. He took a deep breath and walked on down to the Shashi River to wash his face.

5

---

*W*hen James went down with malaria, they put him in a wagon, the heat and sweat oozing the strength from his body and the sudden cold of the fever tautening his muscles. Van der Walt fed him with broth made from kudu and treated the fever as his forefathers had done, in the belief that it was an evil that weak men died from, but strong men lived through if you fed them properly. James was strong when the fever came on, but after four days of the constant twisting and delirium he had become feeble.

"You did well, my friend," said van der Walt, "and despite your soft background and all that education, it is going to take a lot of Africa to kill you. I think this is your country, man."

"I hope you are right, though at the moment I am not so sure," answered James as he rolled his head over to look at van der Walt. "There is nothing very friendly about a country that puts you on your back like a sack of new potatoes and without the strength to lift your arm. Your people must have had a great fight to tame the Orange Free State and the Transvaal."

"*Ja*, man," said van der Walt, "but they were used to that kind of life. The trek was in their blood, like it is in mine. We are always looking for that piece of land where the grass is so sweet and the river never runs dry. It is a dream we have all had for three hundred years. Some of us find these farms, but within two generations we have too many children, and to split up the farm again makes them too small to work, and so the trek starts again to the north. That is why I am with this column. There is no land left for me on my father's farm. I do not want the fifteen gold claims up there, but I do want the two thousand *morgen*. I will sell my gold claims for more land. The land you can see and know if it is good. I can choose the good soil that will give fat cattle and rich crops. The gold may not even be there. Must I waste my effort looking for something else when all that new land is there and ready for the plough? You mark me well and take up the land, and do not get that look of a gold prospector."

"I have thought of this," said James, "but Morgan and I have decided to give the gold six months. To develop a farm needs a lot of equipment, and equipment sent up this road is going to be expensive. If, after six months, we have found nothing, then we will make a farm with our bare hands."

"When you come back I will show you the farming."

"Those words will cost you dearly in time," said James and let his head loll back to look up at the canvas roof while he recharged his strength.

James recovered slowly; it was eight days after the fever had come on that he was again able to walk.

THE COLUMN WAS STRUNG out over three and a half miles when James reached the south bank of the Lundi River. It was a third of the way through the dry season, and the vast river held a trickle of water in its centre. Pools of water were scattered among the boulders of its bed. James went down with the others into one of the large pools of water; not even the thought of crocodiles could keep him out of the coolness. As he floated on his back, he looked up at the tall trees that leaned towards him from the south bank of the river.

Most of the column had laagered when a lone horseman was seen walking his horse along the treeless, short-bushed scrub of the great pan of the Lundi River. James watched with curiosity. The man did not increase his speed and the horse, hanging its head, took its own pace. Selous rode out to meet the man, and James watched the horseman being escorted into the pioneer camp and straight to Colonel Pennefather and Dr Jameson. Major Willoughby, in charge of the police, Major Johnson and three officers commanding 'A', 'B' and 'C' troops were called to beneath the huge tree that spread its bows down to the river at an angle of thirty degrees. They were set apart from the men, out of earshot.

James saw Morgan and von Brand join the party and greet the traveller.

"There is no need for me to introduce Johan Colenbrander," began Selous, when the senior officers and scouts were assembled. "Sufficient to say that we have hunted together for many years, and that I have a high regard for his knowledge and understanding of this part of Africa. He is a man that I have never seen frightened, and the import of his message from Lobengula is therefore the stronger. Those of us here control the destiny of the column, and the lives of everyone concerned. These are not light responsibilities. You must all know that Lobengula has never given exact permission for an expedition, the size of the one in front of us, to enter his country.

"Mr Rhodes's ownership of the Rudd concession, which gives him the right to dig for gold, was meant to be negatised by the Lippert concession, which Lobengula granted a few months afterwards. I know Lobengula and, to some extent, the way in which his mind works. He was sick and tired of the concession hunters, and I must say I do not blame him for his impatience, as there were more than enough of them in Gu-Bulawayo. He therefore took to putting his thumb print and elephant seal on pieces of paper in the full knowledge of their content, and the fact that they conflicted.

"What he did not understand was our method of purchasing concessions from each other, as we do property. Lobengula was amazed when he was told that Mr Rhodes was the beneficiary of both concessions. It was then that he sent two of his senior inDunas to England. When they came back, they told him of the strength of England – they had been purposely taken to Woolwich to see British Army exercises. They also told him that the Queen had granted a Royal Charter, based on the very concessions he had signed. This indicated to him that he was also involved with the Queen and, up till now, it has prevented him from having a direct confrontation with Mr Rhodes. Instead, he became evasive. Even the message Major Johnson received at the Shashi River was ambiguous. It asked a question, to which it received no reply. Now he has sent a white man, whose word he knows I will understand and respect. Mr Colenbrander has come direct from the king's kraal at Gu-Bulawayo with the following message, which I will give to you as a verbatim translation from the Ndebele – 'Go back at once and take your young men or I will not be answerable for the consequences.'

"Mr Colenbrander states that if we do not comply with this order, and even if the king still does not want bloodshed for fear of reprisal, Lobengula will be unable to control his inDunas and their impis. To give pressure to Lobengula's instruction, Mr Colenbrander states that there is a nine thousand strong impi across our line of march, twenty miles on from here. Mr Colenbrander," he said, turning to the newcomer, "will you give these gentlemen your opinion of the situation."

Von Brand looked out over the Lundi and licked his dry lips.

"Lobengula," said Colenbrander, "is agitated, to the extent that he sent me with this message, but the inDunas and their impis are a great deal more militant than the king. Lobengula has always given protection to white men in his country, provided they comply with his laws. He is a patriarch and a despot who has enjoyed bestowing favours on the likes of myself, Mr Selous, Mr von Brand and Mr Morgan. It has therefore given him a sense of power even outside that which he holds over his own people. He enjoys power, and this is the only thing that he considers of great value. He will be generous, and the protection he has given to the white man has never been challenged by his impis, despite their constant wish to the contrary, provided that he is fawned to as the king.

"Suddenly, Lobengula has been confronted by a challenge to his power and, despite the ultimate threat from the Queen, he feels that Mr Rhodes has not honoured his bargain, in that your column is not a small body of gold prospectors, which is what he expected, and probably would have allowed. He sees you as a military force and a direct challenge to his authority. Even more, you did not go to Gu-Bulawayo, to sit there for a few weeks until the king felt your stay was long enough to show your respect. If it had pleased him, you would then have been given permission to go forward. Mr Rhodes knew, as did we all, that a force such as this one in front of us would not have been given this permission.

"The king has shown his good sense by not having your column attacked. He has now given fair warning even though he knows that it is better to attack in the first place. My advice, for the sake of peace and for your own lives, is to go back. You are heading for the most treacherous part of your journey. You have yet to climb up through the mountains to the highveld, and, winding up through the hills, it will be each man for himself. Your cannon and machine guns will have little value against the Matabele assegai. Gentlemen, they can wipe you out to a man. Go back."

There was a silence for some moments, while no one looked at another. Colenbrander looked around him, but they did not meet his eyes.

"You've got the shits," said von Brand, and everyone turned to look at him. His back was still to the tree and its attendant uncertainty. Von Brand's face gave no sign of his normal frivolity.

"You do not agree, Mr von Brand?" said Colenbrander. "You are prepared to sacrifice the lives of those young men over there, and probably that of any European living in Lobengula's country?"

"Ah, now we have it," replied von Brand, "it is not only the column that brings you horsed and spurred from the king's kraal, it is the thought of your hunting ground being unsafe for the likes of yourself."

"Do you challenge my integrity?"

"No, I just mention it in passing." They watched the two hunters, and Morgan looked across at Selous, whom he saw was not going to intervene.

"And what do you propose?" asked Colenbrander.

"To go on as we have always intended," answered von Brand.

"And get killed in the process?" said Colenbrander.

"That is the chance of life, Mr Colenbrander," said von Brand, "and, having faced so many chances in your life, it gives me surprise to find you shrinking from a little danger."

"Are you suggesting that I am afraid?" asked Colenbrander.

They faced each other. There was a twisted humour in von Brand's expression but none in Colenbrander's.

"You make it sound that way to the others who don't know you so well," said von Brand. "I wouldn't say it was so much a fear for the loss of your life, but a fear for the loss of your way of life."

"It never crossed my mind," answered Colenbrander.

"You're lying, Johan," said von Brand. "You wouldn't be human if you hadn't thought of that one. The day of us hunters will be over once this column reaches Mount Hampden."

"I came a long way to give you the warning and an honest opinion," said Colenbrander.

"All right. All right," said von Brand wearily. "Let's have no more of expediency. You've had your say. You have honoured your obligation to king and country, and don't think I don't know that old black bastard as well as you. You are trying to put the responsibility of your prophesized disaster on the shoulders of the few of us here, but your picture of terror has been painted many times before. On the last public occasion we were all, man for man, given the opportunity of taking an honourable discharge. We were told that if we did not have the stomach for danger, then we should withdraw to save ourselves from becoming a burden on others. Oh, yes, and a number withdrew, but the ones that remained have got the stomach. Mr Colenbrander, sir, every man out there," and he pointed at the column behind him, while he stared coldly at Colenbrander, "knows what his dangers can be. Gentlemen," and he turned to them all, "we are not leading an ordinary group of men. Those are not the kind who run home to the strings of their mothers' aprons at the first sign of danger. Those are men who have hacked and sweated, and nearly died, through some of the filthiest country in Africa – and they are still here. Look at them, and you will see that none of them are looking back. Must it be a German to tell an English expedition not to retreat?"

"No one has mentioned retreat," said Colonel Pennefather and Morgan smiled to himself at the guile of von Brand.

"Go and ask them," said Colenbrander, "go and tell them the situation and let them stand justice at their own murder."

"Murder," said von Brand, and paused, "is not a word to apply to a military expedition, under military oath, and in uniform, when it meets its Maker in action. What a war you would conduct, if, every time you attacked you told your men they might die, and that any of them who did not wish to make such a sacrifice should withdraw."

"This is not a war," answered Colenbrander.

"By the sound of your words, it's just this, that the old bastard is trying to make of it," said von Brand and turned to the others. "Those men have thought of death," he went on. "It is just such a challenge that we are now facing that has sent them here. If they must die, they will die fighting, and not cursing their officers for having taken them into odds that could not be defeated. There are nearly five hundred of us against nine thousand heathens. Is this not fair odds? Or rather, are they not the odds that we have discussed between ourselves from Cape Town to Kimberley and Mafeking to the Macloutsi?"

"I have delivered the warning," said Colenbrander, "and have given you my honest, unbiased opinion, despite what dear Willy here would say to the contrary. It is for you other gentlemen to make your decision. Make up your minds slowly. Think really of what you are up against. Do not let the bravado of patriotism make a wrong decision. Your bluff has been called, you know it, I know it, and so does Lobengula. You will never finish your road and, if you go on, the vultures will take but a small time to pick your bones clean. There will always be another way for Mr Rhodes to make his money."

No one spoke.

"Gentlemen," went on von Brand, pleading, "is the situation any worse now than what we have expected for weeks, except that we have been warned? Surely, by this warning, we are in a stronger position than before. If we are attacked, we defend ourselves, and if our methods of scouting are what we intend them to be, we will have some warning, even in the worst country. We must maintain a number of defensive positions along the line of road which will take a few minutes to reach, and at night we must tighten the laager. If the king is so sure of his strength and his position, then why has he left it till now before he threatens? With good order and, yes, some luck, there is always that in life, we will reach Mount Hampden."

They went back to their own thoughts, and no one looked at von Brand. Morgan walked away from the big tree and looked out northwards over the Lundi. The column was making camp, and the activity was similar to many previous occasions. He looked back at the road they had made, and saw where it wound through the lowveld and lost itself in the heat haze. If they turned back, he thought, it would be a sign of weakness, and an encouragement to the impi to take the situation into their own hands. There was far more broken country behind them, even if it was not so dangerous. He knew they had gone too far to go back, but he agreed with Colenbrander that there was a good chance of massacre. He knew the Matabele well enough for the column not to show weakness or even a trace of uncertainty. If the situation was put to the column, the word would reach the Matabele through one of the attendant natives, as would be the case in reverse. He knew what he had let himself in for at the very beginning.

"What do you say, Mr Selous?" asked Colonel Pennefather.

"I was engaged to guide you to Mount Hampden," replied

Selous, "and I will not retract from my obligation. As to the danger – my views are known."

"Dr Jameson," asked Pennefather, "what would Mr Rhodes have to say in this situation?"

"I have never known Mr Rhodes to go back on a purpose or to take the decision of an officer in whom he has trust."

There was a pause while they looked at Dr Jameson.

"Major Willoughby?" went on Colonel Pennefather.

"At the worst, we will be in a position to put up an extensive fight."

"Major Johnson?"

"I don't like walking backwards."

"Captains Heany, Hoste and Roach. Have you anything to add to this conversation, before I make known my decision?"

There was no answer.

"Mr Morgan," said Pennefather to Morgan's back, "as the youngest of the hunters, does your insight and experience tell you anything more than we have heard?"

"It has all been said," said Morgan, turning back to the group.

"Then, Mr Colenbrander, will you be so kind as to convey to Lobengula my reply in the name of Queen Victoria – 'we have not come this far to go back.' I thank you for your concern, and your sincere well meaning. I do not in any way reiterate some of the sentiments implied by Mr von Brand, but I think you two gentlemen know each other sufficiently well to speak as you did without retaining any animosity. You will eat with me, of course, Mr Colenbrander, before you return to Gu-Bulawayo. We will give you provisions for your return journey... And now, gentlemen, I think we have a great deal of work to do. We have taken every precaution up till now – now we will take more. I wish you all a safe journey to Mount Hampden."

6

"*L*ook at them," said Morgan, "they raise more dust than the buffalo."

"They are trying to frighten us," said von Brand. "I have the feeling that Lobengula has still not given his permission for them to attack."

"You could be right. I have never before heard of them moving parallel to their quarry for three days."

Their horses moved forward at the same pace as the marching Matabele, some half a mile distant. The Matabele were not in formation. The black mass of feathered heathens moved forward like a mass of army ants.

LOBENGULA KNEW STRENGTH, and the words spoken to him were not the words of weakness. He had made up his mind, and now he was not sure. The gout was bothering him, and he wished that Mr Moffat was in the Royal Kraal to give him comfort. These white men had their advantages, he told himself, and squirmed in his seat. He had been certain that Colenbrander would turn them back, and then all his worries would have been over. He would have shown strength to his people and he would not have antagonised the white queen.

"Are you sure they will not turn back?" he said in Ndebele to Colenbrander, who sat cross-legged on the hard baked-mud floor outside the king's day hut.

"They do not make words that they do not intend keeping," he answered in the same language.

He saw the king's hands fidget with the faded red piping at the end of the arm of his chair.

"The impi will attack without waiting for my order," the king said violently, hitting the arms of the chair with the palms of his hands. "That will settle it. They will take it into their own hands. Are you sure you explained to your friends that they will all be killed?"

"I explained in detail," answered Colenbrander.

"And Selous heard you well?"

"Yes, he heard me well."

"He is brave, that man," said Lobengula. "I remember him many years ago, when he first came here to my kraal to ask my permission to hunt. He wanted to hunt the lion, and I laughed at him, as he was not much more than a boy. Within a week he was back with the skins of two lions, and I had to let him go on hunting."

A very small, fully grown chicken ran helter-skelter between the two of them. Neither of them gave it any notice. They had been in conversation for hours and Colenbrander was tired. He thought there was a good chance of them murdering him in his sleep, for not completing the king's wishes, but this, he told himself, was a chance he took when his life was in the hands of a heathen. The king moved forward in the armchair, in an attempt to make himself more comfortable, and the vast protrusion of his black, belly-buttoned stomach covered the loin cloth that kept the flies from his genitals. He subsided back into the chair without achieving any further comfort, and the loin cloth came into sight. The king yawned, and showed Colenbrander the dark chasm of his throat for a moment.

"Why did they not listen to you?" he asked. "You know the strength of my impis."

"They know this as well," answered Colenbrander, "but they also know their own strength, and the power of their new machine guns. With one of those, a man can kill hundreds; your impis will not be able to use their assegais."

"We will ambush them before they can use these guns," said Lobengula.

"The white men say their scouts will see your impis before they can spring this ambush, and with the scouts are Selous, von Brand and Morgan, and you yourself know how well they know your country. They can kill buffalo like your impis kill the buffalo, and they too can get close enough to kill with the spear."

"It will be a bloody fight," said the king, "but I have many more warriors."

"So has the Queen," said Colenbrander, and they lapsed into silence.

They were silent for a long time, and the king was asleep when the runner, the last of a line of runners from the Lundi River, came into the king's kraal. Lobengula remained asleep, and the messenger and Colenbrander looked at each other and wondered what to do. The inDuna of the Mbizo impi, in full war feathers, and fully armed, came into the kraal, and walked up to the king. He hit his assegai against his shield, and the sharp crack woke the king, who fumbled to get up in his surprise. His surprise turned to anger. There was no uncertainty in his expression.

"I see you, Gambo."

"I see you, Lobengula, son of the black elephant, most powerful and father of the Matabele."

"What do you want?" interrupted the king.

"The white men go forward," said Gambo. "They have crossed the Lundi River."

"And what does my impi?" said Lobengula.

"They follow," said Gambo.

The king looked at him warily for a moment before responding at last, "There will be no peace while the white men stay in my country. There can be Rhodes or me, and there will not be any Rhodes."

He got up and walked into his day hut. Gambo watched him, as did the messenger and Colenbrander.

AFTER THREE DAYS of parallel marching, the Matabele disappeared and this gave Selous, von Brand and Morgan more concern than before. Both Morgan and von Brand knew that Selous was not certain of the route that would take the column up through the hills to the highveld, a distance of thirty miles. It would take them two days. They would have to camp in the hills, and it would not be possible to make a defensive laager of the wagons. The most successful attack would therefore come in the hills; a good general would have moved his impis ahead, and hidden them from the scouts.

"How well do you know the passes up to the highveld?" asked Selous as the three of them sat round his fire.

"There are many places that look the same," answered von Brand. "On a horse, I have never given it much concern. At the worst, if I found a bad stretch, I could walk with the horse, but a wagon would not have gone through the same way."

"There are many paths up to the highveld," said Morgan. "If we are not sure which one to take then the Matabele will not know which one to trap."

"The day after tomorrow, we must enter the hills," said Selous. "Both of you each take one other man and go up through the hills over there..." He pointed into the dark. "It is not a good direction for an easy pass, but it may avoid the Matabele. Go and search that part of the hills and return by tomorrow night. Gentlemen, once we have them over those hills, they will be safe."

. . .

MORGAN AND JAMES waited until the searchlight had crossed over their heads, then rode their horses out of the gap in the laager. The laager closed up behind them, and they rode off at a good pace into the night. They carried enough water and *biltong*, the dried meat of the Boers, to last them two days. There was no moon, and Morgan guided them by the position of the stars. Ten miles away from the column, and approaching the foothills, they ran the chance of stumbling into the Matabele. They dismounted and went on by foot.

Once up in the hills, they looked back and saw the distant searchlight of the column, playing its light over the African bush.

They searched that night and the following day, finding no trace of the Matabele. Morgan was hopeful that the way would be easy enough for the wagons. For the second night, they camped without a fire and only ate *biltong*. They were camped in the open in a place that gave them good hearing. They took it in turns to stay awake.

They moved off again at first light, and found the column close to the foothills. Morgan left James to unsaddle the horses and walked up the line of the column in search of Selous. The echoing chop of the axes broke over the still morning, and the time between blows was shorter than usual. The second member of each working pair stood watch, holding both of the rifles. The guards constantly turned and searched the bush.

Van der Walt, unable to work without James, stood sentry on the rounded top of a kopje that rose to a height of more than a hundred feet. His view was for miles in all directions.

"Can you see anything?" called Morgan in the *taal*, the language of the Afrikaaner.

"If they are out there," answered van der Walt, "they're lying so still the vultures will think them dead and will do our work. *Ja*, that will save trouble."

Morgan waved his hand and walked on as quickly as he could without giving the appearance of panic. He felt comforted by the cold, blue eyes of the Boer scanning every fold in the bush. The man wanted his farm and was not going to be thwarted. He watched each of them as he passed, and saw in them the same degree of determination. There were only white men, the natives having dispersed the previous day without waiting for orders. The word was that they did not wish to be assegaied by their fellow natives. Morgan smiled, but his eyes were cold. He brought back his shoulders and clenched his teeth. They were not going to be beaten now, he told himself.

He found Selous at the head of the column, pointing out the next trees to be stumped out. Selous broke off from his work and walked away into the bush with Morgan. The sun had been up for two hours and the heat was a strong, hot pressure on their shoulders. The bush, tinder dry all around them, was crackling. There was nothing green; the trees were stark and leafless, and the tall grass brown and motionless, and the earth baked and dusted between the patches of grass that had been pounded by three months of sun and no rain. It was game country.

"Can we try that pass?" asked Selous, when they were out of earshot.

"We saw nothing," replied Morgan. "The pass may present a difficult passage, and if we have to dismantle the wagons it has been done before. At the moment, the pass is not sheltering the Matabele."

"If we have to dismantle and carry the wagons it will take time," said Selous, "and I want to be into and out of those hills before our friends can make up their minds. Maybe Colenbrander was right, and we are all for the vultures. If the Matabele want us, they can get us up there."

"They will have a fight on their hands," said Morgan. "The men back there are determined."

"They may need their determination," answered Selous. "Thank you for your information. We will go up through that break in the hills." He pointed to where they would go. He walked back to the head of the column. Four troopers were waiting impatiently for orders. He pointed out trees for them to cut in line with his pass, and the road took up a new direction.

The trees grew smaller and easier to move as they began to climb up into the hills. The wagons were bunched as close together as possible, and the police patrolled in detachments. If they were attacked, each patrol was to be the local rallying point. The scouts roamed up into the hills that grew into vast, tree-clad mountains.

Morgan took his horse up ahead into the pass. The vegetation had changed and, for the first time, he encountered msasa trees. As he went, he looked for broken twigs, scuffed earth and trampled grass. He spurred his horse to take the incline, and began the climb up the side of the pass. The horse forced itself up the slope and past the thin trunks of the msasa trees and beneath their canopies that, in three months' time, would spring into a ceiling of green and russet and orange and red.

From the top, he looked back down, over the leafless trees, short and flat-topped, spread for the sun, and saw the first signs of the column that was moving into the pass. Up on the slope, it was calm and peaceful, and the blood running through his body pumped hard. He pushed himself up in his saddle and looked around. His eyes focused on an eagle that glided down the slope of the mountain to his left, its wings motionless, and its flight sustained by the upward movement of the warm air. Morgan knew that its small head would be turning from side to side, and its telescopic eyes would be methodically searching the bush for mice. There was great beauty in its flight. He watched the bird go right down into the valley.

Morgan urged his horse along just below the crest of the hill, and then he stopped the horse and watched. More of the column moved into the valley, together with the first of the wagons. They were moving faster than he expected. He let his horse go down the slope away from them and within moments he was alone. There were the hills, and their trees, and the powerful sun above all of them. There was no sign of there ever having been any life on the great slopes of the hills, almost an escarpment, that led up from the heat of the lowveld, to the plateau, four thousand feet above sea level. He searched around for the time allotted to his patrol, and then turned his horse back towards the pass and the column.

The smell of sweating oxen reached him first, and then the straining sounds of physical determination. The first sixteen oxen were plodding forward, dragging at their burden, with a pioneer corps ox driver pulling gently at their leader's head. The front wagon stuck against a boulder, and without any word of command, hard, strong hands went down to pull it away, and the wheels of the big wagon began to go round again, and the spokes turned over and over.

"The police must patrol the slopes and a little beyond," said Morgan, when he found Selous, "there is no point in them keeping close to the column as we can see up to the crests of the hills from here. There is nothing for five miles that will force us to dismantle the wagons. The angle of the climb increases, that is all."

He went on down the column and found James standing guard. Van der Walt's back was just visible where he bent to dig the roots clear from a small msasa tree. The sweat was pouring from his shoulders. They watched him work. He put the shovel aside and took up the axe. The chips of wood flew out of the hole, and within five minutes the tree gently swayed over on its side. Van der Walt cut the tap root free and Morgan pulled the tree out of the hole.

"Take a rest," said James, "and let me fill in the hole."

Van der Walt exchanged the shovel for the guns and ammunition bandoliers. James shovelled rock and earth into the hole, while van der Walt swigged from the water bottle. As he did so, he turned round slowly and scanned the bush and the hills all around him. He put the stopper back in the bottle, and hit the cork home.

"How do you fancy nine thousand heathens yelling their heads off and running down that slope at you?" he asked.

"I don't," said Morgan.

"It would not be nice," agreed van der Walt, and smiled.

"You're a pessimist," said Morgan.

"It was only a thought. Perhaps all those heathens have gone home, hearing Koos van der Walt is after some target practice."

They both laughed, but without conviction.

"We'll laugh better," said Morgan, "when we get out of this bloody death trap. I've been up all over those hills and seen nothing, but they could just as easily be in the next valley with the whole Matabele nation."

"There is nothing else to do but clear the road and worry about our friends when they arrive," said van der Walt.

Morgan agreed and went on down the column.

The road moved up and between the hills. The climb steepened. The oxen pulled and the wagons followed. As they went up, the air grew purer and the piercing rays of the sun more powerful. The humidity dropped away, and their energy increased. They watched and worked and the tension increased as they wound further up through the hills. They had nowhere to retreat to, and nothing to give them protection. Every few minutes, and, they hoped, without the other knowing, they looked up and along the crests of the surrounding hills. They spoke little, and used their energies on making the road as quickly as possible.

There was no place better than another to stop for the night. Selous kept them working until the light faded. Down in their valley, the light went quickly, and the big shadow of night spread over the mile and a half of the column while the colours of a rich, blood-red sunset blazed out from behind the contours of the hills. To the shouts of officers and ox drivers, the column closed up, and, as best they could, they bunched into a bad defensive line.

James took the midnight watch. As instructed, he moved a hundred yards up the slope, away from the wagons. The moon was obscured by the hill that went up into the darkness in front of him. There was no light, and he could not see his hand when he held it out in front of him. Ahead lay two hours of guard duty. He strained his eyes to see, but was unable to make out anything more than the different depths of darkness. The column was silent. Their orders were to make no sound, show no light and make no smoke. The bush around him was alive with small noises that grew in volume as he listened. A leopard coughed in the hills on the far side of the wagons, sending a chill of fear through his body. He gripped his Martini-Henry rifle strongly, and tried to sense if he was being watched. He stood motionless beside the trunk of a msasa tree. A night beetle fell off its piece of bark three feet away from James, and crashed into the dry leaves. He jumped back and hit the msasa tree with his back. He recoiled and stood still. His legs shook and his heart pumped. He clenched the rifle and forced his mind to take over the control of his body. After a while, his control and confidence returned. The leopard coughed again, but from further away.

An hour and a half later, still standing in exactly the same spot, he was certain he was not alone. An instinct he was unable to recognise, and which had lain dormant in his family for centuries, told him the watching presence was animal. He could feel where the animal stood, and noiselessly turned to face the intruder. The bush noises continued around him as he challenged the animal's nerve. His fear had gone, and he stood his ground with a precise, cold confidence. He thought it was either the cat or the buck family. He imagined he could hear it breathing, and then realised it was himself. He held his gun ready and waited for the animal to spring, using the power of his mind to force it back.

Van der Walt gave the recognised cough of the leopard, three times in succession, and when James replied, keeping his willpower concentrated in front of him, he heard the bush rustle and, before van der Walt joined him, he sensed that he was alone.

"There's a leopard close," he whispered. "It moved off when we coughed."

"There are always leopard in hills like this," answered van der Walt. "That's why Selous nominated a leopard cough to warn each other of our whereabouts. Even a Matabele would not find the sound out of place. Let's hope the leopards around here are well fed."

James left him alone to the guard duty, and found his way down to the wagons as quietly as possible. A few moments after pulling the blanket up to his chin, he was asleep.

THE COUNTRY BECAME FLAT, and the column wound its way out of the pass and moved up onto the highveld. Selous called the pass that had given them a safe passage "*Providential.*"

Morgan was seen to gallop his horse out ahead of the column into the new, flat country. They were out of Matabeleland and out of danger. They laagered some distance from the neck of the pass. A new sense of life came over the column, as the sight of Morgan and his horse grew smaller in the distance. Morgan slewed his horse to a halt. He swung himself out of the saddle and planted his feet firmly on the ground. Suddenly he jumped into the air, both feet off the ground, and stamped down. He did it again and again until he was exhausted. He began to laugh. He looked up at the sky, and bellowed like an animal. He felt free for the first time in three months. He looked around and felt a surge of power well up in his stomach, and it made him remount and pull the horse's head round to face the distant laager. He dug his heels into the animal's rump. The horse tried to match the energy of its rider, and froth foamed at its mouth as it galloped back to the wagons.

"The whole Matabele nation is waiting out there," he shouted from fifty yards out.

The men within hearing quickly stopped and looked for their guns. Morgan reined in his horse and vaulted out of the saddle. He stood looking at them, his hands on his hips and his legs wide apart. He began to laugh from the bottom of his belly, and within seconds they were all laughing with him.

"Fooled you," he shouted. "I fooled the whole ruddy lot of you," and they laughed even louder with relief.

PART 2

1891 TO 1893

1

"*N*ow we'll head in the right direction," said Morgan and turned his horse at right angles to follow a thin, well-trodden game track. "There was no point in telling them where to look for the gold. If Willy is not as careful, they'll follow him into the Hartley hills. Even if we don't, the others will think we should know where to find a reef."

The horses took their own pace. The long grass on either side of the track was bent over after the heat of the five-month-long dry season. The msasa trees had burst their buds into russet and orange-coloured leaves, despite the lack of water, and Morgan again accepted the beauty as a miracle. Overhead, the clouds built up into mountains of white cumulus with black depths of water at the base that hung over the bush with ponderous menace and power. The humidity was high. Everything waited for the rains.

Out of uniform, James felt comfortable in an open shirt and breeches, with a bush hat, its brim pulled down at the front, keeping the sun out of his eyes. The bandolier, full of shells, was strapped over his shoulder and across his chest. The butt of his Martini-Henry rifle protruded from the army saddle holster in front of his left knee. The horse followed behind Morgan's in Indian file. Further behind, and at the end of a rope attached to the pommel of

James's saddle, a third horse followed along the track, its head just above the level of the broken grass. It was packed with sleeping bags, prospecting picks, hammers, shovels and pans, spare ammunition, an axe, food and water, cooking utensils, and two bundles of their personal possessions.

"Those are the Mazoe hills," said Morgan, pointing in front of them and slightly to the left. "That's as good a place as any to start to make ourselves rich." He turned and looked over his shoulder at James. "How does it feel to be rich in your own right, Mr Carregan?"

"I'll tell you when we find all that gold," said James.

Morgan faced in front again and they lapsed into the business of following the game track through the bush that led them towards the hills. James's feeling of freedom was greater than his hope for gold. They had all been told there was gold in Mashonaland, but looking around at the dry and endless bush he found it impossible to imagine their picks digging into a thin, elusive reef of gold. Van der Walt had gone in search of his perfect farm, and he had the whole country from which to take his choice.

The rest of the Pioneer Corps, and the police who had obtained a discharge, were spreading out over the country in all directions from Fort Salisbury. None of them had told each other where they were going, except von Brand and Morgan who had a cross stake in each other's fortunes. Carregan, and Fentan, who was with von Brand in the Hartley hills, had smaller shares in the same syndicate.

James and Morgan went on with few rests, as Morgan wished to reach his fortune as quickly as possible. Towards afternoon, they walked with the horses; the heat and humidity were oppressive, and the Mazoe hills seemed no closer. The hills shimmered through the heat haze but stayed out of reach.

"If we want to eat fresh meat tonight," said Morgan, "we had better find ourselves something to shoot."

They took their rifles out of the saddle holsters, put a shell in each breach, and turned their attention to watching the surrounding bush, as the horses walked on in single file. It relieved the monotony. After two hours of fruitless hunting, they reached the banks of a dried up river.

"We'll camp here for the night," said Morgan.

They unsaddled their horses and unloaded the pack horse. James went into the bush to bring in enough wood to keep a fire burning all night, while Morgan took his rifle and walked off down the dried-up bed of the river. Having been watered, the hobbled horses strayed into the bush to find their food from the tinder dry grass, and grazed methodically. James collected the wood, and piled it up beside the place where he would make the fire. The mound grew with his forages deeper and deeper into the darkening bush. He cut grass, cleaned it of pieces of thorn thicket, and made a pile. With a shovel, he cleared a patch of level ground a few feet away from his fire site, and put a thick layer of grass over the dry earth. Without enthusiasm, as they still had nothing to cook besides corn and maize, he cut two forked sticks and a straight one to rest in between. When the dusk grew almost into night, he was still on his own with the horses. He lit the fire and the flames sprang up quickly.

One shot rang out, and the noise spread in a violent rush over the bush.

James sat on his haunches and watched the fire. He became mesmerised by the dancing flames. The thoughts in his mind went on down much further than the hearts of the flames; a jumble of reasons and equations tumbled around inside his mind. For the first time in months, he was able to think without interruption. He tried to apply the practical examples of the life he had experienced since leaving Halmeston to the theoretical knowledge he had been taught at Oxford. Theory and practice were not really the same, he concluded.

He looked back through his memory, at the principles he had been told were the basis upon which he should live, but they were no longer clear. He thought of God but it did not seem to be the same God who had watched over him as a child in the quiet peace of a Norman church; in his mind's eye, he saw the coloured windows, with the leaden outlines of the stained-glass knights, with the rings of holiness above their heads; the sun played beams of light on the wooden pews, and a million flecks of dust danced in the beams.

He could not fit the pattern of such gentle godliness into Africa. In England, there was 'meekness and mildness,' of a type he had learnt in his first prayer. There was the soft heat of summer, and the warmth of a big fire in winter, and the gentle scents of the English countryside. Through the security of his father's money, he had grown to accept them as everyone's heritage. He had been born into a world that for him knew no struggle, and its strict comfort had driven him away. He thought about why he had gone away, and why he had not been content with what he had. He knew, now, that he wanted the new country, and that he had found a depth of purpose for his life, but he realised that this was luck, and not a definite goal he had known in the beginning and gone out to find. He thought, and then felt, that maybe he had gone because he knew what he did not want.

He had been selfish, and he thought about this as well. He considered his father and saw degrees of the same selfishness; his father had discarded his grandfather to further his own aim of climbing in society; his father had made him the one who was acceptable in society and though he knew he should have considered himself to be the beneficiary of this act, he knew that it had not been done for his benefit. His sister, Ester, had wanted him to stay in England, not because she thought he was making a mistake by going to Africa, but because she would be lonely without him. Nearly everything everyone did centred on themselves, he concluded.

He tried to think of the world without himself, and saw that there would be no world as, without his eyes to tell him what it was that he was looking at, there was nothing. If he had not existed, there would have been nothing to relate anything to or from. There would have been no starting point, not even for his imagination. He saw clearly that the centre of life was himself, and yet he knew from his upbringing that to accept this, and practise life accordingly, was wrong. He told himself that his thoughts had not taken him any further forward, and he got up to put more wood on the fire. He threw the branches onto the flames. He called softly to the horses, and one by one they came to him. He took the ropes off their hind legs and tied them to a tree close to the fire; he did not want the jackals snapping their jaws at the horses' legs.

He sat down by the fire and crossed his legs, and his knees stuck up in the light thrown by the guttering flames. The firelight made hollow shadows around his eye sockets that were enhanced by his thick growth of beard. He stretched and lay back on the earth. He could hear Morgan approaching the camp, softly whistling to himself. He looked up at the brilliance of the galaxy of stars. The more he looked, the more he saw, and he wondered how much or how little was out there, and the 'there' was a word in his mind that dismissed the unknown of everything. As he looked, he became uncomfortable with his acceptance of 'there'. He became sure that there was more. They had gone into Mashonaland, and occupied a great tract of Africa in the name of civilisation, but how big, he thought, was this venture in terms of what he saw above? What was he looking at? Was it just a part of the outer core of his world that gave it beauty at night, or were there other eyes watching his world as a star?

"It is a perfect night sky," said Morgan, and James came back to himself.

He sat up. Morgan held up a dead guinea fowl and laughed. The bird had no head.

"Best I could do," he said. "I had to be careful, using a Martini-Henry, to only knock off its head."

They lapsed into silence.

"I wonder how much is up there," said James, and lay back again.

Morgan looked up at the night sky for a long time.

"I don't know," he said, and then looked down and leant his rifle against the tree and patted the neck of his horse, "and neither does anyone else."

The bush was strangely quiet, and the crickets made a soft background of noise to the night. There was a cold breeze that suggested rain. The breeze played on their faces, and then left them to the humidity that was the prelude to rain and storm. It was an expectant night, and they both felt its meaning. They were glad of each other's company.

Morgan sat down, crossed his legs, and methodically began to pluck the feathers from the guinea fowl. James put his hands behind his head and stretched out flat on his back again and searched the heavens for a new star. The firelight caught at the feathers as they fell to the earth around Morgan's legs. The metal of his gun, standing against the tree next to James's gun, shone briefly again and again as the branches burnt, and crashed deeper into the fire, and flared the flames. The pile of feathers grew lightly.

"I would have been married now," said Morgan, "and with five children, and a small house near my legal practice, and a hearth that was warm in the winter nights. Instead of which I am plucking a guinea fowl in the middle of Africa."

"Would you have been content?" asked James.

There was silence.

"Yes, I think so," said Morgan, "... if I had known nothing different. There are probably sides of our character that lie dormant throughout our lives."

"Could you have lived in one house forever," said James, "and grown old, and been buried in the local graveyard with a marble stone telling us that here lies R Morgan, attorney, and beloved father of fourteen children who forget his grave and memory, but for the brief pangs of conscience, and acknowledgement of having been created? A life of little things from the day of birth until the day of death?"

"If you know no better, this can be a comfortable life," answered Morgan.

"This is the lot of the majority of people from our background," said James, "but what can have been the purpose of a life such as that. It is like a plant that grows in isolation, and has no chance of showing the reason for its life to anyone else, and then it dies, and rots, and goes back into the soil to manure its own seed."

"What are we looking for in life?" asked Morgan.

There was silence while he finished plucking the bird. He took some fat from their food bag, greased the bird, and stuck it through the middle with the stick James had prepared. He put the forked sticks into the ground on either side of the fire and put the ends of the centre stick in the forks.

"Peace," answered James, "to enjoy those stars; love, which for you is to enjoy your Annabel. Money, music, ornaments, laughter, friends, home, children."

"Power," said Morgan.

"Health and food, the satisfaction from knowledge."

"And what about sex?"

"I know nothing about that," said James.

"It is a powerful force, maybe the most powerful."

"But they all add up to happiness," said James. "Could you have been happy as a vegetable?"

"Who knows? Nothing is perfect. Here I have the power and excitement of being a man, but it is only part of a life. There must be a woman as well."

"When we have tamed this country just enough," said James, "we will combine the two. Maybe this is what the Boer has, and what forces him to trek when the land of his forefathers becomes safe. When he treks, he always takes his family with him, and the women fight the heathens alongside the men, and the children fight too if they are big enough to hold a gun. Maybe life is a constant search that is only found in parts. The answer," he went on, as he watched Morgan turn the guinea fowl on the spit, "is to enjoy what we are doing at the time we are doing it, and to the fullest degree of our ability. It is good to dream, and even drift away back into memories, but there is no value in nostalgia or bitterness."

"Maybe," agreed Morgan, "there are too many ideals in a civilised world."

"In Europe," agreed James, "we are too far away from our original roots. We have become too involved in petty rights and wrongs, and have built around ourselves a code of behaviour that gives a frivolous purpose to life. I think this is what my grandfather was trying to say on the voyage out to Cape Town. Anyway," he said, sitting up and taking a closer interest in the cooking bird, "here we are right back to the basic needs of hunting, eating and surviving."

"You don't regret," asked Morgan, "having come to Africa?"

"Not one bit. In Africa, there is a whole purpose in itself. Especially the highveld... no, I am happy... I hope I can maintain as much of this happiness in the future of my life."

"It is a great gift to recognise happiness when you have it."

The fat began to drip out of the guinea fowl, and it dripped and splattered and flared in the flames of the fire.

"I shall sleep well tonight," said James, yawning, "after a good meal of that bird, I shall drift off gently into the world of dreams, where every rock will be gold, and the water of every stream will glitter; the sun will be gold, and the sky as well, and everyone will be so rich that to be rich will have no purpose. The great game in that world of wealth will be to get poor and to find, for the first time, the exciting feeling of hunger, the dread of war, and the very ultimate in pain. Let us hope that we do not find too much of your gold, Rhys, as I have this feeling that it will not do us very much good."

"It is much more exciting looking for something," said Morgan, "than trying to enjoy it when it has been found. Except Annabel. I could have gone on enjoying everything about Annabel for the rest of my life."

"But to have been successful in doing this," answered James, "would it not have been necessary to explore all the new things together? I think you might have grown tired of that warm little hearth in the winter."

"You are trying to destroy a dream," said Morgan and laughed.

"Maybe it is better just to have a dream as it cannot be destroyed by other people. I can always imagine what our lives would have been like together, and fit her into any of the worlds that catch my fancy. I have imagined us here in Africa, and in England. The picture is always perfect. We never quarrel or grow old. I wonder how many people, who know me only as a hunter, would laugh if they knew some of the thoughts that go through my mind, when I am out alone in the bush."

"We all have dreams," said James, "but it is only on the odd occasion, and under rare circumstances, that we talk about them. They are the private strength of ourselves, and they have no currency in the outside world."

"What do you dream about?" asked Morgan.

James sat still and tried to piece together the jumble of thoughts that went through his mind.

"For months, my dream was of being here... I wanted to see the unknown, and do something that was not the same as everyone else. It is a selfish, conceited thought, and when I look at it objectively I can see this fault. I suppose I dream of being recognised for my own special quality. For the moment, I have found my dream, and only time will tell whether I have anything to give to it. Yes, I dream of my farm that is ploughed and cropped and goes out as far as the eye can see in all directions. Vaguely, I see a family. In such flashes, I am, of course," and he laughed briefly, "the perfect lover and father, though I have no means to know what it means to be either. I want to improve the lot of the local native but this is again a conceit, as I would do it for my own satisfaction and patronage, and if it gave them pleasure as well, it would be a by-product. I would never admit this to anyone else. How many things that we would loathe to find in others, Rhys, do we think about and secretly enjoy? There is too often the one true self inside, whilst outside the actor plays his part and, if he is good, he receives a measure of applause for his acting. We all take each other in. Sometimes, I have even tried to take in myself."

"There is very little true honesty," agreed Morgan, and turned to the guinea fowl on the spit. He turned the spit, and juice ran out of the carcase and onto the fire, and set up a long note of sizzling. They went back into their own thoughts and remained there for some time. James lay back and closed his eyes. After a while he fell asleep. Morgan heard his heavy breathing, and smiled at the trust of youth. He listened to the bush sounds, but could hear nothing unusual. It was a quiet, peaceful night, like so many hundreds of others he had spent by himself in the bush.

He thought the guinea fowl was ready but let it go on cooking as he did not wish to wake James. He was enjoying being completely by himself. The solitude around him was a tangible thing he could touch, if he wished to stretch out his hand. The horses were asleep. They stood completely still. He took the bird off the fire and balanced it between two branches that stuck out from the pile of wood. He took wood from the other side of the pile and put it on the fire; he watched the sparks rise up into the night; they floated clear in the upward surge of hot air from the fire, and then went out. Other sparks rose up to follow them.

"Do you want to eat?" asked Morgan.

There was no reply.

"The bird's ready," said Morgan, in a loud voice that disturbed the quiet of the surrounding bush.

He pulled a leg off the guinea fowl and went over to where James was sleeping. He held the meat an inch away from his nose, and waited for a reaction. The steady note of the heavy breathing changed, and then the nose twitched. Finally, James jerked his hand up over his face, and would have knocked the leg out of Morgan's hand if Morgan had not pulled it away a fraction faster. James sat up quickly.

"Dinner, your Lordship, is served," said Morgan, and handed him the leg of guinea fowl.

"You sure disturb a man's dreams," said James. "They were a complete jumble, but I know the flavour was good."

James sunk his teeth into the meat and chewed.

"If you eat so quickly," said Morgan, "you will have indigestion, and a nightmare."

James smiled and chewed the meat more diligently, and they went on eating in silence, tearing pieces from the carcase, until they had finished the bird. Morgan burped, and sucked at his greasy fingers.

"We'll sleep with the guns next to us," said Morgan, "but I don't see anything around here to give us trouble. Whoever wakes during the night is to feed the fire. That will keep the jackals away from the horses."

They lay down on the grass beds. Their separate thoughts rambled on and merged into sleep.

The fire died down as they slept through the murmurings of a peaceful African night. A jackal came as close to the fire as it dared, and went away again. The night went on, and they slept without moving. Morgan dreamt of England, and while he slept he lived a normal married life with Annabel. There was no passion or problem but a quiet peace. Gavin had grown to a boy and Morgan was teaching him to swim in a mountain stream in the hills of Wales, when he was awakened by the neighing of his horse. James woke at the same time. They gripped their loaded rifles and crouched, back to back, searching the darkness of the bush. The horse stamped its hooves and fought with the rope holding it to the tree.

"There's nothing there," said Morgan tensely. "The bush is totally quiet. I can't see or feel anything, yet my horse is more frightened than I have ever seen him before."

He stood up and walked slowly towards the horse. James tensed himself.

"My God," shouted Morgan, "it's ants, army ants. They've half eaten your horse where it stands. No, keep back. Quick, cut the horses free."

Morgan pulled out his hunting knife, slashed the rope of the pack horse in one movement and prodded the animal into action with the muzzle of his rifle. James did the same to Morgan's horse and then bent to pick up his saddle bag.

"Don't touch anything," said Morgan. "Come on. If those ants get onto you in quantity they'll eat you alive."

They began to run from the camp and James felt a bite in his leg. He hit at it as he ran. He could hear the two horses crashing through the bush ahead of them. Other noises sprang up ahead of their flight. He thought of the ants and his flesh crawled.

"You can't see which way the bastards are going at night," said Morgan, as they slowed down, their legs torn by the thorn thickets. "They are only dangerous if you are in their path. At night, I take no chances. They'll have cleaned your horse of flesh by now. They swarm over and eat and then the next swarm eats. We'll go back when the light comes up," he said, as they stopped. "Was my horse free of ants?"

"I couldn't see," said James.

"Neither could I see the pack horse," said Morgan. "They are still running, which means they couldn't have picked up so many. Have they bitten you?"

"Only around my ankles," answered James.

"I hate ants," said Morgan. "I hate bloody ants. I've only seen them once, and that was years ago."

Morgan whistled to the horses, but it failed to stop them crashing on through the bush. "We'll look a couple of fine prospectors in the morning," said Morgan. "No horses, no water and no equipment. It may take us days to round up those animals, and if they've been bitten badly we never will."

"We'll have to walk back to Fort Salisbury," said James.

"A fine laugh that'll be," said Morgan.

They lapsed into silence. The night had returned to normal. Morgan re-took his bearings. They found a rock and sat down with their backs to each other.

"You don't think," said James, "that this piece of Africa has any more surprises for us tonight?"

"Not unless you are sitting on a puff adder," answered Morgan and laughed as James surreptitiously moved his backside to try and see more clearly on what he was sitting.

They rested, and after some time they relaxed. Half an hour later they saw the sky behind the Mazoe hills pale to an orange glow that grew to a deep orange, then red and finally a great, blood-red streak spread across the horizon. The sun came up. Morgan waited until he could clearly see the detail of the ground in front of him and then they retraced their steps. The sun yellowed the tops of the msasa trees and shone through the boughs and russet-coloured leaves, while the birds sang in chorus. When they reached the camp, a strong ray of the sun was pointing through the msasa trees at the skeleton of James's horse. The bones were completely clean and dry and the skeleton head was twisted to one side.

They both looked at the remains of the animal, and for a moment Morgan rested his hand on James's shoulder. Their equipment was just as they had left it the night before. A half-eaten bone of guinea fowl was lying where it had been thrown. A few brown ants clawed at the remaining flesh without making any impression; the bone had not been in the line of march of the big, black ants. Apart from the bones of the horse, and the two empty ropes hanging from the tree, there was nothing to be seen of the night's work.

"Would you have been able to find the camp on your own?" asked Morgan.

"Yes. I tested myself carefully. I knew that we would have to find our water."

"A good sense of direction is essential if you want to survive in the bush. There may be more water in that riverbed. Come on, we'll find out."

Morgan picked up a shovel and James followed him down to the dried-up bed of the river. The riverbed was soft sand, and they took it in turns to dig out the hole. The deeper they went, the wider the hole had to be, as the sand from the top kept crumbling. At a depth of eight feet, the sand became moist, and two feet further down the water began to collect. It was clear and sweet, well filtered by the sand. They filled their water containers and left the hole as it had been made. They packed their saddle bags with essentials and, with two water bottles each, they set off on foot to track the horses.

They walked through the whole day, and at nightfall they made camp in the tracks of the two animals.

"We're lucky they stuck together," said Morgan as they ate some of the small buck he had shot earlier in the day.

Throughout the night, one of them kept watch by the fire while the other slept. A strong, colourless moonlight bathed the bush. The moon was brilliant in itself, and the sky a tapestry of stars. Between the stars was a total, indigo blackness. The world, and its heaven, was wrapped in peace.

TOWARDS EVENING THE NEXT DAY, they found the horses. Morgan called to his mare and the animal whinnied in recognition. From lack of water, both animals were unable to go further. They camped beside the horses and watered them little by little. A patch at the bottom of the legs of the pack horse had been eaten away, but it was only a surface wound that had been dried up by the sun and caked by dirt from the bush. Morgan looked at it carefully but found no signs of festering. The horses ate the next morning, and slowly the quartet retraced their steps, the men leading, the horses following at their own speed; a line of four in the endless bush.

They rested the horses for two days beside the water hole whilst they built up a stock of biltong. When they moved out again, the Mazoe hills looked no larger than they had been a week before.

"THERE IS A LINE OF OLD WORKINGS," said Morgan, pointing, "that go from there right along through the valley. They are difficult to see unless you know what you are looking for. They must be over a hundred years old, judging by the way that the diggings are overgrown by trees."

James stood with his hands on his hips and looked down into the depression that Morgan had told him was an ancient gold mine.

"You can see," went on Morgan, "that the hole has a definite line that could not have been excavated by an animal. All the books on gold mining in the Witwatersrand, Australia and America say that the gold bearing ore bodies go downwards. All that the ancients could have taken here would have been surface gold. There must be a reef underneath."

"If there are diggings dotted down the valley," said James, "it could just be surface gold pockets that have been forced up by the water level. The underground water would dissolve the gold, and then deposit it in concentrated pockets on the surface. The books I read spoke of gold in reefs and gold in isolated pockets, where the underground ore body did not contain enough gold to mine, but the water level had pushed up pockets to the surface. Why did the African miners stop at such a shallow hole?"

"Because they didn't know how to mine properly," said Morgan.

"Or because the gold ran out?" asked James.

"Then there must be more of these pockets."

"There are two of us," said James, "and there were thousands of them, over hundreds of years. Maybe they found all that there was to be found in this valley."

"You cheer me up no end," said Morgan. "We'll camp here, anyway, and see who can prove his point. We'll dig out this working, and go down another thirty feet below the underground water level. There must be a reef as the pattern of the workings is symmetrical. I have had my ideas about this valley for seven years, and if my theory is right, the mine will flood when we find the reef and we'll have to bring in pumps. Rhodes sent up a number in the wagons, as he had the same theory. We believe they stopped digging when the underground water flooded them out. Being the end of the dry season, the water level should be lower than usual. I want to prove my point before the rains come, stake a claim, and then open it up next April."

"There is only one way to find out," said James.

They climbed down into the depression and began to dig.

"Look," said Morgan, as he disturbed a small mound with his pick, "here is the place they heated the ore and threw cold water onto it so that it shattered and was easier to crush and pan. The river runs through the valley down there, so there will be plenty of water for use in extracting the gold."

"One thing is sure," said James, "there are no gold nuggets lying around to be picked, my grandfather was wrong about that one."

"You are still sceptical, by the tone of your voice," said Morgan, "as to whether there was ever any gold in this valley. Bring the pestle and mortar, and we'll take some of their shattered ore down to the river. And bring the pan as well," he said over his shoulder, as he bent to pick up a handful of the ore. "This is a conglomerate, by the look of it," he went on, "and the gold is meant to be in stuff like this."

"I'll believe your gold, Rhys, when I see it."

"You're the most optimistic partner I could have chosen," he said, as they climbed out of the depression and began to walk down a gentle slope to the centre of the valley and the river. "If we were both like you, we'd sit up there on that hill and cry. Let's see you enthuse, Carregan."

"How does one enthuse about a handful of slag and a hole in the ground?"

"You use your imagination," said Morgan. "You will the stuff out of the ground, and you conjure up the spirits of the dead diggers to help you."

"You're bush happy. You've been in the sun too long," said James.

They reached the river that was still just flowing despite the lack of rain, and vaulted out over the rocks to where the water ran between two boulders.

"This would make a great place for a farm," said James.

"That comes later, when we've got the gold in our pockets."

Morgan put the mortar on the rock next to the water, quarter filled it with a handful of ore, picked up the pestle and began to grind the conglomerate. When his hand grew tired, he handed the pestle and mortar over to James. When the ore was almost a powder, Morgan poured it into the prospecting pan, with its very fine mesh that would let the water come through but retain any flecks of gold.

"The principle," he said to James as he carefully submerged the pan in a part of the water that was flowing gently, "is to float the lighter ore up the pan and then flick it out. The gold, being heavy, will stay in the bottom rim of the pan. You can see that by shaking the pan in this way I'm making a tail of the crushed ore that runs up the pan. Some of the old-timers on the Rand can run out the trash in seconds. See, the big pieces are rising as I shake, and the powdered, heavy stuff is staying at the bottom of the pan under the water."

He worked methodically until there was half an inch of sludge in the pan. He worked his wrists harder and the sludge edged its way up the pan. He pushed the pan down gently into the water so that the lighter sludge was forced off the mesh and drifted away.

"You've washed it all away," said James as he watched, crouched on his haunches.

"Now we shall see," said Morgan, and pulled the pan clear of the water.

The last of the water trickled out of the pan and sucked at the slender trail of residue that showed a pattern of tail that ran up the pan. As the water left the tail, the glint of the sun on the water changed to a glitter of gold.

"Now do you believe me, you bastard?" said Morgan jubilantly.

"If that isn't gold," said James, taking the pan from Morgan to study it closer, "then it gives a very good imitation."

He looked closely and made out the small flecks of gold lying on the mesh of the pan. As the gold dried, it glittered more strongly. "That's gold," he said softly, "that sure is gold," and as he looked up from the pan at Morgan, he failed to keep the excitement out of his eyes. His eyes went back, and he again looked at the tail of gold in the pan, and his hands began to shake. "Hell, I wish Grandfather could see that," he said, and put the pan down carefully on the rock.

"Now that's a smile on your face," said Morgan, and began to laugh.

James laughed with him. They came close to falling in the river as they shook hands and tried to dance each other round on top of the rock. James kicked the pestle in the water, and they both scrabbled to get it before it went off down the river. Morgan fell into the water first and James followed. They got to their knees in the shallow water, and hit the surface of the river with the palms of their hands, sending sheets of water into each other's faces. They laughed with the water streaming down their hair and beards. Morgan bent his face down to the water, and filled his cheeks with water. Standing up, he fountained a steady stream into James's face. James pushed Morgan firmly in the chest, which made him wallow backwards. He let himself float away with the river as he thrashed happily at the water with his hands.

"Mind the crocodiles," shouted James.

Morgan unsheathed his hunting knife and waved it at James, but went on floating down the river on his back.

BEFORE THE RAINS broke they excavated the digging and went down below the table of the normal water level. The soft rocks were wet, but the water failed to seep into the hole. The conglomerate reef was small but strong, and appeared to run down the valley in the direction of the old diggings. After constant panning, Morgan estimated that the reef held up to half an ounce of gold to the ton.

"Unless Willy has found something better," he finally said to James, "we can open this up as a mine. We'll start with a three-stamp crushing mill, and, if the reef holds, we shall have enough money to bring in something bigger from Johannesburg. We had better get back to Fort Salisbury before the rains break," he said, looking up at the sky. "Willy and Michael Fentan may even be there by now. There will be the whole of the rainy season to make our plans."

<hr />

2

*T*he rains came in a tropical deluge and the road from the banks of the Limpopo River became impassable. One of the last ox drawn wagons to reach Fort Salisbury brought the mail. James and Morgan took their letters into the pole and dagga hut they had built for themselves.

"I wish Willy and Michael had reached Fort Salisbury before the rains," said Morgan, slitting open a letter with his hunting knife.

The rains began again, and the deluge of water battered the thatched roof above their heads.

First, James opened the letter from his father. The light was bad, with the storm building up outside the open door. Lightning flashed at the surface water and the thunder crashed. He could just make out the flamboyant writing. The letter was nine months old, written in reply to the letter of explanation James had sent to his father from Cape Town.

 Halmeston, 4th May, 1890

Dear James,

If you were under twenty-one I would inform the Magistrate. Seeing that this is not in my power, I can only discard you from my mind as an expensive waste of time. You will come to no good. You are looking for the easy way. Life is never easy. You imagine that all these stories of gold in Mashonaland are true. Too many people are gullible. I have it in my mind that Rhodes has put out these stories so that poor fools like yourself will invest money and time in his wretched Charter Company. You mark my words, it will end up like another South Sea Bubble. It is a confidence trick, and you and your grandfather were fool enough to be taken in by it.

Your father,
Ernest Carregan

James folded the letter and looked across at Morgan. He was not certain in the bad light, but when the lightning flashed he thought he could see tears in the other man's eyes. They did not speak and the storm went on around them. The other letters were left unread as there was insufficient light, despite the time of day.

James thought of how it felt to be rejected by his father. He had known before that there was very little understanding between the two of them, but he'd hoped that this had never been his own fault. The iron barrier that had maintained the obedience of his youth seemed so far away. He remembered the few times that he'd tried to speak to his father, and the 'small boy, pipe down' rejections.

He tried to listen to the African storm outside, but his mind would not concentrate. He could not alter the situation; he could not even add anything to the problem. He could, he thought, learn from what he thought was the mistake: rigid, forced discipline is a reactionary force and he saw that maybe the reaction for his father was the loss of his son. James wondered if his father had ever wanted a son and tried to make his mind stop at that. He felt the pressures of being completely on his own. He had never given the feeling of isolated loneliness any conscious thought before. He had always been looking forward. But now he knew that he had accepted Halmeston, however cold the atmosphere, as his home, and, without knowing this, the secure base from which to go forward with his ambitions.

The storm did not help to dispel his feeling of separation. He had lost his father and his home. He knew he could now stand on his own feet, but the certainty of this did not dispel his feeling of separation. He would have to find the home in his own family.

He associated himself with the storm. The crashes of thunder seemed to be inside his whole being, and the strength of the storm ebbed into his blood. He felt better. He decided he would write to his grandfather. The dissociation with his father would only be a temporary thing – time, and age on his father's side, would mellow the situation and, in the end, he might even bring his father out to Africa.

He got up and looked out of the door. The stretch of open ground in front of him was awash. The rain pockmarked the water for as far as James could see.

"I'm glad we are on a slight rise," he shouted to Morgan above the storm.

"We may yet be down the Makabusi with the crocodiles," answered Morgan, but the voice did not show any enthusiasm.

The lightning spaced itself out from the thunder but the pounding power of the rain kept up the incessant drumming on the roof. He went back to his letters and tried to read the dates on the postmarks of Ester's letters. He wanted to read them in chronological order. It was still too dark and he went back to the open door and watched the rain. It was the only opening in the hut and was never closed.

The rain eased and the light improved; white patches appeared among the thunder clouds.

James selected the first letter. With his hunting knife, he slit open the well-travelled envelope, glancing across at Morgan as he did so. Morgan looked away quickly. James unfolded his letter.

 Halmeston, 11th February, 1890
My dear Jamie,

There was a terrible row when Father found out you had gone. He has been very bad to me ever since and says, when he talks to me, which over the last week, since you left, has not been very often, that it is all my fault, and that I should have warned him so that he could have stopped you from going. At first, I said I didn't know how you had travelled but that you had just gone off on a boat to Cape Town. Yesterday, he found out that the only boat that has left for Cape Town in the last month was Grandfather's Dolphin. *It made him so annoyed that when he came home the veins stood out on his neck. The servants are just as frightened, poor things, and it really isn't their fault. I mean none of them even knew you were going. I am still not sure whether the whole thing was such a good idea but I hope you have a safe journey and do be careful with all those heathens. I've read some books on them since you left and they do sound so terrible. I just couldn't face Father if I told him that you had been killed.*

I wonder when and where you will be reading this letter. You already seem so far away and it has only been a week. I think I must find myself a nice, kind husband as this house has become too awful – too awful for words. Oh, I do wish you were here and then you just might be able to calm him down. I know he is going to write to you, as he has made me tell him everything now he knows you are with Grandfather. I don't think it is going to be a nice letter but I couldn't help him finding out about everything, could I, not after he knew that you were on the Dolphin.

I can hear him coming in now, so I'll finish this letter.

Do look after yourself, darling Jamie, and please think of your little sister every now and again. I think of you all the time.

Your loving sister,
Ester

"My father certainly did not approve of my leaving," said James aloud as he put the letter down.

Morgan made no answer, and James picked up the second letter his sister had written and slit it open.

 Halmeston, 18th December, 1890
> *My dear Jamie,*
>
> The Dolphin *came into port today and Father boarded it without getting permission. He started shouting at Grandfather about you, and it seems that Grandfather had him put off the ship. By the look of Father, I think there was some violence but he won't tell me, as you can imagine. Isn't this all too terrible? It must give the family a very bad name, and after all that Father has done to try and improve it. I am sure the story must be right around Liverpool by now and Father will never be invited to all those houses. I think it is rather funny. I mean, can you imagine Father being pushed off a ship by a lot of tar-encrusted seamen? He did not come back with his top hat, so I think that must have been lost in the mêlée. Can you imagine?*
>
> *I was so glad to receive your letter and read that you had been accepted for this expedition. I am sure you were wrong about them not nearly wanting you to go. They could not very well have refused after you had gone all that way to Cape Town. I read in the paper that you started on the last part of your journey some time ago but since then there has been no word. I expect to hear any day now. Everyone is very interested about this new colony and Mr Rhodes's name is on everyone's lips. Apart from Father, the rest of us find it rather nice to say that you are with the column. I mean there is no one else in Liverpool, or Manchester for that matter, who actually has a brother with the expedition. Some of them don't really believe me so I hope you do something spectacular and*

have your name in the paper. I would then cause a sensation at a tea party. Oh, and people do so talk and it would be such fun. When you come back, you must bring me a lion's skin or something. You will be careful though; the papers think the expedition is really rather dangerous despite what Mr Rhodes may say to the contrary. They say this king Lobengula, or whatever they call him, is likely to cause trouble. Some of the papers say he has an army of a hundred thousand. All those heathens against less than five hundred of you is just too horrible to think about. You will be careful, now, won't you?

I think Father is trying to find me a nice, eligible husband as we have been having so many social evenings at Halmeston. Some of the men are very nice and they have good manners, but they don't seem to have very much backbone. I mean, I can't imagine them going off into the jungle with all those heathens. Anyway, these little evenings do pass the time so much better than being alone with Father and, just maybe, the man will come along. It's rather exciting not knowing whether your future husband is just around the corner. I don't know what Father is going to do with this great big house if he is left on his own. He must have realised that his children would leave him one day. It rather frightens me, the idea of being old, there doesn't seem very much to look forward to.

I hope Father calms down as he really is impossible at the moment. Fancy being thrown off the Dolphin! Now you will write and tell me all your news and just exactly what you are doing. I still think of you a lot.

Your loving sister,
    Ester

He put the letter on top of the others he had read and picked up the last of his mail. He did not recognise the handwriting but he knew that it must be from his grandfather. Outside, the sun was trying to shine through the clouds. He put the chair back against the table he had made for himself. Morgan made no move to join him as he went out of the hut into the cool aftermath of the rain. A cock crowed and the water dripped from the msasa trees. He stretched and yawned at the same time. He noticed that Dr Jameson's administration building had a distinct bulge in its brick wall. Behind the building, a closed-up brick kiln steamed as the fire inside drove off the water. Just to its left, and full of water, stood the gaping hole in the side of an ant hill which had been dug open so that the earth could be used to make bricks. Further on into the bush, it was clean and fresh. He smelt the distinct, pungent smell of rainwater on stale wood ash.

"Quite some rain," an ex-trooper called to him.

"Yes," said James.

The ex-trooper passed on and went into the brick building. James walked away from the hut, passed the brick building, greeting everyone he saw. He thought about the rains between Fort Salisbury and the Hartley hills, and wondered whether they had been severe enough to prevent von Brand and Fentan crossing the rivers that lay in between. Von Brand knew more about it than any of them, he told himself; anyway, they had a surprise for them when they arrived. He selected the large stump of a tree beside the proposed main street of Fort Salisbury and perched on the wet wood. He pulled out his hunting knife and slit open the last of his mail. Spread on his knees, the sheets of paper gently ruffled by the wind, he began to read.

 On board Dolphin, *Liverpool,*
22nd December, 1890
Dear James,
It is not my custom to write letters but I think this one will amuse you. I hope you are safe, lad, and that by the time you read this letter you will have done the journey, and that old bastard will not have interfered. My

information was, when we passed through Cape Town on the way back from China, that Lobengula was trying to get his military together. You could have had that fight I warned you about but I warned you then that nothing good was gained easy in life. I have been praying for your safety and I feel myself responsible for you, being in the kind of danger I think you might be.

Your father came on board a few days back and he made a right fool of himself. I watched him climb up that gang plank in his top hat and overcoat, and it was hotter than many days I remember in Cape Town. I didn't recognise him at first. He then bellows a lot of bombastic abuse at his father, all about kidnapping his son, and he didn't quite see my side of the humour when I had the bosun put him back down the gang plank. This time his hat fell in the sea and, the next time Dolphin *came up against the wharf, it got squashed good and proper. Being that the whole thing was seen by the ship's company, it's right round Lancashire now and a lot of laughs they've been having, so I understand, in the business quarter of Liverpool. Poor Ernest, it just doesn't seem right for a man in his position. By the tone of his language, I think he may cut you off, lad, but if you need any help you can always turn to your grandfather. I think Ernest would have quite a surprise if he knew how much his old man was worth.*

I know you wouldn't call on any help unless it was really necessary. I have a lot of faith in you, lad. If you need a partner in any of your ventures, I won't call that help but business. You may need machinery for mining or farming and it wouldn't be much for me to load it on the Dolphin *and bring it out to Cape Town on one of my trips. The old ship has got a good few more voyages in her yet and, if the old skipper holds out, then so will the ship. It certainly dropped a few years off my life seeing Ernest's hat drop down the scuppers.*

Let's hope Morgan taught you how to shoot as you may need it against Lobengula's military. I liked Morgan, and that big German, so give them my regards. I don't like the sound of the newspapers but then you can never trust what they say – all out for sensation to attract the readers. Pity of it is, as I see it, that everyone believes what they see in print, just because it is in print. I say it's got to be written in the first place, same as everything else, so what's the difference? There's a lot less honesty in the world today than there was when I was a boy.

I hope you find the gold and get a farm, lad. If the climate's not too hot for an old man, and Rhodes puts in that railway he's been promising everyone, I will come and see you. I've promised that before, but I mean it, and Mr Rhodes won't have to get his railway as far as Cairo to make my journey possible! I don't think I've ever been that far inland before. Well, we're never too old to try something new.

If you have a chance, write me your news, care of the dock master at Liverpool. He's an old mate of mine and he knows when I'm coming into port.

All the luck, lad,
Your affectionate grandfather

Smiling to himself, James folded up the letter and put it back in the envelope. He slowly retraced his steps to the hut and ducked his head to go inside. Morgan was sitting in the same position. James put his grandfather's letter on top of the pile with the others and glanced back at Morgan.

"Anything wrong, Rhys?" he asked.

"Levenhurst is dead," said Morgan after a moment, but without looking at James.

"Yes," said James, "that would have altered everything."

"If she had only waited," said Morgan. "If we had not contrived to have Gavin. If we had kept it to ourselves and waited."

"It is no good recriminating afterwards," said James, sitting in the chair. "It is never possible to look into the future. If that were possible, we would not enter into most parts of our lives. Did Annabel write and tell you?"

"No, the people who look after Gavin," he replied flatly. "They say the title has gone to a cousin, together with most of the Levenhurst wealth; but in his will he stipulated that Annabel and her husband should always be allowed to live in a wing of Sheldon Hall." Morgan stood up and began to pace the hut. "All that we have been through up till now has been pointless."

"Why don't you go back to England and try and see her?" suggested James. "If the husband is living under her roof, he can't throw you out of her house."

"That is exactly what I will do," said Morgan, brightening immediately. "She could get a divorce under the circumstances. We have Gavin's foster parents as witnesses. I think they would help us, too. First, I must make money and have a home to bring her back to. That's it. By the end of the next dry season, I will have enough. That mine is going to be rich. We will peg out our farms in the valley at the same time and build houses. Some of the bush timber makes excellent material – they say it is like teak – we can build the foundations of granite and thatch the roof – so it will be cool in summer." He stopped pacing. "Think of the view out over the Mazoe valley. If we site the houses correctly it will take her breath away. And the climate is good, despite all the rain this year. Jim, from the money we get from the mine, you and I are going to buy up the whole valley. It will be Morgan and Carregan estates for as far as a horse can ride in one day in any direction." He began pacing again. "We will be just like the Boers and breed ourselves large families. There will be more than enough land for all of them when they grow up. Jim, you are a genius; you have the answer."

He stopped abruptly. "I will not write to her, as he may get his hands on the letter. Next year I will go over myself. There will be the three of you to look after the mine and the farm. Maybe Annabel and I could get married in the new country. You must be best man. It is settled. I wish Willy would get here so we can get on with the plans." Morgan began pacing the floor again. The light faded and it began to rain.

IN THE MIDDLE OF MARCH, von Brand trekked into Fort Salisbury alone, having buried Michael Fentan in the Hartley hills. Fentan had died in the rain and wet, from the cold, wasting dysentery. Von Brand had tried to reach Fort Salisbury to obtain medical attention, but the first river had held them helpless on the far bank. Morgan's enthusiasm subsided. With a cold precision, they worked on their plans to open what they called the Fentan Mine. They hired two of the pioneer wagons and eight of the remaining oxen, and, at the end of April, with no clouds in the sky, they trekked out of Fort Salisbury in the direction of the Mazoe hills.

3

 Fentan Mine,
    8th November, 1891
    Dear Grandfather,
    Since I last wrote, the rains have broken again. We are praying that they will not be as severe as last year, as, if this is the case, the new colony will be stillborn. Last year the expectation of so much gold carried us through the wettest weeks. This year, there can be no such confidence.

    We still have a profitable mine but there is no telling when the reef will peter out for good. It has tapered into nothing twice this summer, and each time it took us many days to find the gold again. As I write, we have paid for the machinery and hire of the wagons but there is very little left for the three of us. Morgan is despondent, as by now he had hoped to have enough money to travel to England to find his girl. If he wishes to bring her to even the bare essentials of comfort, he will have to wait a year, or even two, and that's only if the reef holds out. With the small surplus from the gold, we have started buying up the farming rights from those of us who have had enough. We have purchased two three-thousand-acre allocations for

twenty pounds each and taken up these farms in the valley
here together with our own allocations. Von Brand has lost
some of his faith in gold and has agreed to participate in
our farming syndicate. We have used the oxen to plough
for maize and have planted a hundred acres with the new
rains. It is hard work operating the mine and stumping out
the land for the crop, and then ploughing and planting. We
have found some of the Mashona who are prepared to
work for a wage but they are most unreliable and it is
nearly as quick to do the job oneself. Nonetheless, we are
progressing, if only slowly. It has been a beautiful dry
season and the climate at this time of the year is perfect.

Mr Rhodes was in the country two months ago for the
first time. He visited our mine, as he did many of the others
that are producing gold. We complained bitterly of having
to pay fifty per cent of our gold to his Charter Company
but he explained that it was the price of our opportunity. It
is difficult to disagree with Mr Rhodes – he is very
persuasive. I liked him, but then so did everyone else. He
told us the telegraph had just reached Fort Salisbury.
Provided it is not out by the rains, or the natives, then we
will be able to instantly communicate with the outside
world. It is a great solace and removes some of the sense of
isolation. We can now co-ordinate our efforts if we are
faced with danger.

During the dry season, there was no word of the
Matabele or of Lobengula and we had thought that he had
come to accept our occupation. This was until a few days
ago. Here, on the mine, we are not sure whether it is a
rumour, but word has it that Lobengula has been refused
his annual tribute from a Mashona Chief. They say Chief
Lomagundi felt safe behind the protection of the white men
and thought fit not to make his annual trip to the king's
kraal at Gu-Bulawayo. The rumour is that Lobengula has
sent out a raiding party to exact his tribute from

Lomagundi. What worries me is that this kind of thing can only lead to a clash between ourselves and the Matabele impis. How can we sit back and see these wretched Mashonas butchered? They are also our source of labour, for what that is worth. No, I cannot see us living side by side in peace with Lobengula. I do not think he is looking for war. In fact, up till now, he has done everything to stop any fighting. He has made many gestures that appear hostile but I think they were done to placate his inDunas. Now, he is faced with a direct reproach to his sovereignty. If he allows this one to go unnoticed then others will follow and it is even rumoured that another chief has done just this. On the other hand, if we tell the chiefs to pay their proper tributes, or accept the consequence, they will think nothing of us. They may even become militant. There are many of them and few of us, so we must be careful. It seems to me to be a case of the power of Rhodes or the power of Lobengula.

Something has gone wrong with the mill again. The steady clanking has stopped. That thing was born of Satan. I can hear Morgan shouting my name so I must close this letter and go and help him. I always look forward to receiving your letters.

Your loving grandson,
James

 Halmeston, 3rd June, 1892
Darling Jamie,

I know you will be thrilled. I am going to be married. I am so excited that I can barely contain myself to write this letter. Isn't it all so wonderful? Now you must promise to come home for the wedding, won't you, Jamie? I mean, you've been amongst all those heathens long enough, anyway. It's going to be a large wedding and Father has promised to make it the most splendid of the year. He says no money is to be spared when his daughter marries the only son of a Viscount. Darling Oswald just doesn't have any money but he is such a hoot and I'm sure we are going to be happy. You know, Father changed towards me once he saw Oswald was serious. Father is in such a good mood that he says he will welcome your coming to the wedding. I contemplated asking Grandfather but I thought Father might say that that was taking it too far, and I didn't want to change his mood. He really can be charming to people when he tries.

Oh, Jamie, you will come, won't you? I would even try and persuade you to stay in England after this but, from the letters you write, I can see you are all involved in this new country. It doesn't sound very nice to me, with all those snakes and wild animals. I could see the point of making lots of money out there and coming home rich but this notion of yours to settle, and even bring up a family in Africa, seems funny to me. I mean everyone knows that the white man can only live in the tropics for a few years. Some people say you have to be careful of the very strong sun as it can affect the brain, so there is more than one reason for you to come home for the wedding and look at your life afresh. Father will even pay the fare if you haven't enough money.

The wedding is not planned until late autumn of next year, so you will have plenty of time to receive this letter and make your preparations. We had hoped to be married earlier but you just cannot have any idea of how much there is to do in the planning of a big wedding. Oswald has a number of important relations in India, and they are all going to be given a proper invitation and a discreet suggestion that the Carregans will pay their return passage. People are so funny about money and unless they really want to come, they will never spend money on *pleasing other people. It was father's idea to offer the free passages as he is determined to have all those people at the reception at Halmeston, but I am not sure whether they might not take it the wrong way. I mean, they all have enough money if they really wish to come.*

Immediately you receive this letter you must write and tell me exactly when you will be arriving. A lot of my friends are dying to meet you as all that business of your being on the pioneer column into Mashonaland was very romantic; so there will be lots of entertainment and you will really have a lovely time as well as being at the wedding. My hope is that one of the girls will so capture your heart that you will not wish to go back to Africa; and, oh Jamie, that would be too wonderful.

I cannot wait to hear the name of the ship on which you will be sailing home.

Father sends you his regards.

Your loving sister,
   Ester

Fentan Mine,
   11th December, 1892
   My dear Sister,
   The vagaries of the South African post being such as it is, it took six months for your letter to fall into my hands. What happened was that one of my friends collected my mail in Fort Salisbury, knowing that he would be passing through the Mazoe hills on his way to Shamva. Unfortunately, he was murdered on the road and all his possessions stolen. This was obviously done by the Mashona but we all hope the reason was theft and not political. The police have raided the kraal which harboured

the gang and justice has been done. They found Mason's saddle bag in one of the huts, which is how I came to finally receive your letter.

You will have received my telegraph giving you both my congratulations and every wish for your happiness well before you receive this letter. There might have been time enough for me to reach England before your wedding, but the possible lack of this was not the only reason for my telling you in the telegraph that I would not be able to attend. Of course I would do everything feasible to be at the wedding of my only sister, and a reconciliation with Father would have added to my pleasure, but the whole concept of leaving Mashonaland is out of the question. At the moment, there is a great deal of unrest in the country due to the attitude of the Mashona to Lobengula. I wrote to you briefly before of this if you will remember. A number of Mashona chiefs have failed to pay their tribute to Lobengula and two of them, Lomagundi and Tshibi, along with their families, have been butchered by Matabele raiding parties. Just before I received your letter, an even more dangerous situation occurred, and even though the previous unrest would have prompted me not to leave the country, the latter has made it impossible. I cannot see how we are to prevent ourselves being drawn into a full-scale war with the Matabele.

A few weeks ago, five hundred yards of the telegraph wire were stolen, and as this telegraph is of vital importance to our very existence it was necessary to find the thieves and exact a stern punishment. Accordingly, a troop of the BSA Company Police was despatched to investigate. The nature of the theft being such an unusual occurrence amongst the natives, it caused them all to be talking of the wire and it was easy for the police to not only find the wire but the culprits as well. The theft had been carried out by a petty Mashona Chief, Gomalla, together with others under his instruction. The gravity of his action was carefully explained to him and by all reports he knew well that he was acting as a thief. Accordingly, he was fined fifty head of cattle and the animals and the wire were handed over on the spot. The police withdrew and the case was closed. It now transpires that the cattle, paid as the fine, do not belong to Gomalla, but to Lobengula. As part of each Mashona chief's taxes, he is required to herd and graze a number of the Matabele royal cattle. Each animal must be carefully accounted for and any loss by natural causes must be witnessed by a representative of Lobengula. Immediately, Doctor Jameson, who is now administrator of the territory, heard of the ownership of the cattle and he returned them to Lobengula with a full explanation and extracted his fifty head from Gomalla's own herd.

Whether Gomalla was a humourist or a troublemaker has yet to be seen but, whatever, he has created an explosive situation between his two antagonists and maybe he hopes that he has turned the wrath away from himself. If he has the full sight of the potential of the situation he has so cleverly caused, then he must visualise the sight of his enemies killing each other. It is imperative for Lobengula to take his fullest revenge, as the most sacred possession of any tribe is its cattle. Gomalla has made a laughing stock of the Matabele rule. It is said that immediately Lobengula received the letter from Doctor Jameson, he called in his regiments to Bulawayo and is now reported to be preparing a full scale impi to march into Mashonaland, when the rains have finished, to teach Gomalla and his ilk a lesson concerning the power of the Matabele.

In native terms, Lobengula is perfectly entitled to do just this. The irony of the situation is that Gomalla, who created the situation first, by mocking the Europeans, will find his people being defended by the very police who fined him the cattle. You see, when a Matabele impi becomes incensed, as it is at the moment, and the very pride of the Zulu, their ancestors, has been slapped, it will invade and kill indiscriminately with the greatest carnage. They will kill thousands of the defenceless Mashona all because of one man who became too clever. Gomalla thinks that we will intervene to stop this bloodshed and I cannot see anything else for us to do. We know we have been duped, but the situation seems to me to have gone beyond the point of anyone being able to find a practical solution. If we do nothing, thousands will die, and if we do something, there will be war, a war required no less by Lobengula than Jameson, but beautifully precipitated by a petty chief and the opposing prides of two races.

So you can see that it is for this reason that I am prevented from leaving Mashonaland at the moment as otherwise my friends will see me as running away, and none of us have come this far with our development to do that. These are not heroic thoughts but the common thinking of all of us. It is right to stay and that is the end of it. I am sorry, but I hope you and Father will understand my predicament.

I think we will shortly be asked to join the colours, though war cannot happen until April when the rains have finished. If war comes, it will be before December, during the dry season. I hope your wedding will not be spoiled by a war against the Matabele. Morgan and I are hoping that everyone will keep their tempers, but people are never very good at this once they have been properly insulted. It seems so stupid that thousands of people should die for the sake of five hundred yards of telegraph wire.

I have despatched to both of you my wedding gift of a selection of well cured skins. The animals were shot by Morgan and myself and, even though he has never met *you, he has asked me to send you both his best wishes for your future happiness. We will be thinking of England on November the fourth.*

The mine is still producing gold and this year we have three hundred acres of the farms under maize. We have used most of the money from the gold to buy land and farm equipment. We estimate that the syndicate now owns thirty-six thousand acres and with slow, hard work, and the new equipment, we hope to bring a large portion of the seven thousand arable acres under the plough within ten years. It is removing the trees that takes the time. However, it is a rewarding process and I could never be more happy in my life were it not for the prospect of war. If war does not come, we will build ourselves substantial brick houses during the next dry season. However, if war with the Matabele breaks out, who knows what the outcome will be. There are still very few of us in the new country. Anyway, we are better prepared than in 1890. Unlike Willy von Brand, I do not relish the idea of war.

Please see how sorry I am not to be able to attend your wedding; but how else can I act in these circumstances? My love will go out to you on your wedding day, but of course I will write again before then.

Your loving brother,
James

Fentan Mine,
8th February, 1893
Dear Grandfather,

I received the draft for two thousand pounds with amazement. I have since had discussions with Morgan and von Brand and your suggestion of becoming a partner in the syndicate has been accepted. Under the circumstances, and so that each of us has a clear and written allocation of a portion of the joint wealth, we have decided to form ourselves into a limited company and, in the terms of our original partnership agreement and the new offer of capital, we will allocate the shares. We have accordingly given a value to the mine and to the land we have already purchased. It is difficult to value anything at the moment with this war so close to erupting, but as the outcome, in one form or the other, is without doubt, we have ignored this problem and only looked into the future – if we cannot contain the Matabele ourselves then imperial forces will be sent into the country to protect both life and property. The figure we have reached is eight thousand pounds, and, with your two thousand put into the venture, you will have a holding of twenty per cent. As you stated twice that I must allocate the money as I saw correct, I have accordingly fixed the share issue at this amount. Originally I was not to receive the same share as Morgan and von Brand – if I had prospected on my own I would not have known where to start – but, as they are now both behind my idea of farming they have agreed to split the shares of the original four partners equally. The twenty per cent for Michael Fentan will be held in trust until we can trace his family. We know that he came from the Cape and when one of us is travelling in that part of the country we will make the necessary enquiries.

I remain your affectionate grandson,
James

4

_L_obengula, alone in his day hut, prepared himself to use the full extent of his mind to communicate with his ancestors. The previous night, the February moon had been almost full over Gu-Bulawayo, the place of the killings. There had been a continual activity around the king's kraal as preparations reached their climax for the Great Dance. When the full moon waned, the most important days in the Matabele year would be fulfilled.

Lobengula walked to the door and stood just within the shadow so that he could not be seen from the outside. His father had conquered, and it was not for him to stand and watch the disintegration of so much power and territory. He walked out of his hut and crossed the open space to his armchair, sat down and felt the heat from the last rays of the sun. He would paint himself later, he told himself, but for the moment he would relax and prepare his mind for the great questioning and receiving of the answer. He flapped his loin cloth at the flies and then rested the nape of his neck on the back of his chair. If there was sufficient will and strength of mind, he told himself, then there was an answer to any problem, however great its size and consequence. For him to grow weak of mind and determination was to abdicate his right to lead his people. It was the logic of his experience. He forced himself to relax his whole body. He was the king and the king, he knew, must not forsake his people.

When the sun dropped behind the hills, he got up and went back into his day hut. He was ready to prepare himself for his communication with the spirits. He walked to the far side of the hut and put his hands in the liquid contained in a fourth pot and then streaked the front of his body with black. He slowly walked in front of the three pots that rested on a low trellis of uncut timber. He stood and waited for the beginning of the night.

When the last light of day had given way to the light of the full moon, he felt the presence of the three is-Anuzi. He turned to face them.

"*Bayete Kumalo*," they said to him in turn.

He turned to the first pot and sprinkled some of the liquid content over himself and then, one by one, he sprinkled it over the three is-Anuzi. He completed the ritual with the second and third pots. Their eyes grew accustomed to the blackness. There was silence. They concentrated their minds to go out and seek the spirits. They did not hear the screeching of the crickets in the long grass, or the lowing of the cattle in the royal kraal as the beasts settled down for the night.

"I wish to speak of rain with Umgweni, the inDuna of my father, who always understood the coming of the rain," said Lobengula, in a calm, soft voice.

There was silence in the hut, and then Lobengula repeated himself.

There was silence.

"Will the rains continue late?" asked Lobengula.

"The rains will be short," said a voice from the is-Anuzi of rain.

"How short?" asked Lobengula.

There was no answer and they waited.

"I wish to speak of crops with Gono, the father of my mother, who knows the earth and the way of crops," said Lobengula in a soft but firm voice, and there was silence.

Lobengula repeated himself and they waited.

"Speak to me, Lobengula, son of my child," said the voice of Gono from the throat of the second is-Anuzi.

"Will there be food enough for my people in the season of no rain that will shortly be ahead of us?"

"Yes," said the voice from the is-Anuzi.

"It is good," replied Lobengula, "and we thank our ancestors for their generosity."

For half an hour there was no sound and no movement in the hut.

"I wish to speak of war with Mzilikazi, my father," shouted Lobengula, and he repeated himself again and again.

The sound of his voice bound itself up in the night.

They waited and strained to increase the power of their minds. Lobengula called to his father, and the lapses of silence increased as they took their minds further and further outside of their physical bodies. Lobengula heard the voice of his father in the great distance before the is-Anuzi of war spoke with the voice of Mzilikazi.

"You call to me, Lobengula, my son," said the voice.

"It is with comfort that I hear you talking to me," answered Lobengula. "I will explain to you the riddle that I see as having no answer, but to Mzilikazi, founder of our nation, it will be but a trifle." He paused. "When you lived on the ground between the great rivers, and sent out the power of your great impis to maintain your law, you welcomed and protected the white men who came into your country to kill the elephant. In the beginning, there were but few and they brought with them a knowledge which cured the great pains of your body and has since cured the pains of my own.

"There was good in their coming and they recognised the power of Mzilikazi. Before going out to kill the elephant, they came first to the royal kraal; they brought presents and they learnt to speak the language of our forebears and we heard, in the nights of talk by the big fire, of a new power that came from across the greatest river of them all. This power was greater than that of the Boer and it reminded us of the terrible destruction of Dingaan, our cousin from the south. But you were wise and accepted these people as your friends and not one of them was harmed between the great rivers, and, when you left us to join our great ancestors, I also welcomed the white men to my new kraal here at Gu-Bulawayo, and I gave them the same protection as yourself.

"But as the years have gone by, there have come more and more of these people, and it has needed all my power to stop the young men from my regiments from killing these people, as they have recognised the danger of their growing presence and the young regiments wish to remove the danger before it grows too big. The white man has done nothing to harm us and I have heard that at the back of these people there is a great army that has guns so big that the bravest of our regiments will not reach them with their assegais. It is not fear that makes me see this danger but wisdom, as I know that the weapons with which we fight are not strong enough against so many guns. Therefore, and with this knowledge, I have tried to keep back the white men, but I have never withdrawn my protection. But in all the beginnings of life there is a seed that can become a great tree and so it is that the white man has grown between the big rivers, and now it is that they have an authority of their own and they do not seek the protection of Lobengula.

"For many years, they asked me to let them dig for gold and, until I gave one man that right, they came like the flies around the udders of a cow, and when I agreed to let Rhodes dig for gold it was to make the nation richer in cattle and to remove the flies from the udders of the cow, which was me. When they came to dig for gold, they came as an impi, and I let them come because I thought they would accept my authority, but this is no longer. Many of the inDunas of our tribe are telling me that now is the time to attack before it is too late and there are too many of them with their guns between the big rivers.

"To make sure that I was not hearing false words, I sent two of my oldest inDunas across the great river to the country of these people. They were the eyes of Lobengula, as I knew they would not lie to their king. And what they told me of these people, of the power of the white queen and the great stone buildings and the great size of their regiments and the size of the guns, was of a far more dangerous tribe than ever we had heard of beside the big fire. So I tell my regiments that if they kill one white man there will be ten more to seek his vengeance, and if they kill the ten there will be a hundred until such time as the whole of the Matabele impis will be crushed by their numbers.

"First, they came for the elephant and when they had shot the elephant they came for the gold and next they will come for my land and the great pride of the Matabele will be but as workers for the white men as we will have no one to raid, and the great wealth of our people will have been lost to their protection. And if we raid they will fight us and follow us out of the land of the Mashona into the heart of our people. If we stay we will starve and if we go we must fight them and go on fighting them until they send a big enough army to crush us. I cannot see a way of peace for us but if I do not fight I will have lost my authority over the Mashona and then through my weakness I will lose my power over the Matabele. I, Lobengula, will not have been worthy of so great a father. I have made words on paper with this great white queen and she has told me to trust Rhodes, who is the inDuna of her people in my country.

"Give me wisdom, Father; give me the answer to this riddle and I will go out and change the course of time."

There was a tangible silence in the hut. Lobengula felt the full frustration of his predicament turning over and over in his stomach.

"You are king," said the voice of Mzilikazi at last from the throat of the is-Anuzi of war. "If you need to kill Gomalla, then go and kill him and if any man stands in your way kill him too. At the end of the Great Dance, throw your spear to the East and take your just plunder from the Shona. I have seen the regiments not going there for three years and the Shona have grown fat. They are not giving up their right dues of cattle and grain. It is your right and duty to exact punishment. Be king, Lobengula."

A surge of power went through Lobengula's body. He knew his father had spoken the truth. He had been growing old, he told himself, but because he was old and unable to throw an assegai with power, it did not mean that there were not many in his regiments who held such strength. It was simple, he told himself as he walked past the is-Anuzi and out of the day hut, his movements strong and powerful. He would fight.

LED BY THEIR INDUNA, Gambo, the Mbizo regiment surged up to their king in open line, their assegais and shields held above the feathers from their head-dress. As they stamped their way forward in perfect unison, the regiment of the Nsukamini followed behind in exact copy, and behind them the regiments of the Siziba, the Hlate, the Nyathi and the Babambeni. The feet of ten thousand natives stamped at the dust and sounded like claps of thunder. A warrior emerged from the front rank of the Mbizo regiment and pantomimed the killing of a foe, keeping his movements in time to the stamping feet. The wings of the regiment fanned out to form a half moon around the king who stood in front of his day hut; the grass fence encircling the king, the regiments and the dust of Gu-Bulawayo. The blue jay feathers on his headdress were magnificent, and the jackals' tails hung over his belly and the skin of a leopard hung in penance from his right shoulder. Around his ankles were the small bones of his enemies, in his left hand an ox-hide shield, painted white, and in his right hand the ceremonial assegai that he would throw into the ground at the end of the ceremony to tell his people in which way to raid.

Lobengula felt like the king he was, and he surveyed his regiments with pride. Their discipline was perfect. They would stamp on the white men if they interfered with his raids. He told himself that the power of the Matabele would go on for a hundred years. There was only one law, and that was the law of force. He, Lobengula, had that force and he was going to use it.

The regiments moved on the same spot and the speed of their stamping increased. A sound like the wind started from the far wing of the regiments and, at first slowly, then faster and faster, mounted as the warriors hit their assegais against their shields with ever increasing force until it was a violent crashing; it receded down the line until it sounded like the sigh of the wind and then it came back again, built to violence once more, and died in the wind where it had started. Behind Lobengula, the elder inDunas watched with satisfaction. To their right, the nine Europeans still left in Gu-Bulawayo watched uneasily. Colenbrander recognised in Lobengula what he had not seen in him for years.

Lobengula held up his spear and the movement stopped instantly. The dust settled on sweat. He waited, holding them still. He looked slowly from right to left and then sprang out his left foot to the East and hurled his spear into the ground. They howled in response and rushed at him, the front line waving their spears to within inches of his face. They receded and then came at him again. The assegai remained stuck in the ground pointing directly into the heart of Mashonaland. Lobengula held up his shield and they stopped.

"First we shall feast," he shouted at them, "and then we will take what the Shona have forgotten to give. The power of the Matabele will not be thwarted."

5

"$\mathcal{I}$ shall be sad to see the old chief go," said von Brand and took another sip of his brandy. "I've known him for thirty years and he never did me, or any one of my friends, any harm. The Matabele themselves are a bloodthirsty lot and add little to anyone's way of life. They'll only be getting themselves what they have been giving to the surrounding tribes for seventy years. You can't live by stealing and murdering and not have someone do it to you in the end. It's the law of averages and progress. I don't care about the Matabele but I don't like killing a man who has been a friend for thirty years."

"I agree with you," said Morgan, "but what else can be done?"

"I expect the Charter Company thinks that all the gold is now to be found around Bulawayo," said James. "We certainly haven't seen much of it at this end of the country. Maybe they want war so that they can conquer by force of arms. It would establish the correct legal points for occupancy. I hear the value of the Charter share has fallen to a quarter of the value it held at the time of occupation. There is hope of loot and gold in Matabeleland if Rhodes goes to war. He will be able to increase the capital of the company and attract more money to pay for the police and the railway line and to give him time to produce something of value for the shareholders.

Without gold in Matabeleland, it is going to be a long time before the Charter Company can afford to pay a dividend."

"We were lucky to find enough gold to buy the farms," agreed Morgan. "You were right, Jim, to guide our money into farmland and not into mining."

"*Ja*, maybe you're right," said von Brand. "Maybe Rhodes wants war."

They lapsed into silence and James studied the colours of the sunset in the far distance between the hills. The light was reflected into his face as he sat on the step, taking his first drink of the evening. He was tired, having been in the lands since six o'clock that morning.

"Looks like your sister is not going to get married without knowing her brother is involved in a war," said Morgan. "You were right not to go. You'd have kicked yourself if you'd been in England after the developments at Fort Victoria and the unrest of the last few months. I'm sure Jameson will call us out. He must send us in before the main rains break or otherwise the rivers will be impassable and the supply wagons will bog down in the mire. It's four months since the Matabele began their raids into Mashonaland. I thought we would be called up after that first raid on Gomalla's kraal, but all the diplomacy since hasn't changed the situation. They say the press at home is in favour of Rhodes stopping the indiscriminate killings of the impis. If the doctor has been waiting for the right time he can find it now. He could send a column on Bulawayo and hoist the Union Jack. If Lobengula has any sense, he'll do what his father did when Shaka made it too hot in Zululand, and trek north. He can trek over the Zambezi. The tribes up there won't put up much of a fight against his regiments."

"*Ja*," said von Brand, "it might put him a few years ahead of civilisation. Who's getting up to pour the next drink?"

"It's my turn," said James and got up and went over to the sideboard that he had built out of bush timber.

"I hope we have good rains in the coming season," said Morgan as he held his glass out for a refill. "All we need is a drought."

"*Ja*," said von Brand, "there's either too bloody much rain or too bloody little."

"I think we should plough for next year's crops right after this year's rains," said James, filling his own glass. "That way the moisture will stay in the ground instead of opening up the soil to the sun at the height of the dry season. You saw it happen this year."

"That might help," said Morgan. "We've got a lot to learn."

"I still think this year's maize is going to be better than last," said James. "We've prepared the lands much better."

"If it rains," said von Brand, swigging his brandy.

"It'll rain," said James.

"Why don't we go and see the local rainmaker?" asked Morgan, sitting up in his chair.

"He'd probably put a curse on the lot of us," said von Brand.

"We protect him from the Matabele," said Morgan.

"True," said von Brand. "Well, why don't you go and try him out tomorrow morning?"

"Farming may be unpredictable," said Morgan, "but it is better than following that elusive reef of gold. Jim's becoming an astute businessman; leasing the Fentan Mine was a stroke of genius. If they go on finding gold we receive our cut, but if the reef runs out they're the ones that have bought the new machinery."

"*Ja*," said von Brand, "this is real civilisation, having a permanent roof over our heads. I couldn't remember how it felt to live in a brick house. The roof doesn't leak, either," he added, looking up at the thatch twenty feet above his head.

"As and when we want to," said James, "we can build ourselves houses at various points on the farm. It will be easier to control, since riding to the extremity of the farm from here takes a day."

"I haven't seen half the place," said Morgan.

"We'll need all the land in the end," said James, "and more."

"You're the businessman," said von Brand, taking a drink.

They heard a noise outside and stopped to listen.

"A horse," said von Brand.

"Who the hell's this come visiting at sundowner time," said

Morgan, getting up and leaning over the balcony so that he could see the rider. "Hey, it's a policeman. Either of you two done anything wrong?"

James and von Brand also got up and leant over the balcony to watch the rider coming up the path.

"He's been riding that horse hard," said Morgan, sipping again at his brandy and taking a draw on his cheroot.

"Do you want a drink?" shouted von Brand to the rider.

"A brandy, with lots of water," came the answer.

"Come on, Jim," said von Brand, "you're butler for this round."

"Yes, sir," said James, and went off to find the water.

WHEN HE CAME BACK from the other side of the house, the constable was sitting in James's chair.

"What's all this about?" said James, nodding to the newcomer as he put the glass of brandy and water into the outstretched hand.

"War," said the constable.

"Lobengula?"

"Yes, Lobengula," said the constable. "I'm George Mann, by the way."

"James Carregan. When do we go?"

"Now, if you're ready. The Mashonaland Horse are assembling in Fort Salisbury under Major Forbes. The force is to meet up with Major Wilson's force at Iron Mine Hill. From there, we march on Bulawayo."

"How many of us?" asked Morgan, getting out of his chair.

"We should have over six hundred mounted men together with Maxims and seven pounders."

"Should be enough," said von Brand and drained his glass. "I think we had better sleep tonight and ride out with the dawn," he went on. "It's better to arrive fresh. Give me another drink, Rhys. I can see this may be my last drinking evening for some time and, anyway, it will make me sleep. You'd better sleep here too," he said to the constable, "as that horse of yours isn't going to go any further tonight. You might tell our servant to look after the animal while you're up, Rhys. There's no point in two of us moving around at the same time." He winked at the policeman.

"You," said Morgan, "are the most idle bastard I know."

"Now come off it, Rhys. You know you find it comforting to be of service to others."

They laughed and settled themselves down in their chairs as Morgan left the room. When the light from the setting sun had completely gone they lit the candles and watched the bugs incinerate themselves in the flames.

AT JUST AFTER ten o'clock von Brand stood up.

"The food tonight was good and I don't know when we are going to have Carregan's special cuisine again. To add to it all, I think I am drunk enough to sleep. Goodnight, gentlemen, and pleasant dreams to you all." He wavered a little and made his way to the bedroom.

"Goodnight," they called after him.

"I'll show you to a bed, George," said James to the policeman. "I'm going to turn in too and enjoy a comfortable bed for the last time in God knows how many nights."

"I'll check George's horse again and follow suit," said Morgan, and they all moved out of the living room and left it to the flickering candlelight.

James showed the policeman to a room and then went to his own; he closed the door behind him and groped his way to the window. There was some light from the moon so that he could see the outline and shadow of the farms. The Mazoe hills were dark. The image of light and progress had been removed by the sound of war and the future was no longer clear. He shuddered, despite the clammy heat. He had no wish to kill or be killed and he went to bed with this thought. As hard as he tried, it was some time before he could sleep.

He woke with a start. It was dark. He lay for a moment in his normal state of mind and then a nagging uncertainty took away the calm and he remembered the war. He groped in the dark for his box of matches, lit the candle and picked up the turnip watch from the bedside table and read the time; it was half past four and he thought there would be enough light for the horses to see their way by five o'clock.

He got out of bed, picked up the candle and went to the rough closet he had made for himself in the corner of the room. He pulled back the curtain and took out the uniform of an auxiliary lieutenant in the Mashonaland Horse. There were more officers than men in the force, as the authorities thought that promotion assisted recruitment; James smiled to himself at the ways of men, and put on the breeches and tunic. Lastly, he put on the bush hat, the brim of which was turned up vertically on the left side and held there by the force's badge. He unlocked the chain which held his Martini-Henry rifle and went to wake the others.

"Stop snoring and wake up," he shouted at von Brand.

Nothing happened. James shook him and he woke immediately, fear showing in his eyes, reflected by the light from the candle that James held in his right hand.

"It's all right, Willy," he said softly, "it's not the Matabele."

"I was dreaming they'd put a spell on me," said von Brand, recovering, "and it had a lot a do with a light."

"It's time to go to war," said James.

"Yeh, I thought it must be something like that," said von Brand. "Have you woken Morgan?"

"No, that's my next job."

"Throw cold water over him and he'll pee in his bed."

"Don't be crude," said James, "we're not in the army yet."

He went across to Morgan's room, knocked and was told to come in. He opened the door. Morgan was ready, dressed in an identical uniform.

"Morning, Rhys. Is the policeman up?"

"I think so," replied Morgan.

"I'll make some tea before we go."

"Yes, that'll be good."

"You don't like this war any more than me, do you?" asked James.

"No. I've known that old bastard for too long and I happen to like him. Selous won't have much stomach for this one either, and neither will Johan Colenbrander."

"I suppose it's the price of progress," said James, going out to make the tea.

"Some bloody price and some bloody progress," he heard Morgan say to himself.

TWENTY MINUTES later they rode the heavily laden horses away from the farmhouse. There was just enough light from the dawn to see their way.

"I hope we get back in time to plant the maize," said Morgan. "Did Chatunga completely understand the list of instructions?"

"I think so," replied James, "but it isn't easy for him to adapt to our ways. A couple of years ago he was living up a kopje to hide himself away from the Matabele."

They went on in silence but before they were out of sight of the farmhouse the three of them turned round to take a last look at their house. The policeman glanced back to see what they were looking at but saw nothing unusual.

6

*J*ames moved easily in the saddle and enjoyed the feel of the heavy, well-used saddlery. He leant forward slightly and patted the strong neck of his black horse. He had had the animal for two years. He looked across at Morgan, who still rode the same horse that he had ridden in the column. Von Brand's horses never lasted as long. James looked at the big stallion von Brand was expertly riding and conceded that the poor animal needed all of its strength to carry two hundred and sixty pounds.

They passed the head of the column. Forbes and Wilson were in formal conversation; neither smiled or looked at the other and even Wilson's pure white horse and the smaller, better-groomed roan of Forbes's looked straight ahead.

"Let's go," said von Brand, and they put their horses into a canter and enjoyed the fresh breeze against their hot faces. The sun was over its zenith and the humidity was building up for rain. The country, at first glance, was flat and sparsely populated with trees but, as they moved further away from the column and brought the pace of their horses down to a walk, they could see the country was undulating, with hidden folds in the ground. The grass grew up to four feet in height over large areas.

"We should fan out," said von Brand, and the trio split, with

James going straight ahead and Morgan breaking into a trot to go out on his left and von Brand doing the same on his right. James searched the countryside in front of him but saw nothing except the plains and the grass, taller in some places, and the occasional stunted tree. "Cattle country," he said to himself and pondered upon what the three of them would do with their pay for the campaign – a six-thousand-acre farm and twenty gold claims. Once again, he thought, we're to be paid with the enemy's property before the enemy has been forced from his tenancy. He looked around and saw the others scanning their sector of the countryside. They had seen nothing either; their horses were moving forward at a similar pace as they continued to turn their heads slowly from left to right and right to left. James looked up at the sky and saw that the cumulus clouds were building up heavily; the cores were black and full of rain. When that lot comes down, he said to himself, we'll be changed from a humid stickiness to a cold misery. No matter how hot the day had been, rain made him cold to the marrow.

After two hours they rode back to the column and reported the countryside clear of Matabele for six miles ahead. Forbes took the news, nodding to indicate he'd heard.

"They've probably run out of Bulawayo in the opposite direction," said Wilson. "They will have heard by now that Willy von Brand is on their trail."

They laughed easily and the three of them went off down the column, past the baggage wagons and the pack donkeys, to scout out on the flanks. Willie von Brand knew there was little likelihood of the Matabele having run out of Bulawayo but his ego was inflated to the degree that Wilson had intended. It's stupid, he thought to himself. At my age, I should be immune to flattery.

JAMES TOOK the watch at two in the morning. Shortly afterwards he saw one of the 'black watch' stumbling towards him. The laager opened and let the man inside and James saw that he had been badly stabbed. People gathered while James looked to his wounds.

The man talked, but with difficulty. He had gone down to the river for water and stumbled into the Nsukamini regiment. His two friends had been stabbed to death.

The alarm was given and bugles sounded urgently. James left the Shona to the doctor and joined the others calling to the 'black watch', and the women to come behind the wagons. Officers shouted instructions to their men. Ammunition boxes were ripped open. James distinctly heard the rushing noise of the impi as they ran up to attack. Some of the Shona women and children ran in the wrong direction, and onto the spears of the Matabele. The laager closed, and as James opened fire with the others, he saw a flight of assegais coming towards the laager and tried to make himself small. He concentrated on his aim, lying flat on his stomach under a wagon with Morgan on one side and von Brand on the other.

"Make sure you shoot straight," said Morgan and shot the nearest Matabele dead.

Slowly, James concentrated on killing while the Matabele did their best to kill him. They came at the wagons from around the perimeter of the laager, in waves and on their bellies. The first rush of wild and determined savagery gave way to sniping. Spears were hurled into the inner circle of the laager. The horses had been herded as close to the wagons as possible. James heard a horse behind him dying, but there was no time to look around and find out which one had been hit.

"Don't anyone get out from under the wagons," shouted von Brand. "Their spears are more dangerous than their guns. They are firing too high. They must have set their sights wrong. Don't let any of the bastards into the laager. Pick your target and fire straight and then pick the next. Don't try and shoot three at a time. The Maxims will pick out the concentrations."

As he shouted instructions he kept firing in quick succession, reloading the magazine from the pile of shells next to him. Morgan and von Brand were firing a fraction faster than James but none of them missed their targets. All around the firing was effective and the Matabele were unable to storm the laager; their spears only found ox and donkey flesh. There was no sign of panic in the laager. The stream of instructions issued by the veterans was carefully obeyed by everyone. The firing went on until dawn when the attack fizzled out.

"A bloody good cavalry charge is the answer now," said Morgan. "They've had a bad night not seeing us at all and a charge will break them completely."

"That one is probably in Forbes's book," said von Brand.

Thirty feet in front of James, a Matabele got up onto his knees. James aimed his rifle but the man deliberately fell forward onto his assegai. The spear slowly went into the man's stomach and stuck so that it rolled him over onto his back. James heard Borrow shouting to his troop to mount and, shortly afterwards, sixty men rode out of the laager in pursuit. As the light grew better, James saw that some of the regiments were trying to rally but each time they made the attempt, Borrow dismounted his men outside the range of their spears and fired into them in volleys.

"Which are the regiments?" James asked von Brand, as he counted three different colours of shields.

"The Nsukamini, Siziba and Hlate. The crack Mbizo must be somewhere else. You can see one thing, Jim, they don't know the meaning of fear. They may be heathens but they're brave and well led."

The firing stopped and half an hour later, Borrow and his troop rode back into the laager with one wounded casualty. During the night, one European had been killed.

"If we keep our heads and don't do anything stupid," said Morgan, "we will walk into Bulawayo without any problems. Our fire power from cover last night would have been too much for ten regiments. All we need is cover and ammunition and accurate shooting to stop them getting into the laager. They can only die once and there are only a certain number to kill. Will you pass me the coffee, Jim? For army rations, this stuff is drinkable. When this is all over," he said, turning to James, "I'll be able to sell my gold claims for cash and use the money to go to England. The more I think of it, the more I know it is the right thing to do. If Annabel wants to come back with me to Africa, what can her husband do? He knows about her past with me and relies upon her money. If we let him keep the money, I doubt if he will mind her going. Gavin will be fourteen now and in four years he can make up his own mind whether he wants to stay in Liverpool or come out to the new country to join us."

A moment later, he added, "What are you going to do with the three farms in Matabeleland? I presume we take them up together in the partnership."

"Yes," said James. "My idea is to sell the gold claims for cash and buy cattle. When they split up Lobengula's herd, we should be able to buy at the right price. This type of country looks good for cattle, but not for crops. They don't have as much rain here as we do at Mazoe."

"It's cattle country, you're right," said von Brand, "One of us can either stay on the ranch or we can put in a manager. We won't have any time to play around looking for gold while we still have to plant the maize. The native population is as thin here as it was in Mashonaland. More than half the land is unused. Now that the big herds of game have been shot out, there will be miles of free space to chop up into farms. We'll let Rhys off his share of the cattle, since if we don't let him go back to England and return with his Annabel, we'll never hear the end of it. It might be an idea for Jim to go as well to find himself a wife. Then you'll both have your hands full."

They laughed and lapsed back into smoking their cheroots.

"It doesn't seem right to fight a man and then take his land and his cattle," said James as he stared into the fire.

"That's how he got the land in the first place," said von Brand.

"Two wrongs don't make a right," he answered.

"Who do you sacrifice," said Morgan. "The Matabele or the Shona? Whichever way you look at it, someone is going to develop Africa and it may as well be the British; we usually give more than we take in the long run. If Lobengula wants to keep his spoils, he'll have to kill us now."

James poured himself coffee from the pot that had been keeping itself warm by the side of the fire. 'There is always right and wrong in everything,' he told himself, 'it just depends upon which way you moralise.'

"Hunting teaches you the simple principle of survival," said von Brand. "Life is exactly the same in its every facet, only they don't kill you anymore in the civilised world, they merely starve you to death and despise you for not having been a success."

They lapsed into silence and lost themselves in their own thoughts.

"I'm going to turn in," said Morgan, breaking the silence as he stood up. "I didn't get much sleep last night."

"I hope we do better tonight," said von Brand, "I'll see you at the one o'clock guard change. Goodnight."

"Goodnight," said James.

Morgan lifted his hand in a tired acknowledgement and drew away from the campfire and climbed under a wagon into his sleeping bag.

"I hope he isn't rudely disillusioned in England," said von Brand, knowing that Morgan was out of earshot. "People have their own lives to lead and fourteen years is a long time. He hasn't had another woman to think about, but she has had another man. A nineteen-year-old aristocrat is different to one of thirty-three. At nineteen they don't realise what maintains the family money and position. Then she might have given up her background in exchange for the flush of first love and the excitement. As we get older, we become more cautious."

"But surely, as she had her child by him," said James, "she'll still have a lot of the same feeling?"

Von Brand smiled.

"I wish everyone could stay thinking like you, Jim."

"I don't have any experience of that side of life."

"When you do," said von Brand, "you'll find out the true relationships. Love relationships never end up the way they start. They start with the most powerful expression of feeling between two people, an expression that relates everything to each other. At that point in time the other person is perfect, and the world is beautiful, and you laugh at everything. These are the moments that are never to be forgotten because they are perfect. But it never continues. It may grow into a lasting affection and the unreal may be replaced by a pleasant reality that establishes a home and breeds a family; you feel content with your wife, your home and your children, but you never find again the first elation. More often than not the relationship hits the ground with a resounding crack and you find each other as you really are; and no one is perfect."

"Why didn't you marry?" asked James, "or maybe that's a question I shouldn't ask..."

"No, I don't mind you asking. I have nothing to hide. I married all right, still am for that matter, only I haven't had any reason in the last five years to go back to Berlin to see the old girl. I used to go back every year when I first started hunting. I did my first trip after we'd been married a year and a half. Even then, neither of us thought much of marriage. She didn't really like sex or, if she did, she didn't like it with me. After a year, she didn't bother to cover up her feelings. If we'd become friends, we'd have muddled our lives along together and been the same as most other people, but we didn't even like each other. The young, pretty girl I married, who laughed at my jokes and listened to my ambitions, stopped being the actor and became herself. It was my own fault and I think I knew it in the first place but I was so intent on possessing her body that I lost sight of the fact that I would still have to live with her afterwards. My trips home diminished and became more and more painful for both of us.

"She prefers me being away. I send her money when I have it but she has enough of her own. You can't imagine me in a feminine, civilised household and neither can she. Looking back, it says something for the enthusiasm of youth, that knows a woman for six months in the most refined situations and then promises to live with her for fifty years. When you take one of the biggest gambles of your own life, Jim, I hope you do better than me, because I can tell you that it doesn't matter how much you try and change yourself, and her, to make it compatible; if you don't like each other, it's bloody hell living under the same roof. We were lucky that we weren't able to have any children since, during the last twenty years, they would only have seen their father four times."

"And you think Annabel will have changed?" asked James.

"After fourteen years, I'm quite sure she will have changed."

"Poor Rhys, and he's wasted so much of his life thinking and dreaming about her. Maybe he'll find someone else who is like what he remembers. You make people out to be different to what I thought they were."

"The secret of life," said von Brand, "is to enjoy to the maximum what you are doing at the time. All this looking forward and looking back can leave you with very little in the meantime. I'm tired," he added, getting up. "Killing anyone is a tiring business. I'll see you at the four o'clock guard change." He flicked the stub of his cheroot into the fire. "Goodnight, Jim, and don't lie awake thinking, because it isn't worth it. No two situations are ever the same,"

James sat and finished his cigar. He stared into the flames for five minutes and concluded that he didn't know anything after all, even though he had been through more than most people at twenty-four. He got up, looked at the stars, clear and brittle, and climbed under his wagon and into his sleeping bag, making sure that his rifle and ammunition were close at hand. Within a few minutes he was asleep.

Von Brand woke James at four o'clock and he took up his firing position under the wagon. He watched the sun come up above the bush. The night had been quiet and only broken by the sounds of Africa. To James, it seemed difficult to imagine that men were trying to kill each other. At six o'clock, he stood up and went across to the improvised kitchen to have his breakfast. He was hungry. He hoped that Jameson would come to terms with Lobengula. There was more than enough land for everyone, as there had been in

Mashonaland. He collected his plate of beans and sausage and picked up a jug of coffee and went back to the remains of the previous night's fire. He put down the food and went across to the wagon. He bent down and looked underneath.

"Come on, you idle bastards. It's morning and even the birds have stopped singing."

"Why don't you shut up," said Morgan, and tried to get deeper into his sleeping bag.

"Where's the coffee?" asked von Brand.

"Right here," said James, "but this time I'm not bringing it under the wagon."

"Morgan," said von Brand, "he's forcing us to a fateful decision. I think we are going to have to get up."

With great difficulty, von Brand got out of his lightweight sleeping bag and crawled from under the wagon. "Not a bad day at all," he said, looking around and stretching himself. The camp was astir all around him. He went to the coffee pot and poured from it into his mug. As he drank, he dribbled the coffee into his beard. He patted his large stomach, squeezed his beard by pressing it down with his right hand, gave himself a good scratch and went over to the kitchen to get himself some breakfast.

Morgan climbed out from under the wagon. James was already eating.

"Hell, you're a hard man," said Morgan. "A real nice guy would have brought Morgan his coffee in bed." He yawned, stretched and gave himself a good scratch.

"The way you two scratch," said James, "would lead me to believe you were lousy."

"It's sleeping in your clothes that does it," said Morgan, pouring himself coffee. "Did you see any Matabele?"

"Not a bloody thing."

"They must be getting up to something," he said, and went off to breakfast, sipping his coffee as he went.

.   .   .

THEY WERE four miles from the wagons that were approaching the Bembesi River when they rode into sight of the Mbizo regiment, marshalled in a deep fold in the ground. By the time the Matabele began to fire, the three of them had turned their horses and were over the rise in the ground and out of sight. They gave full rein for a short distance and then James leapt off his horse, took a flare and matches out of his saddle bag, struck the support of the rocket in the ground and lit the taper. He swung himself up in the saddle and they broke the animals into a canter, looking over their shoulders towards the rocket. The Mbizo regiment came up over the rise at a trot, their rifles, assegais and shields held at the ready. They were within fifty yards of where James had stopped when the rocket soared up into the sky. They faltered, but were soon on the move again. James concentrated on riding his horse to prevent it from stumbling.

When the column came into sight, the wagons were being laagered. They reported to Major Forbes.

"We only saw the Mbizo regiment," said von Brand, "but there must be others in the area. They were preparing to attack. They'll be within rifle range in ten minutes."

"Get those wagons inspanned," shouted Forbes. "Here, you, get the Maxims set up. Carregan, tell them to sight the seven pounders before the wagons are circled; there may be another impi nearer than the Mbizo. And tell the Shona to stay inside the laager this time."

The oxen were taken out of the traces and within ten minutes a crude laager was made and the guns re-sighted inside. The Mbizo attacked at an open run and, in the clear light of day, presented perfect targets; only a few ran near enough to throw their spears. Others went down behind bushes and rocks and began firing at the laager with guns.

"Now this is where a good shot can pay for his dinner," said von Brand, as he snap-fired at anything that brought its head up in preparation to firing at the laager. James lay on the right of the trio under the wagon, methodically doing the same thing. The firing started in earnest on the other side of the laager, and the steady rhythm of the Maxims cut into the sound of rifle fire. The slaughter went on for an hour. The Matabele withdrew, leaving hundreds dead around the wagons.

"Anyone hurt?" asked Morgan.

The man under the wagon next to him did not hear; he was dead.

MORGAN, von Brand and James scouted well ahead and out on the flanks of the box formation. They questioned the natives they saw and received a different story each time; it became clear to James that Lobengula was ahead and not in very good spirits.

"It's amazing," said Morgan to James as they rode side by side, "how the blacks can appear to be stupid when it suits them."

"You can say that again," said von Brand, who was riding on the other side.

They scouted for more than two hours without seeing life until twenty Matabele, armed and in full war feathers, stepped out from behind a series of covers. They were surrounded. They stared down at the assegais pointed at them. Their rifles were in the saddle holsters in front of their right knees.

"This doesn't look too good," said von Brand quietly, and tried to edge his horse forward.

"Where the hell did they spring from?" said Morgan.

"Come with us to Gambo, our inDuna," said their spokesman in Ndebele. "He wishes to speak to you."

"That may be true," said von Brand in the same language, while he tried to push his horse forward at the assegais, "but first we must have permission from our own inDuna who is just through the trees with a thousand white men. We will come back when we have spoken to him."

The Matabele hesitated and von Brand led Morgan and James through the circle, keeping the horses to a walk until they were twenty yards away when they broke the animals into a gallop to cover the three miles back to the column.

Their horses were blown when they reached the box formation. They rode straight up to Forbes. Everyone sensed the danger. Raaff, Wilson and Colenbrander joined Forbes.

"Two things we've learned," said von Brand, "and one is that despite our scouting they can surprise us at any time they wish. Secondly, I know Gambo and he's a big, proud Zulu and he's not afraid to fight. The Zulu war tactic is to surround the enemy and slowly close in on him and attack at a chosen point. I would say that, right now, we are being surrounded."

"There is still nothing they can do against the Maxims," said Forbes.

"We didn't have time to draw our rifles," said von Brand in answer.

"It's another reason why we should send back the wagons while we can," said Wilson. "The Maxims are mounted on gun carriages and can be towed fast by a horse. We've got to go and get Lobengula. The longer we fool around in this dripping forest the greater the danger. I know you can see a long way through the trees and it makes you think that no one is there but, as Willy has just found out, it isn't true."

"All right, Major Wilson," said Forbes, "we'll try it your way for three days and if we don't catch up with the king we will be forced to return to Bulawayo, as by then our rations will be almost exhausted. We will take the pack mules and the Maxims. We will not be able to carry enough ammunition to fight for days but if we capture Lobengula we shall have finished the war. Will you please choose the best of your men and the best horses. I require a force of one hundred and fifty men. The remaining one hundred and fifty will escort the wagons back to Bulawayo. I wish us all the luck, gentlemen."

"It'll work," said Wilson.

"I hope so Major Wilson, I hope so," said Forbes wearily.

Von Brand, Morgan and James immediately volunteered for the forward party. The flying party was assembled and one hundred and forty-seven men moved out at the pace of the pack donkeys and the horses pulling the two Maxims. The guns, one out in front of the box formation and the other behind, bounced awkwardly behind the animals' rear quarters. Further behind, the wagons turned about and started a wide curve to return to Bulawayo, from where Lobengula had fled three weeks before. Wilson rode at the front of the flying column, trying to draw them ahead at his own speed.

"I think we're asking for trouble," said Colenbrander as he rode out ahead with von Brand.

"The Matabele know far more about fighting in these conditions than we do, and Gambo is the best general they've got."

Captain Napier rode in from Wilson's party. He reported that Wilson had made contact with Lobengula but had withdrawn half a mile when the king's bodyguard had prepared to defend the king. Wilson asked that Forbes's force move up immediately in preparation for a pre-dawn attack.

"When in doubt," said Morgan, "it is better to attack."

"If attack were possible," snapped Forbes, "I would be first to go forward. But it is necessary to consider the probabilities. Do you imagine we can move the guns and pack mules through a rising river with the enemy waiting on both sides of the water?"

"We can't leave him there now they know where he is," said Borrow.

"What do you suggest?" said Forbes.

"That if we can't send the whole force we send reinforcements."

"You have my permission to pick twenty men. Take as much ammunition as you can carry. Captain Napier will lead you back to Major Wilson. We will move forward with speed at first light. Wish Major Wilson goodnight and good luck."

"Rhys, will you come with me?" said Borrow. "I need one scout and your horse is the best."

"We'd like to go as well," said James.

"I'm sorry Jim. Just one scout."

"But we travel together," said von Brand.

"Forbes will only let me have one scout," said Borrow. "If you two go it will only leave Colenbrander to guide the main force."

"Right," said Morgan. "I'll get my horse."

"Why don't you let them take one of the Maxims?" said Raaff to Forbes, annoyed that he had not been given Borrow's job.

"Because they may have to swim the horses across the Shangani," said Forbes. "Napier says the river is rising fast. There was a storm upriver."

"He didn't have to swim his horses," answered Raaff.

"Commandant Raaff, I am doing the best that I can for Major Wilson, in the light of safety for the whole column. In daylight we will have a greater chance of judging the river and moving the guns safely to the other side. I cannot risk losing a gun. If Wilson had done as he was told, it would not be necessary for us to contemplate such a risk. He was told to return with his troop before dark, which was five hours ago."

"It may be too late," said Raaff.

"I hope not," said Forbes and walked off to supervise the despatch of Borrow's troop.

Five minutes later Morgan rode out at the head of the troop, beside Borrow and Napier.

"We'll see you tomorrow morning, Rhys," said James, and Morgan turned round in the saddle and waved.

Morgan used all his bush craft to find a quick route once Napier had explained Wilson's exact position. He had hunted many times along the banks of the Shangani River. As they rode, it began to rain heavily and the water trickled down his back. It was impossible to see further than ten yards and Morgan suggested that they make for the Shangani River. The horses changed direction and followed each other, two abreast with five-yard intervals behind each pair. At any moment, Morgan expected the Matabele to attack.

"What do we do if attacked?" Morgan asked Borrow as they rode at the head of the troop.

Borrow turned to the man behind him. "If we're attacked," he said, "run for the river, cross it as best you can, individually or in groups, and make your way upriver. Keep going until you meet up with one of the officers. Tell the man behind you and tell him to pass back the word. You and I, Rhys, will have to move upstream fast; that way we will have some chance of bringing the troop together again. If we break in all directions it will confuse the Matabele and the darkness will be in our favour. I wish we could ride faster."

They rode on in silence; the only sound above the rain was the jingle of bits and the creak of wet saddles.

After quarter of an hour, they found the Shangani River and travelled along the west bank. Shortly afterwards they found a suitable ford and led their horses down the sandy bank into the water. The water was rising fast and by the time they had reached the middle it was up to their chests. Mosquitoes bit them incessantly.

"Forbes was right," said Borrow, when he and Morgan had climbed with their horses up the opposite bank. "We would have stood a good chance of losing the Maxim in that current. A pity, I'd have felt safer, but if the regiments are behind us, Forbes will need the fire power."

They waited for the twenty horsemen to assemble and then headed the troop along the east bank of the Shangani River.

"It's about as wet here as in the river," said someone from the back.

Along the bank of the river, they found a clear run and let the horses break into a trot. An hour later, Napier led them into Wilson's camp on the Pupu stream.

"Are we glad to see you," said Wilson. "Where's the rest of the column?"

"Forbes didn't want to risk it at night," said Borrow as they shook hands.

"He wouldn't," answered Wilson.

"If he had been attacked, he would have lost the baggage."

"I suppose so," said Wilson, "but it's good to see you anyway. Make yourselves as comfortable as you can. With luck we'll have this over with tomorrow. I assume that Forbes will move up at dawn."

"As quickly as possible," answered Borrow.

"Good," said Wilson, "then there is nothing we can do but settle down and wait for the dawn and make sure we are not surprised during the night. Lobengula is only lightly defended. We can pull him out with the force we have here."

"We've been told," said Borrow, "that a large impi has fanned out behind the main column."

"Well, all the more reason for making a pre-dawn attack on Lobengula's camp. Before we withdrew, someone, whom I think was Lobengula, shouted at us that we had taken his money and yet we still wished to fight. I don't know what he meant but they sounded more like the words of surrender than defiance. If there is a large force of Matabele on this side of the Shangani they will attack anyway, and I prefer to have the element of surprise on my side. No, tomorrow morning we will finish the job, and then we can all go back to our farms."

Morgan tethered his horse to a tree, leaving the animal saddled in case they needed to move out quickly, and sat down on a fallen tree. There seemed to be no way of sleeping and he gave up any thought of trying. He was wet and hungry. He got up and took his last tin of bully beef out of his saddle bag and, with difficulty, opened the tin.

"Do you want some?" he said to Borrow, who had sat down next to him.

"Thanks. I always get hungry sitting around. How many people do you think are watching us?"

"More than a hundred," said Morgan, munching the bully beef.

"I'll be glad when the dawn comes so we can see where they

are," said Borrow, his mouth full of bully beef. "This stuff's not bad," he added.

When they had finished the meat, there were still three hours of darkness before dawn. They sat and waited in silence. Morgan heard jackal and hyena. He wished himself back in the days of hunting when he could build a fire and cook meat. He wondered if Lobengula felt as cold as he did, or whether he had managed to stay in his wagon. His body was tense and he wanted to shiver. Probably, he told himself, most people feel like this when they are about to fight; he would shout at Lobengula that there was no point in fighting; maybe the old man would recognise his voice and he would have the chance of talking to him, not killing. He lay back and rested the nape of his neck on the tree. He moved about and got himself comfortable. Fleetingly, as the storm clouds scudded across the night sky, he could see the stars. It was Africa and it gave him pleasure. Annie would like the country, of that he was certain, and so would Gavin. The country was free in space and convention. He looked around and saw men waiting, like himself. They would each have their thoughts, and Morgan wondered at the ability of man to think and understand.

AN HOUR before dawn they were called to saddle up. Morgan mounted. Cautiously, they moved in on Lobengula's camp. For a mile, they passed through thick bush. The sky paled. As they moved in to attack the camp it was light enough to see that the place was deserted.

"Damn," said Wilson, "he's got away again."

A rifle fired from the bush.

"We are here to kill you," shouted a voice in Ndebele, which Morgan quickly translated to Wilson.

The bush came alive with advancing Matabele and Morgan recognised the shields of the Mbizo regiment.

"It's an ambush," shouted Wilson and began to fire from the hip.

"Withdraw to last night's camping site. There must be hundreds of the bastards here."

Morgan turned his horse about and quietened the animal as it shied at the volley of shots being fired into them from the surrounding bush.

"I've been hit," shouted the trooper next to Morgan.

"Hold onto your horse and we'll get you out of here," said Morgan, as he moved his own horse nearer so that he could catch the man if he fell. He used his rifle with one hand and fired without sighting.

"Come on then," shouted Wilson over the noise, standing up in his stirrups, his white horse a magnet for the Matabele rifle fire. "Let's get out of here." He broke his horse into a canter, stopping a short distance ahead to urge his troop past, then he followed. They were sniped at; there were as many Matabele in front as there were behind. Two others were hit as they fled through the trees and long grass. They reached the Pupu stream and milled around.

"We'll have to stand and fight," shouted Wilson. "That way we'll keep them off until Forbes arrives. If we keep retreating like this we'll be picked off among the trees. Burnham," he shouted above the noise of the rifle fire, "will you, Ingram and Gooding get back to Forbes and call up reinforcements. We need those damned Maxims. You three have the best horses. Everyone else dismount. If your horse is hit, kill it and use it for cover. Form a laager. Make the best of every bullet. Ammunition is short. Fire individually when you have a target."

Morgan swung off his horse and patted its neck to quieten the animal. He heard the three horsemen crash their way into the bush behind. He began rapid firing at the advancing impi over the saddle of his horse until it shied and he was forced to use both hands to bring the animal under control.

"Keep firing accurately," shouted Wilson, "and we'll have them yet. We must have killed fifty already. If your horse won't stand still, shoot it." His horse went down and he sank to his knee behind the animal and continued to fire at the constant waves of advancing Matabele.

Morgan heard a man cry out in pain and saw that another, further away on his right, had stopped firing, the man's head resting against the flanks of his dead horse.

"Christ," said Borrow, "it sounds as though the main column is being attacked. That's gunfire to our rear and it can't be Burnham, as it's too far away." He kept firing as he spoke. "It's Forbes," he said, a moment later, "I can hear the Maxim."

"We'll have to look after ourselves," said Morgan, and saw the man at whom he had fired stop and stumble forward. An assegai came at them from behind and buried itself in the neck of Morgan's horse. The point of the spear stuck out the other side and blood gushed from both wounds. The animal sank to its knees and fell on its side; its flanks heaved in long struggles as though the animal were trying to force air into its body. Morgan brought his gun down and fired one shot into the horse's head. He felt the pain of tears behind his eyes. A bullet smashed into his left shoulder and forced him to his knees and the cover of his dead horse. Painfully, he propped his rifle on top of the horse and began to fire across the fifty yards of open space on his side of the surrounded troop. Behind them was the mopane forest. Rifle fire came at them from all directions.

"If you run out of ammunition," shouted Wilson, "take it from a man who can't fire anymore. If we keep up this accurate shooting they'll have to withdraw."

A wave of assegai and shield-bearing Matabele came out of the trees on the far side of the glade in front of Morgan and began to weave their way towards the twenty white men who were still able to fire. Morgan started on the left and had stopped four of the screaming Matabele before they were close enough to launch their spears.

The flight of spears came at them and Morgan braced himself to get out of their way. He watched, horrified, as the assegais glided towards them and sank into horses and men. Morgan looked around and saw three of his friends with spears sticking into their bodies. One was trying to pull the metal head out of his leg by its shaft, but the other two were still.

There was a lull in the shooting. No one came at them out of the trees. Morgan tried to hold back the blood that was oozing from his smashed shoulder. He forced himself not to faint. "We are going to kill you all," shouted a voice from the trees, but Morgan did not translate.

The firing began again and another wave of Matabele came out of the trees and began weaving towards them, bent double and holding their shields as protection against the bullets. As they ran, they shouted obscenities. Morgan shouted back in Ndebele and fired at them as quickly as he was able to with one hand. He noticed that their own firing had slackened. He again heard the firing from far behind where Forbes and the main column were fighting.

"Keep it up, everyone," said Wilson. "Forbes will have sent a relief column immediately he heard the firing. Keep shooting straight and don't let the bastards get up to us. How's your shoulder, Rhys? I see you can fire as fast with one hand as two. Why don't we try a song while we fight?"

Wilson broke out into an obscene music hall ditty which was taken up by those with air in their lungs. Morgan did not know the words but he desperately hummed the tune as he fired at the Matabele who were closing in on them from all sides, their threats in rhythm with the speed of their advance. They came on, leaping over the bodies of the dead. Wilson sang louder; he was the only one who had not been hit. Just short of the laager, the Matabele threw their spears. The rifle fire opened again from the mopane forest. Morgan was hit in the neck and blood gushed from the wound. He sank behind his dead horse and lay on his back with his head propped against the saddle. He painfully reached for his pistol and pulled it out of the holster. Wilson was the only man standing. The others had stopped firing.

"Right, you bastards," Wilson shouted at the forest. "I'm coming out after you." He pulled out his pistol and took another from a dead trooper. Morgan watched him climb over a dead horse and run at a wave of Matabele. He kept on firing until he dropped to his knees. A flight of spears hit him.

Morgan looked around in the silence. He was able to move his head but he could see no one else alive. The Matabele began shouting. Four leapt over the dead horses into the laager. Morgan saw they were sweating; he noticed their war feathers were crooked. They went from trooper to trooper, stabbing each in turn. One came to Morgan and lifted his spear. Morgan brought up the pistol and fired into his face. The man's expression turned from bloodlust to surprise. They rushed at Morgan but his strength was gone. He saw the assegai go into his stomach and then he passed out.

7

*L*obengula sat in his faded, red armchair that had one side tilted where the springs had broken; the end of the tassels at the bottom of the chair hung limply on the wet of last year's mopane leaves. He let the sun soak into his body and eased his gout-ridden foot a little forward to relieve the pain. It made no difference and he continued to suffer in the sun as he had done in the rain during the previous weeks, since driving north with his wagons and away from his kraal at Gu-Bulawayo. Gambo and Magwegwe sat on their haunches in front of him, but none of them looked at each other. Lobengula shifted his weight again and closed his eyes to see if it would relieve even a small portion of his pain, and after a while he felt better. He opened his eyes and looked at Gambo.

"I see you, Gambo," he said in answer to the traditional greeting he had received from his commander ten minutes before.

"The white men have gone," said Gambo, "and they will not come back for many months. Maybe they will go away, back to the land of the Shona. They are brave men," he finished. "The ones we killed died fighting to the last man and their inDuna came out at us from the horses with his pistols. They sang as they died."

"Were there any of them that we knew?" asked Lobengula.

"Morgan," said Gambo. "He was the last to die. We thought he was dead but he killed once more with his pistol before we drove the assegai many times into his body."

"Did you open up their stomachs to let out their spirits?" asked Lobengula.

"To everyone," said Gambo. "They killed many of us."

"To be killed in true battle is to go straight to our ancestors," said Lobengula. "You have done well, Gambo."

"They were men of men and their fathers were men before them," said Gambo.

"That is why you have done well. To defeat the Shona is nothing."

"The main party got away," said Gambo.

"You did as instructed," said Lobengula, "and prevented them from reaching my person. It is good for them to go back as then they will be able to tell their friends what it is like to fight with my impi. We fear no one, and this they have seen. Go back to your impis, Gambo, and tell them that Lobengula has seen their will to die for him."

"What must they do now?" asked Gambo.

"Rest, and I will send word where we are and where they must bring my cattle."

"We will not go back to Gu-Bulawayo?" asked Gambo.

"We destroyed Gu-Bulawayo. My kraal was destroyed. But soon I will send word for you to build me a new kraal."

Gambo rose and picked up his shield and assegai. His war feathers of blue jay were perfectly straight and the sun shone on them so that Lobengula could see the fine tracery of the feathers and the translucence of their quills. They looked at each other for some time, and then the pain of his gout returned and he closed his eyes. He heard Gambo move away. He looked a moment later and saw his chief inDuna walk out of the glade and into the mopane forest.

He was a great king, he told himself, if men like Gambo could follow him and continue to live and not go against his is-Anuzi, making it necessary for them to smell him out, and for Lobengula to have him killed with his family, servants, cattle and livestock. Lobengula agreed that Gambo had done well. He let the sun warm him and stopped his mind trying to think of what next he should do. He knew he was tired, of that he was certain, and he knew he was old and that his gout hurt him, but for the rest he did not wish to think. He closed his eyes again and ignored Magwegwe as he had done all afternoon. Magwegwe wanted to speak to him but he did not wish to speak to Magwegwe.

Finally, he went to sleep and the pain in his right foot was lost and he began to dream. When he woke the sun had gone down behind the mopane trees and he was unable to remember his dreams. There had been glimpses of so many things, of that he knew, but he could not remember any of them distinctly and, because of this, he told himself, there had been no omens for the future. His camp was astir but Magwegwe was still sitting on his haunches in the same place where he had been all afternoon. Lobengula saw that he had slightly moved his position. He smiled to himself. Magwegwe was getting old. They were both getting old.

"I see you, Magwegwe," said Lobengula in reply to the question he had been asked when the sun was right above his head.

"Where do we go?" said Magwegwe.

Lobengula thought about this for some time, and looked around at the glade and the tall mopane trees and the long, fresh grass and the newly killed eland that hung between two trees at the far side of the glade. They had been there for five days. Lobengula liked the place because he knew that when his wagon started to move again the pain in his foot would be unbearable.

"Why not let us stay here?" he said. "It is a peaceful place and the rain has gone. Tonight we will make the fire here in front of me and I will not have to move. We will roast the eland and talk of when we were young, when the white man came to the royal kraal and we kept them waiting for weeks and they never complained."

"How long shall we stay here?" asked Magwegwe.

"How do I know," answered Lobengula, irritably.

Magwegwe held his tongue. He watched the flies trying to work their way under the king's loincloth; they had been trying to do that all afternoon. He remained on his haunches in the same position and waited for the conversation to turn in a direction which would allow him to tell Lobengula all that was in his mind. After a while, the light of day began to fade and he thought the king was asleep.

"Go and tell them, Magwegwe, to make the fire here," said Lobengula suddenly. "I can still feel the cold from the rain. Tell them to make a big fire so we can see all the memories of our lives in the dancing flames; the big, dark flames of war, and the small dancing flames of red and orange that are the flames of beer and laughter. Make the fire big. We will eat well. We will drink beer. The white man has been driven away and I have done this. Why do you sit there?" he shouted, and Magwegwe got up quickly despite his age and the time he had sat in the one position. "Do you think I tell you things for them to be ignored?"

He glared and when Magwegwe had his back to him, he got out of the chair and stood on his feet with care. He rubbed his bare buttocks to return the circulation, and sat down again.

Magwegwe shouted at the king's bodyguard and, within moments, they ran out with dry grass and twigs and then large boughs of trees. They laid the big logs next to where they would make the fire so that when it was hot they would place the big logs in the flames, and the fire would burn all night. Lobengula watched each move and every time they put something down they backed away from the king, lightly clapping their hands in front of them and avoiding the eyes of the king. Hot coals were brought from a small fire that was kept burning in camp, and, as the new fire burnt up in front of Lobengula, the light of day went out, and the shadows were made by the dancing flames, and the mopane trees receded into the darkness of night. The night sounds of Africa became predominant; the guinea fowl screeched deep in the forest as they flew up to roost in the trees. A lion roared and Lobengula sat up and listened. A troop of baboons chattered at each other and he could see one of them at the top of a mopane tree, where it was silhouetted against the last light of the sunken sun. In that moment he made up his mind, and he felt sad that he must end all this, but he was the king and the king had responsibilities to his people.

"Bring me beer," he said to a boy who was tending the fire. His voice was gentle. He looked at the boy to see if it was one of his own sons, but despite the bad light he concluded that the boy was not his own. He could not remember all of them. In the same way, he found it difficult to remember his older wives who had fallen out of favour. Tonight he would drink, he told himself, and he was pleased with the speed with which a gourd of beer was offered him. He took the large gourd and drank and afterwards ran a large red tongue over his lips and up to the tip of his aquiline nose where the white liquid had smeared his face. He drank again, and then balanced the gourd on his belly and sat back in the chair.

"Tell Magwegwe to come and drink with me," said Lobengula to the boy. He did not like to drink by himself.

A FEW MINUTES later Magwegwe sat down on the ground in front of Lobengula and crossed his legs. He accepted a gourd of beer from the boy and, as Lobengula lifted his gourd to drink, he did the same and they watched each other over the tops of their gourds and Magwegwe could see the light of the fire dancing in the eyes of the king. They drank the first gourd and, in silence, accepted another. They watched a haunch of the eland being covered in fat and placed on the green-wood spit over the fire and the fat dripped into the fire and the flames flared and the sound blended into the sounds of the night.

"I can still drink as much as I could when I was young," said Lobengula, as much to himself as to anyone else. "The beer is good."

"The beer is good," said Magwegwe, and they lapsed into silence.

"Why did they take my money and still want to fight me?" asked Lobengula.

"The two white men stole the money and did not deliver your message," said Magwegwe. "It is said that these men are gambling with your gold sovereigns."

Lobengula thought about this for some time.

"There is no one you can trust," he said. "Maybe it is best this way. I might have talked to them as they asked and gone back with them to Gu-Bulawayo."

"Are we going up over the big river?" said Magwegwe.

"The people will do this," said Lobengula, "when they have found a new king."

"But we have our king," said Magwegwe in surprise, generated by fear. The choosing of a new king was a dangerous time; but he did not understand, because the king was sitting in front of him, drinking his second gourd of beer and, when they had finished the fifth gourd, they would eat the meat and talk of the great hunts of the past and he would once again hear how Lobengula had killed his first lion. No, he was getting old and his ears were not as sharp as they used to be and he had heard the king wrong; the best thing to do was to pretend that he had not heard what the king had said.

"I am too old to go far," said Lobengula, but Magwegwe did not answer him. He waited for some time and then Lobengula spoke to him again.

"When the wagon moves it hurts my feet and the pain is too great. And where could we go, Magwegwe? I am tired of fighting. I have been fighting for too long. We can go on forever through this forest. To make ourselves strong, we must fight many times, and this is the job of a young man. The impis did well, but nearly a quarter of my best men lie dead or unable to fight again. We cannot fight the white men anymore. In the end, they will have killed us all with their guns. Next time, if we let them have a next time, they will not make the same mistakes. They are wise and brave men and there are too many of them and we are too few.

"The tribe must go north, Magwegwe, with a new king who will re-found our nation, as did my father, Mzilikazi, when he left Zululand. I have lost his lands, but there are many more for the taking. The nation is still one and they must stay together and go out and take together. You find it strange for me to be talking like this but I have thought out all the answers. There is too much pain in my body to go on enjoying life. In my kraal at Gu-Bulawayo, I could sit in the sun all day when my feet were hurting and I only moved into the wagon to sleep. But this constant travelling is no good for me, Magwegwe."

Magwegwe said nothing, as he was not sure whether the king was being serious or whether he was testing him so that at the first sign of his being in agreement, the king would have him killed and his family killed and his cattle killed if they could find them. No, it was dangerous talk and he must be careful and remain seated on the ground, and drink his beer, and say nothing.

"You think I am tricking you," said Lobengula, leaning forward and glaring down at his silence. "But I'm not." His voice was tired and slowly he sat back in his armchair and took a long drink at the gourd.

The haunch of venison was turned on the spit and the smell of meat drifted up into the night air. There was a gentle silence in the glade that was only broken by the hissing of the fire as the fat dripped onto the hot coals of the wood. It was the first hours of night before the prowling began and there was a sense of peace over everything. The air was still and the tops of the mopane trees stood sentinel against the night sky and the moon was halfway full but had yet to bathe its strongest light over the forest.

"Do you remember the days of my father?" asked Lobengula.

"Yes," answered Magwegwe and felt that the subject was more to his liking.

"He ran away as well," said Lobengula, as though he was talking to himself. "He ran from Shaka and then from the Boer, Potgieter. There is nothing wrong in running away when you cannot see any means of winning." His voice pleaded with himself. "It is a stupid man who fights only to lose, and they have shown that in the end we cannot win. At first I thought it was only the guns, but now I can see that they are not afraid to die."

His voice was flat and he leant forward and looked hard into the fire.

"You must come north with us," said Magwegwe, and bit his tongue for having spoken.

"Do you think I should?" said Lobengula, with interest. By the light of the fire, Magwegwe saw the inner brightness of his eyes.

"It will be a new country with new places to raid," said Magwegwe.

"Do you think so? Yes, maybe you're right. We will conquer again. Yes, that is it. We will carve out a whole new tract of country. The cattle will be fat and so will the women."

"And within a few years," said Magwegwe, warming to the subject, "we will be stronger than ever before and the spirit of your father will look down upon you with pride."

"And we will hunt again like we used to," said Lobengula, sitting up and looking at Magwegwe. "It will be like it used to be when I was a young man and first king. The impis will come home from every direction and all will be bringing me rich rewards. And there will be many strong young men winning the right to take their brides and no one will stop dancing for the whole of the three days of the Great Dance. There will be a new king's kraal, much bigger than Gu-Bulawayo, and I will take myself another six wives to celebrate. It will be a new and stronger nation and it will grow faster than ever before.

"And I will be king. I will be fair, yes, but I will be strong. If anyone displeases me I will have them killed with all their family, but that is only justice that the king shall wield. It is my right and I will always have my right. The king must have his right." He drank hard at his beer and with impatience brought it back to rest between his knees.

"The food looks good," he said. "Maybe you should carve a piece off from the outside for me and I shall be able to see how it is cooking. Here, take my hunting knife. It has done the final killing of many eland in its time and now it will kill many more. When my feet are good I will ride out on the hunt and stalk the game on my horse. It can be done. Selous told me that once. Now, where is Selous?" The enthusiasm left his voice. "Oh, yes. That was Gu-Bulawayo with Selous, and Baines and Hartley: now there was a big man. He liked me. I think they all liked me. Feared me, yes, but liked me as well. Those were good days, Magwegwe... I enjoyed myself in those days."

"And you shall again in the new country," said Magwegwe, handing him a piece of the venison on the end of the hunting knife.

"Do you think the new country will be good?" said Lobengula, with just a little interest.

"It will be better," said Magwegwe.

"You think so," said Lobengula, and put the whole piece of venison into his mouth. "Why?" he asked pleasantly, with his mouth full, but Magwegwe saw the trap and tried hard to think of a way to answer. "Why?" asked Lobengula again, as he leant forward and stared down at his inDuna. "Why, I ask you, will it be better?"

"Because you will make it better," said Magwegwe with relief, having carefully considered any trap that such a remark could present.

"Maybe so, maybe so," said Lobengula and swallowed. "If I was young and my feet did not hurt me and I could run with the best of my impis. But, can you see that now, Magwegwe? Look at me. What do you see?" He paused for a reply. "So you prefer not to answer me. Be careful, Magwegwe, as I still have enough power to have you smelt out."

"You will always have that power," replied Magwegwe.

"A power, yes," said Lobengula in disgust, "to rot in the sun and not be able to do a thing but suffer and complain. You do not know what these feet are like," he said pleading. "It is a slow, hungry pain that eats into every one of my vitals, so how can the new country be better?"

"The raiding parties will be more successful because the tribes to the north have not been raided by us before," said Magwegwe hopefully.

"But maybe others have raided them," said Lobengula. "You see, you cannot be sure. No one is ever sure of anything he does not know. No, it will not be better and you and I will never have again what we have had in our youth. Nothing can be repeated. We have been wandering now for over a month. We could go on wandering. Maybe the forest never ends and goes on even after the crossing of the big river. Must I lead my people on forever and, when I grow too tired to go on, have them sit me down in the glade of the mopane forest for me to suffer my feet and the pain of our wealth growing smaller? If Gambo succeeds in war he will want to be king, and when he sees me as I am, he will laugh in my face and my power of king will have gone, and I may not have the strength to do what I am going to do now. Now, I still have my power and even Rhodes has seen our strength. He forced me away and I forced him back and now we wait to see which one of us has the power to roar. I have not lost my father's lands. Not yet. It is better to die before they can spit in my face."

"But who will lead us over the big river?" asked Magwegwe.

"Not you or I, old man. We have thrown our last spear. It will be the task of the inDunas of the regiments to choose their king."

"But you can lead us over the big river," insisted Magwegwe. "It is for you to go and the whole tribe will follow. Now that they are scattered, they will only follow you. Otherwise, there will be many kings with little power. There is no need to throw a spear. We will listen to your wisdom. You are Lobengula, king of the Matabele, and there is no one else who can be king."

Lobengula avoided his eyes and sank back into apathy at the back of his chair. He had lost interest in his beer; it rested precariously on his left knee.

"Maybe I no longer have the heart," said Lobengula.

Magwegwe waited in silence and felt his life begin to flow away from him. What the king had said was true and he knew it as well as Lobengula, but it frightened him to see another side of the man he had feared most of his life.

"It is no good, old man," said Lobengula with a sigh, "our day has come and gone. For the likes of us there are only memories. Let us drink well, Magwegwe, and forget about the future. The meat looks good and soon we will fill our bellies. There are few nights during the season of the rains that are like this, so let us make the best of it as it may be our last. Drink hard and then they will bring another gourd."

Magwegwe watched carefully to be certain that he finished his beer at the same time. He was too old not to be careful. He knew that in the morning the pain in Lobengula's foot would be gone and Lobengula would be driving them along the trail and talking of the future.

"Let's talk of the past," said Lobengula, as he finished the beer in his gourd and waved the empty skin for more. "Do you remember raiding that village at Chedza, and how I bet you your life that you could not rape ten virgins in one night and, to spite me, you raped all twelve in the village? And you had fought hard that day. You had done a lot of killing."

The new gourd was presented to them and they drank.

"No, that I will not forget," said Magwegwe, "and the next day I could not make up my mind which was more sore, my stabbing arm or my penis."

Lobengula laughed violently and crashed back into his chair and spilt some of the beer before bringing the gourd up to his mouth.

"We could do anything then," said Lobengula in his best humour. "Cut me another piece of that venison. The last piece was good but could have been better. I like to taste the smoke in the meat. Yes, those were the best times, when we were young and strong and nothing like this to carry around."

He slapped his paunch and laughed, and Magwegwe watched carefully and judged that he should laugh as well and added his lower volume of laughter to the raucous guffaws of Lobengula.

"And when we raided a Shona village, they would all run away like long-legged chickens and they never fought. They were so easy to rob, but it was our right to rob them. And do you remember how I kept you all in suspense for years after my father died, while they looked for his brother, and only when I was sure that I had enough regiments behind me to kill anyone who challenged my rule did I allow them to make me the king. And what slaughter there was afterwards. There was a smelling out almost every day. Three, four, sometimes, depending on my mood. There was always something to do in those days." He accepted the piece of venison that Magwegwe had been offering him for some time, chewed four times and swallowed. "Not bad," he said, "but we still have time for two more gourds of beer." He drank in an effort to wash down the venison that he had not chewed sufficiently.

More wood was put on the fire and the sparks floated up into the night with each new batch of wood. There was a dome of night above them of indigo, and the moon had gathered its strength and was throwing a pure, colourless light over everything. As the big fire flared, they could see the entrance into Lobengula's sleeping wagon that faced them where they sat around the fire, with the haunch of venison cooking steadily just above the flames, a small boy waiting motionless beside it, only coming to life when he turned the handle of the spit and the haunch changed its position with a fierce hiss of burning fat.

"Let us drink," said Lobengula, watching Magwegwe carefully to be certain that he also finished the contents of his gourd. As they finished, new beer was presented to them. Lobengula put the new gourd to his mouth and drank and Magwegwe followed each one of his movements.

"We can still drink," said Lobengula, when he had half-finished the contents of the new gourd at the first attempt. "Now, where were we? What were we talking about?" He stared hard at Magwegwe and watched him cringe. "I said what were we talking about?"

"The smellings out," said Magwegwe unwillingly.

"Ah, the smellings out," said Lobengula with relish. "How could you have possibly forgotten what I was talking about?"

"It must be the beer," said Magwegwe. He tried to smile.

"It must be," said Lobengula.

Magwegwe said nothing and looked down at his crossed feet

and hoped that the cloud would pass and that Lobengula would want to talk about a more pleasant subject. He felt he was being stared at and he slowly brought up his eyes and looked back at Lobengula.

"Are you frightened?" asked Lobengula.

"No," said Magwegwe.

"Well, you should be," said Lobengula, "as tomorrow we are going up into the caves, and you and I are going to die for our tribe." He laughed louder than at any time previously but Magwegwe was unable to join in his laughter, as much as he tried. He was sure that the king was not serious, but it was not a subject that he liked to joke about. He had worked hard in the past and now he was an inDuna. He had received a great deal of *lobola* for his many daughters and he wished to go on enjoying the ease and comfort. Lobengula stopped laughing abruptly and drank thirstily. Magwegwe carefully matched his drinking.

"You don't laugh, Magwegwe," said Lobengula, waving his empty gourd and throwing it at the boy, who presented him with his fifth gourd of the evening. "Why don't you laugh?" he repeated, leaning forward.

"I am quite happy living," answered Magwegwe. He hoped that his voice sounded natural.

"Well I am not," said Lobengula slowly, "and it is my wish that my old friend should die with me."

"I am sure it is an honour," answered Magwegwe after a moment.

"I am sure you are right," said Lobengula, and began to gulp at the full gourd, spilling some of it onto his paunch. He wiped away the beer from his stomach with the palm of his hand and sneered at Magwegwe.

"When we have finished this gourd," said Lobengula, "we will eat, and we will go on eating until it is impossible for us to swallow and then we will be sick and then we will be able to eat some more. It is a big haunch, that one, and I am sure that it is going to be a delight to eat, and the haunch is just for you and me. You will cut the pieces and we will eat piece for piece and be certain that you do not give Lobengula the larger piece or Lobengula will be upset. For the first time in a month, my feet are sufficiently bearable as to have them as part of me.

"So, tonight, for the last time, we will enjoy ourselves and tomorrow we shall take poison in the caves, and the Matabele will be able to choose another king for themselves who will be young and able to lead them out of their troubles. They will choose the king as I, Lobengula, will have no say in it, either for the sake of my children or for the sake of my favourites. This I will do for them who have had me as their king for thirty years. It is my gift to them." He sat back and brought the gourd to his mouth and drank it down.

Magwegwe cut two large pieces of meat off the haunch and he was pleased to see the way it cut and the way the juice rose. It took his mind off the caves and the poison. He offered the smaller piece to Lobengula and before he took a bite of his own, the saliva rose in his mouth and he satiated it with the meat.

"Perfect," he said to Lobengula with genuine pleasure.

"It is one of the best," answered Lobengula. "A young beast, but not too young so as to be without flavour. Cut us each another piece and we will see if the second is as good as the first. I will have mine from that burnt part near the knuckle. On a young eland, that can be the best."

Magwegwe cut two pieces from near the knuckle. They swallowed the previous piece, bit again and chewed.

"Even better," said Magwegwe, and popped the other half into his mouth. By the twentieth piece he had had more than enough and would have happily lain back near the warm fire and gone to sleep.

"Now I am really hungry," said Lobengula. "Now you will cut large pieces. Those little titbits have sharpened my appetite. We will drink beer with the meat and in that way it will be well washed down and there will be plenty of room in us both for the whole haunch."

The new gourds were presented to them by the waiting boy and they took a long drink. Lobengula then balanced the gourd on his left knee and belched.

"Now," he said, "now that we have the wind out of the system we can do good justice to the meat."

He took the large piece of venison offered to him by Magwegwe and tried to stuff it all into his mouth. He pulled it out, gnawed off a chunk and chewed. He nodded his head at Magwegwe in appreciation and, with the back of his hand, wiped the grease off his face. Magwegwe tried hard to swallow but his throat refused to function. His belly was as tight as a drum and he wanted to relieve himself. The king watched him carefully.

"Don't you like the meat?" said Lobengula. Magwegwe was unable to answer with his windpipe blocked by the venison.

Lobengula eased himself forward and put his weight onto his feet with caution, grunted with pleasure in the fact that they were holding him up without any unbearable pain and took four paces forward, raised his large right hand and brought it down with tremendous force on Magwegwe's back. Magwegwe lurched forward and swallowed. Lobengula cautiously made his way back to his chair and eased his buttocks into it, grinning with pleasure.

"You still have another piece of meat in your hand," said Lobengula in a soft, friendly voice, "and mine is finished and I am hungry."

Magwegwe bit his meat in half and began to chew diligently, with Lobengula watching him impatiently. Magwegwe tried to chew faster and slopped a little beer into his mouth, which only made it worse.

"You do not look as though you are enjoying my venison," said Lobengula threateningly. "I am growing hungry from all this waiting. When I ask you to drink and eat with me, I mean it, and there can be none of this laggard in you."

He held Magwegwe's eyes with his own and Magwegwe tried to swallow, but without success. Menacingly, Lobengula began to ease his buttocks off the chair; with clenched teeth, Magwegwe forced the unwanted meat to go down.

Lobengula eased himself back into the chair and smiled. Magwegwe tried to smile in return.

"Now the rest," said Lobengula. Magwegwe stared at the meat in his hand. "Come along," said Lobengula.

"I think I am going to be sick," said Magwegwe.

"Well, have it out of you and then I might get some food."

He watched him get up with difficulty. Magwegwe had not gone halfway to the mopane trees before he began to retch and relieve himself at the same time. Lobengula clucked his tongue and watched until nothing more came out of Magwegwe. He saw the old man shudder twice before turning round. He slowly re-traced his steps to the fire.

"I think you have had enough," said Lobengula. "Just cut me another piece of meat while I go and relieve myself." He got to his feet. "I like to see people trying hard and you did your best, and if I stuff you with food anymore," he went on, as he walked four paces away from the fire and began to relieve himself, "you will not be able to tell me good stories."

It took him some time to finish. When he had, he belched and retraced his four paces, turned round and eased his bare buttocks down onto the chair. He lay back, panting with the effort, and accepted the piece of venison from the end of Magwegwe's knife.

"Tell me a hunting story," said Lobengula as he finished the meat and rested his head against the back of the chair. "Make me amused."

"Well," said Magwegwe, feeling that he was once again in control of himself, and began to recount the great hunt of Shaka. Before he was halfway through the story, Lobengula's mouth dropped open and the king began to snore.

MAGWEGWE WATCHED HIM ALL NIGHT, as he had not been given permission to leave and he knew what the penalty would be if Lobengula should wake in the night and find him gone or asleep. He liked his life and he fought all night to keep awake. The dawn came in the sky as beautifully as the sun had left it the previous night. All manner of birds began to sing to the new day and Magwegwe wiped the slight dew from his cold arm. The fire had gone out an hour before.

Lobengula woke, but kept his eyes shut and remembered carefully what he had decided to do and, in the cold of morning, he was again certain. He was stiff but the gout was a little better and he judged it sufficiently eased to let him ride. It would be his last ordeal. He opened his eyes and looked at the dawn and the cool light of day that showed him the leaves on the most distant mopane tree. He smiled at Magwegwe, who was watching him.

"Will you follow me?" he asked Magwegwe.

"Why do you ask a question when you already know the answer?" Magwegwe replied.

"I want you to collect together as many of my inDunas who can be here within the time it takes for the sun to come up over the trees. We will then find the big hill with the caves. I will ride my white horse and you will ride the second horse and the others will follow on foot. You will enquire the quickest route to the caves but, first, give me a slice of the cold venison."

Magwegwe cut the meat and gave it to Lobengula before going off on his errands. Lobengula ate slowly and prevented his mind from thinking of anything else except the task he had set himself. He finished the meat and got up. He was determined to forget the pain in his feet and walked with strength to his wagon. He climbed up into the front and went inside. He found what he wanted and went back to the entrance.

"Bring me two gourds of beer," he shouted, and waited there until they were brought to him. Then he went back into the wagon and poured the poison equally into each gourd and shook the contents. Satisfied, he sealed the gourds and waited for the sun to come up over the mopane trees. He sat on the driver's seat of the wagon and looked out on the bustle of the camp. He had sat many times on the same seat in Gu-Bulawayo, from where he had dispensed his justice. He sighed as he waited for the sun to come up over the mopanes. He saw people arriving from the forest. The last to arrive, just before the sun tipped the trees, was Gambo. Lobengula stepped down from the wagon and walked steadily across the glade to where his white horse was tethered to a mopane tree.

"Have you found us a guide?" he said to Magwegwe.

"This man says he knows the caves well," replied Magwegwe.

"He had better," said Lobengula, "as he will not be given a second chance." He looked around before attaching the two gourds of beer to the saddle of his horse and, with a supreme effort, swung himself up, leant forward and untethered the animal from the mopane tree.

"We are ready," he said to everyone. "Gambo, go and bring my shield and my assegai. We need nothing else."

Each of his inDunas was looking at him with the same intense mixture of curiosity and fear. They had been told of Lobengula's intention by Magwegwe, and they all agreed that it was one of the king's ways of testing them, and this was made certain by Gambo being given the honour to carry the king's assegai and the king's shield as Gambo had defeated the white men.

Gambo returned from Lobengula's wagon with the shield and assegai that Lobengula used each year at the Great Dance.

"Come now, guide," said Lobengula. "You are the one who knows the way. Lead us there, as the day will not live with us forever.

Following the guide, Lobengula led them into the mopane forest. Magwegwe followed on a brown horse, certain in his mind that he was about to be tested by the king and that he would do exactly what he was told and not show a trace of fear. The sun filtered through the trees and dappled his horse, and despite the amount of beer that he had been forced to drink the night before, his head was clear and he felt younger than his years. He looked behind at the other inDunas and smiled at them imperiously from his position of height and favour. They tried to ignore him but he could tell what they really thought of walking behind Magwegwe while he rode the king's horse. He was not sure about using the stirrups, so he let his feet dangle like Lobengula.

They went on for three hours before they found the caves. Lobengula dismounted, took the two gourds of beer from his horse and led everyone into the largest cave. The sun was streaming in behind them and clearly showed the fresh spore of lion on the dust of the floor, which Lobengula chose to ignore. No one dared mention the fact, as they were convinced that they were about to see a very bad smelling out. They looked around the cave for the is-Anuzi but saw none.

"Place my assegai and my shield in front of me on the floor," Lobengula said to Gambo. In each hand he held a gourd of beer and he waited until everyone was watching him.

"You have known me all your lives," he started, "and in those years you have never seen me do anything which I did not consider to be in the greater interest of the Matabele nation. We have fought together and shared each other's dangers and, in the strength of our youth, we were always victorious. The youngest of you here, Gambo, has been victorious again and against the most dangerous enemy that we have fought. He won that fight because he was young, and there are many other young men of equal fight and youth, and it is these people that must lead you when your need for a leader is greater than ever before.

"If you did not fear me so much, you would have done to me many years ago what I am about to do to myself, and maybe even then it would have been in the interest of the tribe. I am going to kill myself and you will bury me here with my assegai on one side and my shield on the other and with me dead will be Magwegwe, and you will do the same to him, and then you will block the entrance to this cave and tell no one where I am buried.

"You will then go out among the nation and, in the traditions that we brought with us from the south, you will choose yourselves a new king and he will be young and able to lead you without a body that is always in the most terrible pain. He will have many alternatives to offer you but the greatest three are these. He may either choose to fight Rhodes, to accept Rhodes or to go north. You have your wisdom and your years and you will be his inDunas, so counsel him well.

"Come, Magwegwe, and drink a gourd of beer with me, and we will go and find our ancestors and later talk to the tribe through the voice of the is-Anuzi."

Magwegwe stepped forward and took the gourd with confidence and without any sign of holding back, as he had watched Lobengula's tricks for many years and he knew that the only way to be a chief and stay alive was to do exactly what Lobengula told him to do. He took the gourd up to his mouth at the same time as Lobengula, and began to drink at the same speed, and they watched each other closely as they drank and, as he reached almost the last of the beer, he saw Lobengula pitch forward and heard the cry of the inDunas and then a violent pain gripped his stomach and he realised that there was no trick and that he was going to die.

PART 3

1894

1

"*I* was right," said James to von Brand as they looked out over the acres of tall maize, each stalk carrying more than one cob, "the maize this year is the best we have grown. We will make a good profit." He walked into the maize land to inspect the cobs and was immediately lost to sight. "We will be able to buy more machinery with the money," he called from amongst the maize, "and more cattle for the ranch at Bulawayo. After this crop, we will be financially safe and the gambles will have paid off."

James came out of the maize and into the sun. His bush-hat, without the badge of the Mashonaland Horse, was pulled down in a full brim over his face and his slate-blue eyes looked at von Brand from behind the shadow made by the rim and the sun. He had shaved off his beard and the sun had driven a deep tan into his face; the smooth appearance of youth had given way to a slight pinching at the cheeks, his chin was sharper, and his eyes had a knowledge that had not been there the year before.

"You'll make a farmer out of me yet," said von Brand as they began the long walk up the path towards the farmhouse. Von Brand's beard was completely grey and had changed colour at the same time as his hair, after they had returned together from Bulawayo. The sight of the greyness had shaken him far more than his friends. When he looked into the mirror he saw an old man; the years in the sun and the cases of brandy had written their story.

The farm was not the same with two of them; they had found that to exchange a stream of antagonism at table required three. Life had lost a portion of its flavour and von Brand was no longer even able to look forward to a change in the future as he had now come to the end of his wanderings. He had found a home and he would stay there, as the joints in his body were not as flexible as they had been before he went to Bulawayo. He put it down to weeks in the wet, and though he had spent many such weeks before in his hunting days, he blamed the war and not his age.

They walked slowly, side by side, up the slight incline of the path and von Brand took a sidelong glance at James, whose eyes were looking out over the maize and seemed to von Brand to be looking even beyond the distant hills that shimmered in the heat of the day. By looking at him, von Brand could not even remember the boy he had met four years before. Then, he had been the leader, but now he knew he was being led. Von Brand sighed to himself but more from contentment than frustration. He felt that he had reached the stage in his life when he wished to slow down. He was now quite happy to let a younger man take up the responsibilities of planning and thinking. He yawned, without bringing his hand up to his mouth, and enjoyed the feeling of the good stands of maize on either side of the path. It was the first time in his life that he felt that he belonged to one place. His instinct to wander had been satiated.

"There is a farm for sale at the end of the valley," said James. "The soil is not as heavy as it is here but the rainfall is the same. It is a small place of five thousand acres but I am determined that we should own the whole of the valley. I have put in a bid. He is asking six hundred pounds to which I have agreed provided he takes one hundred pounds a year for six years at no interest. I think he will take it, as there is no one else in the market. It is a fair price. The man wants to go back to England. I think he plants his crops upside down, as nothing grows. I checked the soil and it is no different to what we are using on our eastern boundary. There are a number of these farmers going bankrupt who want to stay in the country and I have a plan. You and I, Willy, cannot possibly cover the whole of Morgandale because it is too big and, unless every farm job is carefully watched, it is not done properly. We have trained a number of the Shona to do the ploughing, hoeing and reaping, but they must always be watched if the job is to be done to our satisfaction. What I have in mind is to employ ten European managers and split the farm into ten sections. We will supervise the overall programme but we will no longer be held up by having to stand in the lands all day. If we give them a small salary and pay for their food it will be enough, provided they each receive a percentage of their section's profit at the end of the year. In the good years they will do well, and so will we, and in the bad years we will not have laid out the capital. With the present crop, we can afford to set up the scheme straight away, provided you are in agreement."

"It sounds good to me," said von Brand, "provided you've worked out the figures correctly. I'd like to look at it on paper when we get back to the house."

"Well, that's settled," said James with a smile. "The theory is good, Willy. I've spent two weeks working it out from every direction. It will give us proper control and profit."

"I can see there's some of your father in you," laughed von Brand.

"I hope I never take it to his extremes. You know, Willy, it's a wonderful thing to have a partner who's not jealous of the other man's ideas."

"If I think the idea is bad I'll tell you soon enough and explain every one of my reasons. You forget that it is something to see a pupil running to form."

"At a future stage," said James, going on with his main line of thought, "I would like to trek some of the cattle up from the Bulawayo farm and fatten them here. I'm sure they'll eat the maize stalks after we've reaped the cobs. When Fort Salisbury is big enough, we'll get a good price for beef in the town."

"Don't you ever stop thinking ahead?" said von Brand, his voice full of humour.

"I think farming is a case of keeping one jump ahead, if one is to compete with the elements."

They lapsed into silence and continued to walk slowly.

"How do your heels feel?" asked von Brand.

"They don't hurt as much now. In another few months they'll be normal."

"I've never seen feet in a mess like that before," said von Brand.

They walked on and, half an hour later, the farmhouse came into sight.

"I think I shall go to England when the maize has been reaped," said James. "By then, we'll have found some of the section managers."

"You are right to go," said von Brand. "You have a lot to do and, at your age, it will do you good to see civilisation. You must find yourself a woman."

"I don't know so much about that, but I certainly have a lot of business to complete. I'll visit the farm machinery factories and tell them our problems. They may be prepared to adapt some items for our use."

"I can see," said von Brand, chuckling, "that you will not be wasting any of your time, but take a tip from an old man and enjoy yourself while you're over there. I think you may have some surprises in store for you, Jim. Your looks and background are going to cut quite a dash amongst the wealthy society of Cheshire."

"I'll write to the family now," said James, ignoring what von Brand thought was in store for him in England.

They reached the farmhouse and James went on towards his study.

"Don't you want a drink?" called von Brand, to James's back.

"I'll join you on the veranda when I've finished the letter. By then, the sun will be going down and we won't be cheating with our drinking hours."

As he opened the door of his study, he heard the bottles rattle and smiled to himself. He went inside and closed the door behind him and crossed the room to his desk. The desk faced the window and he looked out at the sweep of the Mazoe valley, most of which they now owned. He looked around inside at the shelves of books that he had built up himself; he was quite certain that he had everything he wanted. He sat down at his desk and pulled Ester's last letter out of the pigeon-hole to read it again so that he could answer it properly.

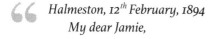

Halmeston, 12th February, 1894
My dear Jamie,

I am so glad that you are safe. Even Father took a serious interest in the fighting and found a close contact in the War Office so that he was even more up to date than the press. I think he was genuinely upset when he learnt that your friend, Rhys Morgan, had been posted missing, presumed killed. He was very relieved when he found out that you had not even been wounded. It was the first time that I can remember him showing any genuine emotion.

I think in some ways it was all a good thing as it helped to take his mind off the fiasco of the wedding. Afterwards, he found that some of the right people were very interested in what was happening in Matabeleland and, with Oswald living in the house as well, a number of people came to call, ostensibly to see Oswald but in fact to ask Father about you and the war against Lobengula. It has partly made up for all Oswald's relations snubbing us at the wedding. It really was terrible, as we knew nothing about it until we got to the church. Oswald knew, but he said afterwards that he was too embarrassed to say anything about it and, when we walked up the aisle, there were masses of people on the Carregan side of the church but none on the Granthams' worth speaking about.

The only one who really enjoyed the joke was

Grandfather, who, once Father had given me away and gone back to his pew, kept looking around and nudging Father. When we walked into the vestry to sign the register, Father was purple in the face. Grandfather insisted on coming in as well, as he said he was the next closest relative to the bride after the father and, with you away at the war, he was quite right, but it didn't improve Father's colouring. Oswald thought it was an absolute hoot and I became a little annoyed with him at that. The weather was really quite mild and the reception was done very well except that there was too much of everything as less than a third of the guests actually turned up. Oswald found out afterwards that it was the Carregans offering to pay all those fares back from India that finally turned Viscount Grantham into a terrible rage. He made them all accept, receive their tickets and then just not turn up. So poor Father spent a lot of money and saw nothing for it in return, as he couldn't really expect a refund from the steamship company as none of them had actually cancelled their passages. Father didn't dare start arguing about the return leg of the journey as he had sent them all open tickets, and, anyway, there was nothing to have stopped them making the journey without attending the wedding.

Nevertheless, we are married and having Oswald in the house makes everything so much easier, even though he has refused to have anything to do with the Liverpool and Maritime, but it doesn't really matter. So long as some of Oswald's friends come to Halmeston, Father remains in a good mood, though every now and again I see that old look, especially when dear Oswald is being really rather silly. I wonder how long the arrangement can last? I wish Father would give us a proper allowance so that we can live as we want; Oswald might then find something to interest himself as it isn't really right for a man to be around the house all day and not do anything. He doesn't like Father talking about you, as Father always emphasises that it is not necessary to be born with money to, as Father puts it, 'do any good in life' and I think that Oswald feels that Father is criticising him. Anyway, we have been to some very good parties in just the best places and everyone treats me exactly the same as Oswald.

Please write soon, and when are you going to visit us now that the war is over?

Your loving Sister,
    Ester

James looked out of the window and saw that the sun was three quarters of an hour from setting. He took up his pen and a clean sheet of paper and began to write.

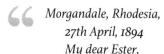

Morgandale, Rhodesia,
    27th April, 1894
    My dear Ester,
    Thank you for your letter of the twelfth of February which I have just re-read. I am glad that the wedding ceremony was successful. I would not worry too much about all those people not turning up. People who do childish things like that cannot be worth very much. You ask in your letter, 'When are you coming to England?' and, as we have had a very good crop this year, I intend to begin the journey next month. I have business in Cape Town, so I am not sure which boat I shall take, but I will have them wire you my date of arrival. Time is short, I must be back on the farm within eight months, so I shall take one of the new steamboats of the Union line; don't tell Grandfather, as we will end up in an argument on the commercial merits of sail. You must agree, having met him,

that he is a wonderful man, but you do not say anything in your letter. I shall write to him care of his agent in Liverpool, as I would very much like to see him again during my stay in England.

The local newspaper called itself the Rhodesia Herald *and the first name seems to have stuck to the country. As Mr. Rhodes controls the newspaper, I wonder how much he had to do with the coining of the name? Nonetheless, he was the person to make the country possible so, along with Bolivia, we are one of the very few countries to be named after an individual. The war, I think, brought us all together and we have come to call ourselves Rhodesians. The country is quiet at the moment and though we never actually defeated the Matabele it appears that the impis have disbanded. Doctor Jameson is carrying on with the government and the division of Lobengula's wealth as if they did not exist, though I have the feeling that we have not heard the end of them yet. It is rumoured that Lobengula is dead, but no one can be certain. Jameson has found the two policemen who embezzled Lobengula's peace offering and the two men have each been sentenced to fourteen years imprisonment. If they had delivered their message, we would have had none of the fighting and Rhys and the others would still be alive.*

Three weeks ago, Willy von Brand and I made a special journey to Bulawayo, and there is no doubt now that Rhys died with the others where he stood and fought. Just before we arrived in Bulawayo to make enquiries, two traders, Dawson and Reilly, returned from having buried the remains of Allan Wilson's patrol. They had spoken to the leaders of Lobengula's regiments who were still living in the forests, and it is quite clear from many of them who fought against Wilson that the party was annihilated to a man. All the stories agreed.

We took our horses along the same trail that we had fought along. The rains had finished and the mopane forest was cool and there was no one watching us in the night. It took us four days to find the place that Dawson had described to us. We enquired often on our way and it was curious to talk to the people who, only months before, had tried to kill us. They were perfectly friendly and willing to talk and they all confirmed the story that Dawson had given us in Bulawayo. The Matabele seemed to be living in small groups and there was no sign of militancy or of them having any leader. I found it difficult to imagine the same people repeatedly storming our laager. In the end we saw the place where Rhys died. It was a small glade in the forest and we found it late in the evening. It was so peaceful. Three bushbuck were feeding at the other end of the glade and, before the light began to fade, we found the tree under which Dawson and Reilly had buried the bones of thirty-four men. Dawson had carved the inscription 'To Brave Men' on the tree and there was nothing else we could do for Rhys except take off our hats and remember one of the best men we will ever meet, and the friends that died with him. Except for one set of bones a little way from the main laager, Dawson found all the other remains in one place. There were no bones of the Matabele as they always remove their dead from the field of battle. I have never felt so sad. We did not stay there long but left them in peace and made our way back to Bulawayo.

It is for Rhys that I am coming to England but I will tell you all about it when I arrive as I may need your help and that of your husband. The next time that you hear from me will be via a wire telling you when I will arrive. It is a long journey, as I have to travel by horse to Mafeking and take the train from there to Cape Town. The railway is reaching towards Umtali but the constructors are having a terrible time with malaria and sleeping sickness.

Willy will look after the farm, which we have named after Rhys, while I am away, though we are going to employ ten section managers on Morgandale and I hope to have some of them installed before I leave for England. We have a large tract of land now, some fifty thousand acres at Morgandale and another twenty thousand just outside Bulawayo. It will take us many years to stump out the trees and use all the arable land; but I am young and I intend to see the whole of the red soil in this valley under crops. It is the kind of challenge I enjoy.

Give my regards to Father, and say how much I am looking forward to seeing you both after five years, and to meeting your husband.

Your brother,
  James

2

*J*ames began his enquiries about Michael Fentan at the Harbour Tavern but Hennie had never heard of the name. He sat and drank brandy for half an hour before he remembered that Michael had started off with them from Cape Town; the Charter Company must have a record of his next of kin; if he died in company service they would have wanted to know where to send his valuables and any pay that might have accrued.

"Have the Charter Company an office in Cape Town, Hennie?" he asked. "I know the Head Office is at Kimberley but with Mr Rhodes here as Prime Minister they must have something."

"Why don't you go and see his private secretary?" suggested Hennie.

"First, I'll have another brandy and then I'll work that one out," said James. "I can't find a berth to England for ten days so I think I have more than enough time. If the worst comes to the worst, I can telegraph the Charter Office at Kimberley now that I'm in Cape Town. When the means of civilisation are at one's disposal, life becomes very much easier."

The barman moved away to serve another customer and James looked around at the long bar with the benches and tables and lanterns overhead. The place brought back too many memories. He swallowed his brandy in one gulp, thanked Hennie, and left the bar.

He took a cab back to the Vineyard Hotel and used the telephone to call the Prime Minister's office and within ten minutes he had the address of a Mrs Fentan. She lived some way out of town on the other side of the mountain to the Vineyard. He went up to his room, put on a clean shirt and the latest fashion in trousers, jacket and cravat that he had bought that morning and looked at himself in the mirror. He could not remember what it felt like to be properly dressed and, at first sight, he burst out laughing. They were the clothes all right, but inside was a definite bushranger with long, unruly straight brown hair that curled well over the collar of his grey jacket, and with the face went the burnt, hard skin and the sun-bleached eyebrows. He stood up straight to his full five-foot-ten and turned sideways to see what kind of fool he looked from that direction.

"You could put on some weight, James," he said to himself and patted a flat stomach. He noticed that the end of his sideburns were a shade on the ginger side and, despite the haughty looks he had received at the tailor, his jacket hung smoothly over his shoulders and dropped down his back without a crease. He was glad he had shaved off his beard. Satisfied, he walked down the stairs to the foyer to see if his transport had arrived.

"Are you Mr Carregan, sir?" enquired the hall porter.

"Yes, I'm waiting for a cab," he replied.

"It's ready for you, sir, if you'll come this way."

James followed the man as instructed. He climbed into the cab, gave the driver Mrs Fentan's address and sat back in the small carriage, taking a cheroot from his cigar case, the end of which he chewed off and spat through the open window.

Looking out of the window, he could see the harbour in the distance. Many more buildings had been built since 1889. The houses spread right around the foot of the mountain. The air was fresh and a strong wind came off the sea from the southwest. The tensions of running a farm had left him, and, for the first time since he had arrived back from the Shangani Patrol, he felt his nerves and body at peace with one another. He enjoyed the cheroot and the faint taste of the brandy that lingered at the back of his mouth.

"How long will it take us, driver?" he asked.

"About ten minutes. I know the house. It's not a wealthy area."

The cab came up over the rise and began the descent towards the bay that was flanked on one side by the giant cornices of the twelve apostles and on the other side by the Atlantic Ocean. The sun sparkled on the calm water but, out to sea, where there was no protection from the strong wind, white horses ran quickly over the choppy waves. The cab entered a small street and wound around the open side of the bay, between small, wooden houses.

"That is the one, sir," said the driver. "The one with the red gate on this side of the road. Do you want me to wait?"

"Yes, please. I shouldn't be more than ten minutes. She may not be at home."

"Right, sir. Take yer time and I'll be waiting."

"Thanks," said James.

He got out of the cab and crossed to the small, red gate. He leant over, unlatched the catch and pushed open the gate. Everything, including the fence, was in a bad state of repair. He glanced up at the mountains before walking up to the faded front door, its paint peeled by the weather. He banged with his knuckles on the wood; there was nothing else to use. The door was opened by a young woman with long, smooth black hair that ran down behind her back. Her skin was the colour of a thick, smooth olive with red highlights at each cheek.

"I'm sorry to stare," he said, "but I was expecting Mrs Fentan to answer the door. Do I have the right house?"

"Yes," said the girl. "Won't you come in and sit in the lounge. I'll tell my mother that you are here. Your name is?"

"Carregan. James Carregan. I'm down from Rhodesia."

"I've heard your name before. You were one of the pioneers we heard about in connection with Michael."

James followed her from the small hall into a lounge cluttered with trinkets and ornaments.

"My mother and father used to collect them," she said, as she watched him look around the room.

"I can see that."

James looked at her and they laughed.

"My name is Sonja," she said. "Please sit down and I will see if my mother feels strong enough to talk to you. Since it must be about Michael, I think she will. Her English is not very good, so I will translate. I was born in South Africa but my parents came from Estonia. They were fifteen when they married and neither of them mastered the English language, not even mother after twenty years. As she has grown older, she has forgotten the English she learnt. She is only fifty-seven but you would think her much older. We Jews had a hard time in Russia. There was always some new purge. Those of us that did not die had to move from one place to the next. I'll get her for you, Mr Carregan. I'm sure you do not wish to be bored with the family history."

"She knows about Michael?" he asked.

"Yes. We made enquiries. Mr Rhodes helped. Michael died in the Hartley hills while looking for gold... I'll go and get my mother."

James was left by himself. He gazed out of the window at the sea, and the contrast of freshness and colour was as startling as Sonja. He heard them talking further inside the house, but in a foreign language. He sat down in the largest chair and waited, remembering his manners and stopping himself from lighting a cheroot. He smiled at the restrictions which society imposed upon itself. After five years in the bush, he would have to give himself a refresher course in etiquette. Men grew into bad habits on their own, he told himself. His thoughts were interrupted as the women came into the room. He got up and walked towards a frail lady. She was no more than five feet tall. She stooped. Her hair was white and a few strands straggled over her face.

"This is my mother," said Sonja as they shook hands. She said something to the old lady and he heard his name mentioned.

"Please, let us all sit down," said Sonja.

"I'm not sure where to start," said James and cleared his throat. "Maybe if I tell you everything that I know, you will be able to translate at the end. To begin with, Michael and I met on the train that took us to Mafeking; a number of the pioneers had entrained at Cape Town. After that, we saw each other on the march from the banks of the Limpopo River until we raised the Union Jack at Fort Salisbury. My partner, von Brand, knew Michael better than I, but even to Willy, Michael said very little about his background. There were a lot of us, however, only looking forward; the past had happened and was not of interest. Von Brand had known my other partner, Morgan, for many years. They took Michael and myself as their respective assistants, and, when we reached Fort Salisbury, they asked us to join their syndicate to look for gold. As they knew the country and the old gold diggings of the Mashona, it was a good proposition.

"They were not sure whether the most likely place was the Hartley or Mazoe hills. We went in two parties, Michael with von Brand, and Morgan and myself. Morgan and I found gold at Mazoe, but soon after we returned to Fort Salisbury to register our claim the rains broke and von Brand and Michael were cut off by the rising rivers. Michael contracted dysentery. When we opened up the mine, we named it after Michael. The Fentan Mine is still producing a trickle of gold. My own partner, Morgan, died on the Shangani Patrol. I am on my way to England to tell his people."

Sonja turned to her mother and translated. Twice the old lady nodded her head, and once she raised her hands upwards in an expression of acceptance. James sat back in the chair and watched the girl. He caught her eye once and for a moment she seemed to stop, then looked away to go on talking to her mother. At the end, she put her hand softly on her mother's arm. She turned back to James.

"My mother thanks you," she said.

"There is something else," said James, "that may help you a little. When we formed the original syndicate, it was agreed that each of us would share in any find, irrespective of which pair found the gold. Afterwards, I convinced Morgan and von Brand that we should use our money from the gold and put it into farmland. You see, the gold reef was too irregular and I could not see that it was sensible to spend a large amount of money on machinery, unless we were certain that there was enough gold in the ground. In the end I was proved right, as the Fentan Mine has only half paid for the new machinery installed by the lease owners, and that is over three years.

"In the meantime, we have accumulated fifty thousand acres in Mashonaland and twenty thousand in Matabeleland and we are already reaping good profits. Some time ago, my grandfather offered us two thousand pounds in cash to put into the farms and, at that time, we valued the assets of the original syndicate at eight thousand pounds and formed the whole into a limited company with each of the partners holding an equal fifth share; the original idea of Michael and me holding a smaller share was discarded. I therefore have in my hotel a blank share certificate for two thousand fully paid up one-pound shares in Morgandale, which I will issue to your mother when I have her full name.

"The certificate has already been countersigned by von Brand. The shares are worth more than their face value, I think. So far, we have not paid a dividend as we have used the money to buy more farms, but there is no reason why we should continue this practice in the future. The shareholders who do not wish to receive their dividend in cash can loan it back to the company at the normal rate of interest. I would estimate this year's dividend at two hundred pounds per partner, though the total profits will be much higher than a thousand pounds. We still have a number of long-term commitments and we require machinery and cattle.

"If you would both like to dine with me tonight at my hotel, I will give you the certificate and we can agree where to pay the half yearly dividends. We will be able to make a telegraphic transfer from the Standard Bank in Fort Salisbury to the Standard Bank in Cape Town, if your mother will open an account."

Sonja translated. There was silence for a moment and then the old woman spoke.

"My mother is surprised that Michael left us his share," said Sonja. "Before he went with the column my mother was angry with him. You see, Jewish families are meant to stay together for the strong to help the weak and we only have this house and the few shillings a week interest that we receive from my father's investments. We have no other relations in Africa. When Michael insisted on going north, my mother said she would never speak to him again and now, through you, he has given us more than we ever could have expected had he stayed and worked with the shipping company in Cape Town. Did he leave a will?"

"No," said James, "but that is not necessary, as when he died there was no company and no certainty that the Fentan Mine would yield sufficient gold. The issue of the shares to your mother is the conclusion of a verbal agreement."

"Did Michael ask you to find us?" asked Sonja.

"That I don't know, because I was not with him when he died. I am confident, however, that he did as, no matter how bitter the argument, you are his only relations."

She talked again to her mother. James got up and looked out of the window to make certain that his cab had not driven away as he had already been longer than ten minutes.

"I hope we are not keeping you," said Sonja.

"On the contrary," said James. "I was checking my cab as I did not wish to get lost walking back to my hotel."

"My mother says that, as much as she would like to have dinner with you, she is not strong enough. She suggests that I take her place. It will be the first time I have been allowed out alone with a male escort."

"Well, then," said James, coming back from the bay window, "it will be something for both of us, as I have been in the new country for five years and I have never taken a lady to dinner. I only hope I will know which knife and fork to use. May I call back at eight?"

"I hope my clothes will be correct," said Sonja.

"I only have this suit myself," said James. "I thought I had better let my father help me with a wardrobe in England. Everything seems to be different to what I remember. Please say goodbye to your mother and thank her for allowing me to take you to dinner. Say that I am sorry she will not join us."

James smiled to Mrs Fentan and shook her hand and then followed Sonja out of the living room into the small entrance hall.

"I will look forward to tonight," she said, and opened the door for him to go out.

"So will I. Eight o'clock then."

James went out down the path, and turned to put the catch on the gate. He looked up and, as she smiled, he waved and turned to the cab. The driver held open the door and he got inside.

"The Vineyard," he said.

James took his watch out of his pocket, looked at the time and told himself there would be time for a drink in the cocktail lounge, a bath and a shave. He rubbed his hand along his chin in contemplation and then relaxed back in the comfort of the leather seat. 'My, my, Carregan,' he said to himself, 'the best things grow in the strangest places.'

He tried to remember everything that he knew about the Jewish people. Before, he had never thought of anybody being anything else but Church of England or Catholic and the Catholics usually kept it pretty much to themselves in Cheshire. He knew von Brand was a Lutheran, but von Brand could not remember the last time he had gone to a Lutheran church. Somehow, the religion of England did not seem so close to him in the African bush, but he had no answer as to the reason. He tried to remember where the Jews had appeared in his history degree, but he could remember few parts that were relevant. The Old Testament and the Gentiles and God were the same, but the rest he had never seriously thought about.

'It probably doesn't make any difference,' he told himself and took a cheroot out of his case, chewed the end and spat it out of the window. He bent down below the line of the wind to strike the match. He puffed hard and the heavy tobacco burnt well. He sat back, cigar between his teeth.

SITTING at the bar in the cocktail lounge of the hotel, he looked down into a half-empty glass of Cape brandy and soda. He drank it down and got off the bar stool. He went out to the reception and was told where to find the *à la carte* restaurant.

Upstairs, he explained his problem to the *maître d'hôtel* and tipped him five shillings. Satisfied, James went back down to the bar and drank his second brandy and soda more slowly. He found it difficult to relate his surroundings to the previous five years and he was glad that he would have ten days in Cape Town to accustom himself to the rules. He looked at his watch; it was six thirty. He had time to relax in a hot bath with taps that ran hot and cold water.

At twenty minutes to eight he got into the cab, a cape held loosely over his shoulders. The air was cold. It was almost dark and clouds obscured the setting sun. He felt clean and comfortable. He held the remains of his post-bath cheroot between his teeth. Half an hour later, Sonja opened the door, but there was insufficient light for him to see anything more than her outline and the fact that she was also wearing a cape.

"Mother has gone to bed," she said, "so, if you are ready, we can go now."

"I have the papers in my pocket," he said. "All I need are your mother's full names."

"Can't we do that over dinner?"

"Yes, of course." He stood back to let her pass as she closed the front door. He followed her down the narrow path and held open the gate.

"Thank you," she said, picking up her cape and dress as she stepped into the cab through the door the driver held open.

James climbed in the other side and they sat next to each other with little space in between.

"Is the air too cold for you?" said James.

"No, it's fine," she said.

They remained silent as the horse jogged them back to the hotel. For twenty minutes neither spoke and James began to wonder what kind of an evening they would have after all.

"In which hotel are you staying?" she asked, and her voice showed none of the strain that might have grown from the silence.

"The Vineyard."

"Don't you find it expensive?"

"I don't know," said James, feeling the tension leave him. "I haven't yet had the bill."

The cab turned into the hotel entrance and they jogged up the long driveway through the oak trees. When the cab stopped, James stepped out first and paid the driver. When he turned to Sonja she was standing next to him.

"The doorman let me out," she said.

"Come on then. It's time for a cocktail downstairs and then we'll go up for dinner. They have two violinists who play while we eat. The *maître d'hôtel* promised the food was the best in Cape Town."

"May I take your coat, Madam?" said the doorman as they entered the hotel.

"Carregan," James said to the bellboy. "You can put them both together." He turned to indicate to the bellboy the coat held by the doorman.

Sonja had her hands clasped loosely at arm's length against the front of a yellow dress that flared out and dropped down to the floor. Her sleeves were long and lightly ruffled at the cuffs. The dress flared easily from a firm waist and ran up through a bone bodice covered by the same yellow material. Her shoulders were bare and the deep olive skin plunged down to a wide cleft between her breasts that were held up firmly by the dress. Her hair was brushed to a black velvet sheen and worn as he had seen it that afternoon. She wore no jewellery except a small Star of David that hung below her throat on a silver chain. They smiled at each other. He held out his right arm and she took it gently.

"Let's go get a drink in the cocktail lounge," he said.

. . .

"ONE ALWAYS TRIES to make it look as though one is at home," said James when they were seated in the restaurant, "but I must admit that I find the bars in Fort Salisbury a little less frightening. Now that we have ordered, you must tell me all about yourself. Downstairs, we didn't say very much."

"Oh, where does one start?" said Sonja. "I'm Jewish, as you know, though not orthodox or I would not be able to eat non-kosher food, and I was born in Cape Town. My name is Sonja but I am always called Sonny. My parents came from Estonia. Michael was born there as well. People don't really like us Jews, and there is always someone trying to move us on. We've been wandering for thousands of years. We were very poor in Estonia, but then so were our friends. It took my father many years to save up the fare to South Africa. When he arrived here he was over forty. There is a Jewish guild in Cape Town and they helped him to set up in a small clothing shop. Despite the language barrier, he did very well and repaid the four hundred pounds, together with the interest, in three years. The next year we bought the house that you saw this afternoon and, if it had not been for Father dying only four years afterwards, we would now be wealthy. What we obtained for the business paid for mine and Michael's education and keeps Mother and I alive at the moment. You see, that was why Mother was so disappointed in Michael, as he was given all that education and we expected him to become a lawyer or a doctor but, once he had left school, he didn't have the inclination to learn anymore and went into the shipping company, saying it was to give us more money. And then he gave it up."

The oysters were put down in front of them, the shells resting on seaweed. The *maître d'hôtel* squeezed lemon into each oyster. He then poured a little of the wine for James to taste.

"That's nice," said James. "I'm sure you'll like it. It is not too dry and you can taste the grapes."

The glasses were filled and they each sampled an oyster.

"I like them," said Sonja.

"I think this is all beginners luck," said James.

He finished his oysters and looked around at the room that had begun to fill up. The two candles on either side of their table framed Sonja's face. The brandy and wine had warmed him.

"Go on," said James, when she had finished the last of her oysters. "You were telling me about your family. Then I want to hear about you."

"Well, of course, it was a long time ago that Michael left. I was only thirteen at the time."

"That makes you eighteen now," interrupted James.

"Yes."

"Well, I think your mother is even nicer to have let us go out," said James.

"We have not met many honest people in our lives, outside our own relations," said Sonja. "It would have been just as easy for you and Mr von Brand to forget Michael Fentan and even Mr Morgan."

"No, Sonny. You don't know quite what we went through together. They would both have done exactly the same for Willy and me."

"Are you sure?"

"Quite sure. You see, we all had something in common and it made us understand each other."

"What was that?" asked Sonja.

"We were individuals," said James. They lapsed into silence for a moment. "Go on," he said, gently. "I have found out that you are eighteen and I am impatient to learn the rest."

"Father had made Mother promise," went on Sonja, "that if any of us wanted to go to university she would use the capital. He said that in the end, the best investment was in the children's education, and, with Michael gone, I thought I would have to support Mother, so I'm reading medicine at Cape Town University. I have done six months so far, and it will take another four and a half years before I qualify, but when I do, I will always be able to earn a living. I am on vacation at the moment, which is why you found me at home today."

"You all seem to have had a difficult time," said James.

"Not so difficult now, thanks to you," replied Sonja. "Two hundred pounds a year is a lot of money."

"Within a short time, I hope that it will be very much more."

"Now let me hear about you," said Sonja, as the waiter put down her plate.

As the couple ate, they could hear the two violins being played gently on the far side of the room.

By the time they had finished the Chateaubriand and the half bottle of red wine, he had told her a little about himself and Morgandale.

"Would you like strawberries?" he asked her as the waiter removed their plates.

"I can't eat another thing," she said.

"Maybe coffee?"

"Thank you."

"Coffee it is," he said to the waiter and turned back to her. "Do you mind if I talk business for a moment and complete the share certificate? After all, it was the excuse for asking you to dinner."

"Then we had better do it." James called for pen and ink and completed the document, countersigned von Brand's signature, rolled up the certificate and gave it to Sonja. They finished their coffee in silence, listening to the music.

"Will you have lunch with me tomorrow?" he asked.

"Yes."

"I'll collect you at twelve."

"That will be fine."

"We'd better go now."

"I suppose so."

"I want your mother on my side."

"That's wise."

"Come then," he said as he signed the bill, "they'll find us a cab downstairs."

3

$\mathcal{J}$ ames stepped out of the cab that had brought him from the station and looked up at the house and the imitation battlements. The cab went off down the drive and he looked down the avenue at the elm trees, which were green and lush, and at the rockeries, which were coloured with summer flowers. A bee droned in the gentle warmth and the scents of an English garden came up to him. He looked out over the river Dee towards Wales and Denbigh and he thought how strange it was that he and Morgan should have been born so close and met so far away.

He climbed the steps up to the large front door of Halmeston, pulled down on the handle and heard the bell ring inside. He waited and thought of Sonny.

The butler James had known all his life opened the door and he bent to pick up his two cases.

"Can I help you, sir?" The butler looked straight at him as he stood up with a case in each hand.

"Yes, Jennings, you can tell my father that I have arrived."

"I'm so sorry, Mr James, but I didn't recognise you. I knew you by your voice. You have changed in five years."

"Yes, I suppose I have," said James, and walked into his father's house, looking around at everything that was familiar and which had not changed in the smallest aspect.

"There's no one in at the moment," said Jennings.

"Am I expected?" asked James.

"Oh, yes. They have a ball arranged for you on Saturday. The kitchens have been preparing the food. It's just that it's Thursday afternoon, and Mr Carregan is at the office and Mr and Mrs Grantham are horse riding. They left just after lunch. The other servants are off duty so I'll carry your cases. You're in your usual room. My, but you have changed."

"Yes, you said so," answered James.

"How long are you staying, sir?"

"Until the end of August." They began to walk up the stairs. "I can't find a convenient boat passage to Cape Town before then."

"I think they are hoping you will stay permanently."

"Yes, well, I'm afraid that's impossible."

"It's been a lovely summer so far," said Jennings.

"Yes, and it's a lovely day. We have been lucky too. The rains were good at home this year."

"Oh, but surely you still regard this as your home?"

"No, Jennings. My home is my farm."

"But you won't live out there all your life, will you?"

"Unless anything prevents me," said James, and opened the door into his old bedroom. He looked around. Everything was exactly the same.

"Will that be all, sir?" asked Jennings.

"Yes, thank you."

"I will tell them you are here when they return. And welcome back to Halmeston."

"Thank you."

The door closed. He took off his travelling clothes and unpacked. He put on a silk dressing gown and lay down on the bed. Within a few moments, he was asleep. He woke to the sound of horses in the courtyard. He lay where he was for a moment and then got up and looked down from the window. He recognised

Ester. She was talking and laughing with the groom but the man with her was not part of the conversation. Even at a distance, James could see that he was tall and lean, with a long, thin face. The man stooped slightly and affected a dangling motion with his riding crop.

James went back to his wardrobe and changed. He opened the door and walked down the stairs and was halfway down them when his sister walked into the entrance hall from the west wing of the house. She was followed by her husband.

"Hello, Ester," said James softly. She looked up and put her hand to her mouth and then ran to the stairs.

"Jamie, it's you, it is you," she said, and ran up the stairs to meet him. She flung her arms around his neck and then held him out to look at.

"But you look so different," she said in a startled voice, "and your skin is so dark."

"It's five years and too much sun," said James, and laughed, and as he did so he looked down at his brother-in-law in the entrance hall. The man was looking at him.

"Hello," said James, and, holding his sister across the shoulder, he led her down the stairs. "You must be Oswald," he said, putting out his hand, "I'm James." They shook hands, James gripping hard and Oswald returning no pressure.

"We've just been for a ride," said Ester. "When did you get here? Have you had any food? Is your room all right? Oh, but it's lovely to see you again."

"And seeing you," said James. "Come on, let's go and have a brandy and soda to celebrate. I think I may need one before Father arrives."

"I don't know whether it is quite the right time to drink alcohol," said Oswald. "I should have thought tea would have been more appropriate for the time of day."

"Come on," said James, "I've had the stuff for breakfast before now."

"Have you?" said Oswald and kept his mouth closed for a moment.

"Oh, I don't mind," said Ester. "I mean it has been five years."

"It's just that your sun doesn't go down at the right time," said James, as they reached the sitting room.

"Bring me a tray of drinks," said James to Jennings, "and put a tall glass on for me for brandy and soda, and whatever the others drink." He shepherded them both into the long room with the high ceiling and long windows that looked out over the lawns, then took his cigar case out of his hip pocket.

"Do you smoke, Oswald?" he asked, and offered him a cheroot. "It's the best Cape tobacco. A bit strong, but it keeps the flies away at night. No? Oh, well. You don't mind if I smoke?" He felt his pockets. "No matches and no cutter," he said with the cheroot between his teeth.

"There are matches over here for the guests," said Ester. "No one else smokes."

"Well if that's the case, I'll have to bite the end off."

He bit the cheroot and spat the end into the dark gap just above the fire guard. Ester put her hand to her face to stop herself laughing. A servant came in and put a tray of drinks on the trolley beside the fireplace.

"What are you having?" said James, turning to the drinks with the well-lit cigar held in his teeth.

"I'll have a small dark sherry to celebrate," said Ester.

"And Oswald?" asked James, as he looked for the sherry bottle.

"Well I suppose I'd better have a brandy and soda as well."

"Good," said James and poured the drinks.

"Try these," he said. "Cheers, and I'm sorry I couldn't come to your wedding. Lovely to see you again, sister. Five years is a long time."

"What are your plans, Jamie?" asked Ester as she put her arm through his.

"First, I wish to see a woman by the name of Annabel Crichton.

I thought you might be able to help me, Oswald. She was Lord Levenhurst's daughter."

"As it so happens, I have invited her to the ball on Saturday," said Oswald.

"Goodness, well that helps to solve my problem. And yes, I've heard about the ball. Then I have an address to find in the not so prosperous end of Liverpool, and I have to go to Wales. I also wish to take a train to Birmingham to visit some factories. Willy and I are not farmers, so we've had to learn. Rhys was brought up on a sheep run in Wales but that didn't help much either. I also want to see Grandfather and give him a report on the farms. There are other things as well, but they're not as important. My other important job was to find Michael Fentan's relations, which I did in Cape Town. What do you know about the Jews?"

"Not very much," said Oswald. "I keep away from them myself."

"Why do you keep away from them?" asked James.

"Oh, I don't know. Everyone says they're different. They don't think the same as us. They only think of money."

"Are they the only people who think of money? Maybe if you knew one of them you would change your mind."

"Doubt it," said Oswald.

"Why this talk about Jews?" asked Ester.

"Because I'm thinking of marrying one."

"Oh, you can't, James," said Ester quickly, drawing away.

"You haven't even met the girl."

"But she's Jewish."

"So what?"

"Well, you just can't. It's not done."

"Neither is running off in the middle of the night to go to Africa," said James, and smiled.

"That was different."

"It is now, because it was a success, but it wasn't at the time. Anyway, I haven't finally made up my mind, since I have no comparison of women, but I don't think Willy will let me back onto the farm without a wife."

"We have a lot of girls waiting to meet you," said Ester.

"I shall enjoy meeting them."

"But I don't think any of them will go back to Africa with you."

"Well then, they can't marry me in that case."

"They could, if you stayed in England."

"But I am not going to stay in England, Ester." He looked from one to the other and there was no sign of laughter in his eyes. He turned and poured himself another brandy, put the glass under the soda siphon and pressed the lever.

"Why do you want to see Annabel Crichton?" asked Oswald.

"She was a friend of a friend of mine," answered James.

"Anyone we know?"

"I doubt it. He was killed on the Shangani Patrol."

"One of the officers?" said Oswald, with a more relaxed tone to his voice.

"Yes, he was," said James.

"Funny, she never told me anything about it, and it was all the rage at the time. You weren't actually on that patrol, were you?"

"No, but I was close enough to hear the firing."

"Well, why on earth didn't you go and help them?" asked Oswald.

"Because we were fighting for our lives at the time," said James.

"Oh, I see. Well, that's different."

"I think that's Father now," said Ester as a gig came up the drive. "They must have telephoned him at the office."

They drank in silence until Ernest Carregan walked quietly into the long room. To James, he looked much older. They looked at each other without speaking for a moment, then Ernest said, "Hello, son."

James shook his hand. "It's nice to see you again."

"I hear you've been in the wars?"

"It always sounds worse than it is."

"I'm sorry about your partner, Morgan. Ester told me he did a lot for you at the beginning."

"He's one reason why I'm here. I have to tell his relations."

"The War Office will have done that," said Ernest Carregan.

"Not all of them. I hope you don't mind me drinking your brandy but I coaxed the others into a small celebration. Won't you have one as well?"

"Why not? Five years has been a long time. I'll have the same as you. You don't look the same but we won't go into that. You've heard about the ball? Oswald's idea really, but we all think it's a good one."

James poured the brandy, gave it a splash of soda and handed it to his father.

"Your grandfather will be coming. He should look something in evening dress."

"He'll come in uniform. Evening dress is something I'll have to buy. Could you help me to choose a few things in Liverpool?"

"I'll introduce you to my tailor. He's expensive but first class."

"I have a good amount of my own money," said James. To James's surprise, his father laughed and then they laughed together. The only one who did not smile was Oswald.

"You making money out of those farms?" asked his father.

"We had a good season this year," said James.

"Must be damn hot."

"Only just before the rains. The winters are dry and pleasant."

"Well," said his father, having again looked at his glass. "Cheers. You proved me wrong, James. Didn't think you had it in you, but then you don't look the same boy that ran away. Your grandfather said you'd make it, but then we had a row and I never got to hear his reasons. We'll have a family dinner party tonight and then you can tell us."

4

———

"*Y*ou'd better see whether the orchestra know what they are doing, James," said Ernest Carregan. "Most musicians are stupid."

"Can I take them a drink?"

"Good idea. It will brighten them up. They're meant to be good but they always say that. It'll be another half an hour before the guests arrive. Can you see anything wrong with my dress?"

"Don't ask me," said James. "I'm used to riding breeches and shirts that haven't been washed for a week. But it looks fine."

"Oh well, we're only expecting three hundred tonight and some of them won't arrive. They accept everything and then choose their fancy at the last minute. You'll find champagne in ice buckets down the window side of the library. When you're finished, come to the billiard room and we'll have a glass of wine together before the guests arrive."

"Right. I'll only be a moment."

JAMES WALKED BACK from the orchestra stand, away from the music of Bach, and passed underneath the four chandeliers that showed up the frescos on the ceiling. Around the tops of three walls, above the picture skirtings, were hunting scenes.

"I've a bottle waiting for us," said his father as he joined him. "Oswald was right, for once. They can play music."

"It is like discovering music for the first time," said James, as he followed his father into the billiard room.

"Sit down. We can hear the music from here and it's not too loud to stop us talking. We haven't really said much to each other since you returned. I thought it better to let you find the atmosphere yourself. You go ahead and open the champagne. It hurts my thumb. Things have changed around here. When you went away, I thought you were a boy and I treated you as such. You were twenty-one and I should have seen that I couldn't hold you down, but it's hard to change a habit. When you went to Africa, I didn't want anything more to do with you. Everything I had built was to give you the social chance that I never had. That's it, pour the champagne to the top. But when I thought about it, I realised that if I had been in your place I would have gone too. Anyway, that's all over now and we can talk. Cheers, son," he said, lifting his glass, "to you, and I'm glad they didn't kill you out there." They drank together. "I followed it, you know. I never wrote, but it was mostly pride. Maybe I'm getting old. I don't see things so right and wrong anymore."

They listened to Bach. James sipped his champagne and puzzled over his father. But there is good and bad, he told himself. If he had had everything as a child he would have had no ambition to do anything for himself.

"I haven't brought you in here to persuade you to stay in England," said his father. "You have your own mind and your own responsibilities. I've learnt a lot in the last five years. You know that, for me, just making money wasn't enough. I wanted position. I succeeded with Ester. She will not only become gentry but nobility, and her son will be a Viscount. But what a price to pay. Oswald has nothing and his father little more. All they have is the title from an ancestor. No, a man must make his own life. Since you came back to

Halmeston I have seen that, and I was able to compare you with Oswald. My father came up from nothing and so have we. I'm not going to offer you money as you don't need it and you wouldn't take it. From what I've heard about Morgandale, it's more of a business than a farm, and that's maybe where I can help. I've had experience in more than insurance."

"Any suggestions are welcome," said James, sitting forward and taking a cheroot out of his case. "You never know all the answers in farming." He bit the end off his cheroot and spat it out over the end of the billiard table into the fireplace. "Farming depends on so many things outside one's control. You cannot afford to lose a penny by mistake." He lit the cheroot.

"There's a cigar cutter on the table," said Ernest Carregan, looking at his son.

"Sorry," said James. "Force of habit. Anyway, we were talking about the farms so I felt at home."

"You talked of export markets," said his father, "and I'm sure you're right, as with all that land you're soon going to overproduce for the local market. What we have to cost is the best way of exporting. Years ago they herded the cattle to market and lost half their weight. Now they send them by train, but you can't send your cattle from Bulawayo to Europe. I think you have to can the stuff. Make bully beef."

"None of us have thought of that," said James and took a drink.

"I have an interest in a canning factory, which brought it to mind. It will need paperwork to prove the costing, and marketing to find the price at which it will sell, but it seems to me the simplest way of getting meat out of Africa. If the costing is right, we'll make you a proposition, subject to a director of the canning factory visiting Rhodesia. We'll set up a plant under your company's direction with us holding half the common stock."

"You've been talking to the canners already," said James.

"Of course. I'm a businessman and I'm not averse to making money out of my son."

They smiled.

"That's the way I hoped we'd talk," said James.

"Right. We'll go and see the canners on Monday. Come on, here are the first guests. I can hear the horses. Put the bottle back in the ice. We may be able to come back for it later. Some of the women you'll meet tonight talk so fast that you get out of breath just listening to them."

James put the half-empty bottle back in the ice.

"We can't have them calling us 'nouveau riche' to our faces," went on his father as James followed him, "and there is something about the host greeting his guests when they arrive. You will find that all the women over thirty, and a few of the men like Oswald, will spend their whole evening looking for points of social error. Whoever is arriving is five minutes early, so we can gain points at the moment."

They walked through the library and back into the hall where Oswald and Ester were standing, waiting well back from the entrance and on the side nearest the library, while Jennings stood on duty at the door, ready to announce the guests. James looked out of the front door onto the drive, to where his grandfather was trying to get the first mate out of a cab.

"Come on cabby, give me a hand with him," James heard his grandfather say as he and his father joined Ester and Oswald. "He's more frightened than drunk. I've seen him drink all night and still take me money at cribbage. Come on Hal, me boy. No one's going to bite ye, and if I've timed it properly we're the first to arrive. That's me boy."

Jennings remained expressionless. James looked at Ester and they caught each other's eye. The veins in Oswald's neck were pulsing and Ernest Carregan was waiting for the worst. They waited.

"Straighten up, lad," they heard him say in a softer voice. Then they heard the pronounced tread of two men coming up the steps.

From his angle, James saw the first mate come into view as Jennings bent and spoke to them. The man was fully in control of himself through force of discipline, but he was drunk.

"Captain Carregan and Mr Fincham," announced Jennings in a loud voice.

"Come on, ye can leave that out. If me own son doesn't know his father, it ain't going to help by you introducing us now."

They came forward, dressed in the monkey jackets of their respective ranks in the Merchant Navy, each with a row of medals hanging from faded ribbons. James wondered which wars they had been in together; he had never heard his grandfather mention them before.

"Ah, there they are," said the captain.

Ester moved towards them.

"Hello, Grandfather," she said, and kissed him on the cheek. He patted her hand.

"Hello, lad," he said to James. "Some change from Cape Town station. Hello Ernest and Oswald. The invitation said bring a partner so I brought my first mate, Hal Fincham. He wasn't very willing."

Hal went along the line to be introduced.

"Ernest, me son. James, who yer've met. Ester, me granddaughter, and Oswald Grantham, her husband. I went to the wedding."

"Come and have a drink," said James.

"Somewhere away from the crowd," said his grandfather, "so that Hal can find his land-legs."

As James led them away, he glanced back and saw an expression of incredulity on Jennings's face.

White-gloved servants stood at convenient corners in the library and James signalled to one of them to follow him into the smoking room. The sounds of Bach continued. He sat the seamen down and ordered three brandies and soda and then gave his grandfather the latest financial position of Morgandale.

"You had a good partner in Morgan," said his grandfather when he had finished.

"And a good friend," said James. "I hope to have another Morgan on the farm in three years. Rhys had a bastard son who I saw yesterday. He's fifteen, strong, and well educated on Rhys's money. I've told him he must finish his education before he comes to Rhodesia. He wanted to leave now and bring his foster parents with him."

"Well I never," said his grandfather. "You got any bastards, Hal?"

"None that I know of," said Fincham.

"Ye look well, lad, and it's nice to see ye again. They say the railway line will be through to Fort Salisbury by the end of next year. I'll bring the *Dolphin* into Beira then. It'll be something of a pleasure cruise as with all these steamships there isn't the lucrative trade for us. I saw it coming but I was too old to learn steam, and Hal and I have had a good run together. By the end of next year we'll both be seventy and we don't find the *Dolphin* as easy to run anymore. We'll come ashore. We've enough to live on and Hal has a wife when he chooses to remember her. I'll have plenty of time to look over Morgandale."

"Why don't you retire to the farm?" said James. "The climate is good."

"What with the bastard's foster parents, and ageing grandparents, ye won't have much room to move," said the captain.

"It's a big farm and Willy will like it," said James. "He'll have you doing more work than on the *Dolphin*. Anyway, you own a fifth of the place and without your cash, which bought the machinery, we'd be five years behind where we are at the moment."

"I'll come and see first. I've got me friends here, and old seamen like to talk about themselves, and the best listener is the one who's going to talk next."

"Yes, I suppose so. Think about it. I must go and meet the other guests."

"Right lad. Go and keep them happy. Yer something of the prize canary tonight. They've all come to have a look at ye to see whether ye look the same as them, and to get as near as possible to your war without hurting themselves."

"Could be," said James. "I'll be back later."

"Don't drink too much," said the captain.

James smiled as he let himself out of the smoking room, leaving both doors open so that the seamen would become part of the evening. He walked through the library and into the hall where his father was shaking hands with an elderly woman whose skin hung loosely from her throat. She wore a tiara and her eyes watered. James took his place on his father's right.

"This is my son, James, Mrs Hargreaves. James, I would like to introduce you to Mrs Hargreaves. You must remember the Hargreaves of Cheshire. They have been in the same house for generations."

"How do you do," said James, and shook her hand.

"We have heard so much about you," said Mrs Hargreaves before passing onto Oswald. "Oswald, my dear, how are you?" she said. "What a simply lovely evening. The weather is so perfect. Ah, this must be Ester. What a lovely girl."

"This is my son, James," said his father, this time to a young lady. "James, I would like you to meet Miss Lettice Tenant."

"How do you do," said James, and shook her hand.

"Weren't you at Oxford?" she said. Her voice was girlish.

"Yes," said James.

"How interesting. Hello Oswald, darling. How are you? So nice to see you, and such a lovely evening. I'm sure we are all going to have such a lovely time. There's a midsummer ball next week at Sheldon Hall, but I am sure you know about it. It will be lovely to see you there."

"Are all the girls like that one?" whispered James to his father, as Lettice Tenant joined Mrs Hargreaves on her way to the garden.

"Most of them."

Half an hour later, James had shaken hands with fourteen girls, all of them similar to Lettice Tenant, and all but two of whom had asked Oswald whether he was going to the midsummer ball at Sheldon Hall.

"Mr and Mrs Edgar Crichton," announced Jennings, and James looked over to the door.

"Is that Levenhurst's daughter?" he asked Oswald.

"Yes, of course. Haven't you met her? She's giving the midsummer ball. Always does things in just the right way. Hers are the most sought after. Only throws one a year. Weren't you waiting to meet her?"

"Yes," said James.

Annabel took her husband's arm and began to cross the hall. James watched her carefully. She was at ease and seemed to expect everything that was done for her. James studied her face that was no longer young. Her neck was long and she held her head erect. Her husband was bald and fifty. Ernest Carregan bowed slightly and James tried to equate her with the boy he had met the day before, but there was nothing that suggested their kinship.

"This is my son, James. James, may I introduce you to the Honourable Mrs Edgar Crichton. Mrs Crichton's father was Lord Levenhurst."

"How do you do," said James, holding out his hand. "We may not have met but we have a friend in common." He saw her expression flicker for a moment and then return to its formal poise.

"How nice," she said. "I cannot imagine who it could be but you must find me during the evening and tell me the secret. Hello, Oswald," she continued as she moved on, "it's so nice to see you. Oh yes, this must be your wife. How do you do, my dear. I am so very pleased to meet you."

James watched them go into the library, pausing for a moment to take a glass of champagne offered to them by a waiter. Then they were lost among the throng of people.

"I think that's most of them," said Oswald. "Anyone coming later will prefer not to be noticed arriving. Annabel always makes her entrance at the last moment that's still correct."

"Good," said Ernest Carregan. "Let us go and join our guests."

"Did you see all those pretty girls?" asked Ester as they walked towards the library.

"They are very pretty," said James. "But you are right. I cannot imagine any of them in Rhodesia, and I'm afraid that none of them compare with Sonny."

"But at least they are the right religion and background, old boy," said Oswald.

"I think Sonny herself makes up for the deficiencies you consider to be important."

"Your father won't like it," persisted Oswald.

"Funnily enough, if he met her, he would," said James, and took a cheroot out of his case.

"Please use the cutter," said Oswald. "There are a lot of my friends here tonight."

"You're safe," said James. "Tonight, I especially remembered to put one in my pocket." He expertly cut the end off the cigar and accepted a light from the waiter.

"Now for a drink," said James, and made his way through the crowd towards the smoking room, puffing at the thin cigar that was held in the corner of his mouth. He looked at no one despite a number of gestures from people whose hand he had shaken. He turned into the smoking room and ordered a brandy and soda from a waiter. Around his grandfather were a group of people listening with interest. The waiter put the drink in his hand and his grandfather looked up and winked and they smiled at each other. He took a long drink and put his cheroot back in his mouth. He listened and then his mind went back to Cape Town, and to watching the sun go down from Chapman's Peak and the richness of violent colours, and Sonny, a person as strong and as colourful as the vision of power that spread out over the sky and seeped into the depth of the sea.

"You don't mind my coming to talk to you, do you?" said Lettice Tenant. "I mean, we were properly introduced and I'm sure you must be the most interesting man here this evening, so I thought I must come and talk to you before all those hundreds of people take up your evening. Now you must tell me about all those natives. I mean they must be terrifying and I'm sure that I would have fainted if I'd seen one of them. The papers said there were a hundred and fifty of you against more than ten thousand of them and it was just a miracle that you managed to get away. We all knew you were on the expedition and it did make it more personal knowing the brother-in-law of someone who was there."

"Yes, it must have done," said James.

Lettice Tenant put her head on one side, smiled, and twice let out a feminine laugh. James smiled back but kept his cheroot clenched between his teeth.

"Yes, well I'm sure," she said. "I must go and find Aunty. You must really tell me about Africa when you have the time."

"It will be my pleasure," said James.

He began to circulate amongst the guests. They asked him many questions, but rarely took any notice of the answers. The orchestra played Mozart, and the dancers left the floor and James saw a few faces who understood what they were hearing. Midnight passed. He looked around for Annabel without any success, and then began a careful search of the house and grounds. He had drunk enough to face his task, and he hoped that by that point of the evening it would not be too painful for either of them to talk about Morgan and his son. He found her at a table on the lawn outside the ballroom. He counted seven people listening to her conversation. He crossed the lawn.

"But my dear Henry, everyone must appreciate the value of society," said Annabel. "Everyone must have something for which to strive. If there were no rich, the poor would be miserable."

"But they must be given a basic standard of living," said Henry.

"Of course," answered Annabel. "And, as the profits rise, so do the wages, but if there is no profit, or you destroy the machinery for making that profit in an attempt to placate your poor, there are no wages, and the result is starvation for everyone. There must be a leader and that leader must be rewarded. If you remove a Levenhurst you have to replace him with somebody else. You cannot have a leaderless society. The argument is not rich or poor, but who leads the poor, and how well can he alleviate the poverty. The sweeping change is a worthless gesture. There has never been an instant utopia. Give England time. She is doing well. The empire may yet keep the world at peace. Don't you agree, Mr Carregan?" she said, looking up at James.

"There is good and bad in everything," he answered.

"When I arrived, Mr Carregan said he had a message for me from a mutual friend. Very mysterious. Who is the friend, Mr Carregan?"

"I would prefer to give you the message in private," said James.

"Nonsense. We have nothing to hide from our friends." She swept her gloved hand around to include everyone and waited for his answer.

"Rhys Morgan," said James.

"I don't think I know anyone of that name," said Annabel, "but maybe if we walk together in the grounds of your father's lovely home, you can refresh my memory. Come, Mr Carregan. It is a beautiful evening, and Mozart can sometimes be the more beautiful for a little distance."

They walked away, towards the driveway.

"Rhys was my partner," said James. "I spoke to your son yesterday, telling him everything except the name of his mother. Have you really forgotten him?"

"No. I read about his death in the paper. I suppose it's why I am here tonight, to see you. How strange. So you became his partner."

"He was coming to England this year, to ask you to go back with him," said James.

"Poor Rhys. A romantic, really. Did he believe that after fourteen years I would run away with him?"

"Yes."

"But we are different people now. How could I leave all this, and my children? They need a mother."

"He had not thought of that. He thought you had married without love."

"A patient man can do wonders. No, in his funny old way I am very fond of Edgar. I loved Rhys because I loved life, but I understood none of its responsibilities. The Levenhursts have not retained their money and position by running off with university students. As I grew older, I learnt to be responsible. Mr Carregan, you will be doing Gavin and me a favour by not telling him the name of his mother. For the sake of my other sons and my husband, I cannot afford to remember. If I did what my instinct dictated, I would go with you now, and find the boy, and sit for a week with you both while you told me about his father. But I can't. I made a mistake once, but it cannot relive itself. I will call my carriage. Tell my husband I will send it back for him." She began to walk away and he followed. "Don't come with me. The coachman will be there... He was a good man wasn't he?" she asked.

"Yes, he was a good man."

James watched, and a few minutes later saw the coach drive away. The elms threw a dark shadow across the driveway. He thought of Sonny, and smiled to himself and walked back to the house for another drink. The music played over the thoughts that began to run through his mind.

CARREGAN'S CATCH (BOOK TWO)
CONTINUE YOUR JOURNEY WITH THE PIONEERS

Is gold worth gambling for when death is at stake?

A fragile peace is broken and James Carregan is called to action. All thoughts of finding a suitable wife evaporates. Months later, the Shona rebellion quelled, James finds himself crossing paths with power-hungry Gavin Morgan, the son of his old friend, Rhys.

With an irresistible proposition, James and his new acquaintance leave the Morgandale Estate for Cape Town. Becoming the toast of the town, Gavin hosts a series of bacchanal parties attracting high-ranking British officers and beautiful women alike... Including the scintillating Sonny, James's love interest.

But despite his new-found fame and fortune, Gavin senses a war brewing between the British and Boers. Young Morgan makes plans to deal with both sides... Treason punishable by death if discovered. As tensions mount and fighting breaks out, Gavin and James are forced into a series of lies and deceptions to hide his complicity.

In matters of love and war, fortune favours the brave. But with

Sonny waiting in the wings, James must decide if his loyalty to his old friend Rhys justifies betraying his country...

PRINCIPAL CHARACTERS

∼

The Carregans
James— Main character in *Morgandale*
Ernest — James's father
Captain Carregan — James's grandfather
Ester — James's sister

Other Principal Characters
Annabel Levenhurst (Annie) — Rhys Morgan's sweetheart
Captains Borrow and Heany — Baggage Masters of the Pioneer Corps
Captains Hoste and Roach — members of the Pioneer Corp
Chatunga — servant to James, Rhys and Willie
Edgar Crichton — Annabel's husband
Gambo — one of Lobengula's inDunas
Gavin (Morgan) — Rhys's bastard child by Annabel Levenhurst
George Mann — a police constable
Jennings — butler to the Carregans
Johan Colenbrander — hunter and advisor to the Pioneer Corps
Koos van der Walt — a soldier in the Pioneer Corps

Magwegwe — one of Lobengula's inDunas
Michael Fentan — an assistant, like James Carregan, to von Brand and Morgan
Rhys Morgan — Pioneer Corps scout and close friend and business partner of James Carregan
Sonny (Sonja) Fentan — Michael Fentan's sister
The Honourable Oswald Grantham — Ester's husband
Willie von Brand — Pioneer Corps scout and James Carregan's business partner

Historical Figures
Colonel Edward Pennefather — the first commander of what became known as the British South Africa Company Police in Rhodesia
Cecil John Rhodes — co-founder of the southern African territory of Rhodesia (now Zimbabwe and Zambia), which the British South Africa Company named after him in 1895
Dr Leander Starr Jameson — was for a time an inDuna of one Lobengula's regiments as well the leader of the infamous *Jameson Raid* in South Africa
Frederick Courteney Selous — was a British explorer who agreed to be a guide for the Pioneer Column
King Lobengula — king of the Matabele people and son of Mzilikazi
Major Frank Johnson — an adventure and head of the Pioneer Corps
Major Allan Wilson — an officer in the Pioneer Corps and leader of the Shangani Patrol
Major Patrick Forbes — commander and leader of the Mashonaland Horse

HISTORICAL NOTES

~

Lobengula

The depiction of Lobengula's death described in *Morgandale*, is fictitious. The actual details surrounding his death is unknown. However, it is known that he became extremely unwell after the battle at Shangani and the cause of his death sometime in early 1894, was inconclusive.

The Matabele

The Matabele tribe are decedents of the Zulu people of the Natal region of South Africa, led by Mzilikazi, who fled north during the reign of Shaka, the King of the Zulu. Mzilikazi a lieutenant of Shaka, had fallen out with Shaka and went on to found the kingdom of Matabeleland, formally known as Mthwakazi, in today's southern region of Zimbabwe. Lobengula was his son and successor.

The Pioneer Column

The Pioneer Column (Pioneer Corps) was a force raised in South Africa by Cecil John Rhodes and his British South Africa

Company in 1890. The column's purpose was to annex and colonise the territory of Mashonaland in the northern part of Zimbabwe, that was once Southern Rhodesia. Once the Pioneer Column had been disbanded, each member was granted a tract of land to farm.

The Shangani Patrol

The Shangani Patrol (or Wilson's Patrol) was a unit of the British South Africa Company that in 1893 was ambushed and annihilated by more than 3,000 Matabele warriors in Matabeleland during the First Matabele War. The unit was led by Major Allan Wilson with the patrol being attacked north of the Shangani River. The event is sometimes called *Wilson's Last Stand* and none of the British soldiers survived the onslaught.

The Shona

The Shona tribe are located in the northern part of today's Zimbabwe which was one of the regions originally divided up when occupied by the Pioneer Column in 1890 as Peter Rimmer describes in *Morgandale*. Mashonaland, as the region was known, was constantly raided by the Matabele, until the region came under the control of the British.

DEAR READER

∼

Reviews are the most powerful tools in our kitty when it comes to getting attention for Peter's books. This is where you can come in, as by providing an honest review you will help bring them to the attention of other readers.

If you enjoyed reading *Morgandale,* and have five minutes to spare, we would really appreciate a review (it can be as short as you like). Your help in spreading the word and keeping Peter's work alive is gratefully received.

Please post your review on the retailer site where you purchased this book.

Thank you so much.
Heather Stretch (Peter's daughter)

PS. We look forward to you joining Peter's growing band of avid readers.

ACKNOWLEDGEMENTS

~

With grateful thanks to our *VIP First Readers* for reading *Morgandale* prior to its official launch date. They have been fabulous in picking up errors and typos helping us to ensure that your own reading experience of *Morgandale* has been the best possible. Their time and commitment is particularly appreciated.

Hilary Jenkins (South Africa)
Agnes Mihalyfy (United Kingdom)
Daphne Rieck (Australia)
Andy Gentle (United Kingdom)

Thank you.

Kamba Publishing

Manufactured by Amazon.ca
Bolton, ON